Wreathed

Curtis Edmonds

Scary Hippopotamus Books
Trenton, NJ
http://www.scaryhippopotamus.com

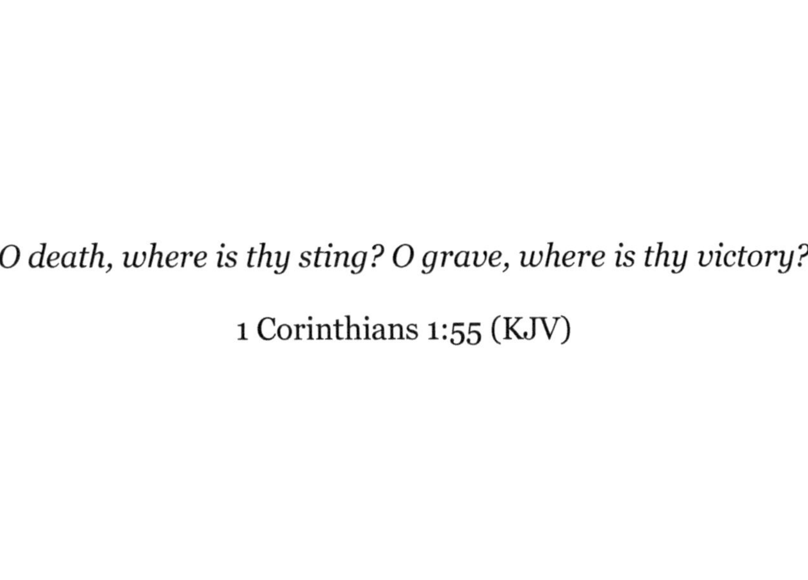

O death, where is thy sting? O grave, where is thy victory?

1 Corinthians 1:55 (KJV)

For
Ellen

who
read
the
last
pages
first

Chapter 1

It was seven o'clock on a Tuesday evening, and I was stuck at the office. I had been working ten hours a day since my last vacation, four months ago. This was just as pathetic as it sounds. I could have been having a nice dinner with friends, or using my long-neglected gym membership, or even sitting on my couch in my pajamas watching real estate shows. But I wasn't. I was at my desk, staring at a computer screen, engaged in the necessary but mind-draining and butt-numbing chore of proofreading legal documents. Just another fun-filled day in the life of Wendy Jarrett, Attorney at Law.

The advantage of working this late was that it minimized distractions. But after three straight hours reading page after page of legal boilerplate, I found myself glancing at my phone, hoping that it might generate a distraction or two. Maybe an old friend from college was in town for the evening and wanted to hang out. Maybe a cute guy had seen me walking across the courthouse square this afternoon and was about to text me and to take me out for drinks and conversation and maybe a little romance. Maybe the anonymous creeper I had been dominating in *Words With Friends* over the last month was secretly a gorgeous billionaire who was waiting downstairs to whisk me away to a life of luxury and ease. None of these potential distractions were, shall we say, *realistic*, but at that particular moment anything had to be better than sitting all by myself in an empty law office in Morristown, New Jersey, and comparing two separate sixty-page wills for typos and inconsistencies.

I did get a distraction in the form of a phone call from my mother. That could only mean that something horrible had happened.

I do my best to keep in touch with my mother, but that means that I'm the one who has to call her nearly every single time. This is partly because she has a misplaced sense of old-money frugality about long-distance phone calls, but mostly it is her passive-aggressive way of getting me to communicate with her more frequently. So I call her on alternate Sunday afternoons, unless I'm on vacation, or unless I'm snowed under with work, or unless I drank so much chardonnay the night before that I lose the ability to claw my way out of bed. We have a nice little conversation, which occasionally touches on topics of parental concern such as why I drink so much chardonnay. Then I hang up, and she hangs up, and that's it for parent-child communication for another fortnight.

The only reason my mother ever breaks this pattern and calls me is if something horrible has happened. I couldn't imagine another reason why she would call me at work at seven in the evening on a random weekday. It meant that someone was in the hospital, or someone was dead, or aliens from Alpha Centauri had landed in central New Jersey looking for Orson Welles. And the only way to find out the nature of this particular disaster was to pick up the phone.

I looked at the phone. I looked at my computer screen. Whatever it was that had gone so badly off the rails that it had prompted Mother to call me couldn't be that much worse than having to read another line of boring legalese. I picked up the phone.

"Hi, Mom," I said, not without some trepidation.

"Hi yourself," she said. "Are you at work? I tried calling you at home, but the call went to voicemail."

"Yes, I'm still at work. I have clients coming in tomorrow for an estate-planning meeting and I'm just proofreading the new version of their wills to make sure everything matches up."

"So you haven't eaten," she said. It wasn't a question.

"I have a hot date with a frozen dinner."

"I know you're busy, dear daughter, but could I impose on you to take me out to dinner? Nothing on today's menu is looking good to me."

My mother lived in an exclusive senior community in central New Jersey, about twenty miles south of Morristown. "Senior community," for most people, means a place where you warehouse old people and make them play shuffleboard and serve them gray institutional meals. This place was more upscale, with organized bus tours and nature walks and what I guess you could call a political action committee. And the food, at least to hear my mother talk about it, was impressive. They served healthy, nutritionally balanced meals that were accompanied by gooey cheesecakes and crispy apple strudels and large, soft mounds of ice cream. I had never, not once, heard my mother issue even the smallest complaint about the food, which was so unlike her that I suspected that the kitchen staff had developed an amazing magical cooking prowess unknown to the rest of humanity. I wished I knew their secret—not so much because I wanted to learn how to cook, but because I wanted to know how to insulate myself from maternal criticism.

"Are you feeling all right?" I asked.

"Of course, dear. Why do you ask?"

"I don't know," I said. "It's just that this seems kind of an unusual time for you to call me, that's all. I thought something might be wrong."

"Nothing's wrong," she said. "I just can't bear the sight of my fellow residents here for another minute, and I don't feel like imposing on your sister right at the moment." When Mother retired, she'd moved to the same town where my older sister, Pacey, and her husband and twin sons lived. Pacey has many fine qualities, but she's not much of a cook, and I could understand why Mother would rather have me take her out to a restaurant instead.

"As much as I would like to join you for dinner, I'm right in the middle of something," I said. "If I stop now, I am going to obsess over it all night and then have to start all over in the morning from the beginning."

"Wendy, please listen to your mother for once. Whatever these people are paying you, they are not paying you enough to sit around and proofread paperwork at seven in the evening."

I thought about explaining, once again, the economics of law firm billing, but I kept my mouth shut. One of my mother's less endearing qualities is the ability to filter out explanations for things that she does not want explained to her. That encompasses any excuses I might have for not going out to dinner with her when she wanted to go out to dinner with me.

"All right," I said. "You caught me at a weak moment. Let me close up everything here and I'll be there in half an hour or so. Think about where you want to go eat."

"That would be lovely."

This all sounds too easy, I thought. *Something else must be going on, or there is some ulterior motive she's not telling me about.* I had no idea what it could be but at least I wouldn't have to eat that rubbery microwave lasagna that had been hanging in the back of my freezer for months.

"OK," I said. "See you in a few."

Five minutes later, I pulled my Audi out of the parking garage, made my way through Morristown, and headed south on the highway. Traffic was sparse, so I shifted gears and merged into the fast lane, passing the slow-moving trucks like so many barges in the wake of a speedboat. Not that I had a speedboat. I had a ten-year-old German convertible and a studio apartment and a giant heaving mound of debt from law school.

The Audi was not my first choice. My first choice had been a MetroCard, and a small apartment in a good neighborhood in Manhattan. After graduation, I'd spent four months looking for a job with a Wall Street law firm. My plan was to work my way up to the kind of job and the kind of office that Michael Douglas had in *Wall Street*. I'd been in two great summer associates' programs in 2007 and 2008, and I imagined I was well on my way up the glittering path to a rewarding career, easy money, and a cute boyfriend who looked like a young Charlie Sheen but who didn't do drugs or sell out small regional airlines in insider trading scams. But the economy cratered during my last year in law school, and all of the smart, engaging, helpful people I'd met in Manhattan during my summer programs were too busy trying to keep themselves afloat to help me get a job. Then I made the stupid mistake of taking the New York and New Jersey bar exams at the same time—and when I passed New Jersey but failed New York, I ended up stuck looking for work on the wrong side of the Hudson.

The best job I could find was with a boutique firm in Morristown, doing wills and estate planning. I was lucky to get the job in the first place, and I was lucky to still have it five years later. I gave up on Manhattan and the small apartment in the good neighborhood and the MetroCard. I found an apartment five minutes from my office, and a used convertible with a hairline crack in the windshield and a big chip of paint missing on the trunk lid.

I didn't need the car and I didn't need the additional debt that went along with it. But if I couldn't live in Manhattan, I at least wanted to be able to cruise down Seventh Avenue or the Jersey Shore or a narrow country road in the Poconos. I wanted the freedom to drive away as far and as fast as I could go anytime the mood struck. For the first couple of years, it worked out all right. But lately, I spent more and more of my weekends stretched out on my couch, catching up on sleep or work or whatever else was more important than getting in my car and driving somewhere and having fun. Worse, even if I did find the energy to drive somewhere and have fun, I didn't have anyone to have fun with.

I kept the Audi in high gear until it was time to decide whether to exit off the highway and keep driving somewhere else. I wanted to keep dodging traffic until I had outrun all my problems. But I knew it wouldn't work, and anyway, I was hungry. I pulled off the highway and made my way south.

Chapter 2

When I picked up my mother, she was wearing a long, plaid skirt and a cable-knit sweater, just as though she were golfing in Scotland. Most of the women at her retirement complex wore tacky, sequined sweatshirts and stretch pants, which is what I aspire to wear if I ever get that old. Either Mother hadn't been there long enough to downgrade her wardrobe, or she'd refused to change the way she dressed just because the rest of the world had gotten sloppy. I decided I would buy her a "World's Greatest Grandma" sweatshirt for Christmas, just to check.

I offered to drive us to a nice steakhouse in the next town over. I didn't want a steak, necessarily, but I figured there might be a chance that she'd spring for a nice bottle of chardonnay and I knew this place had a good cellar. She decided it would be easier to go to the closest chain restaurant. I didn't argue with her, on the grounds that I would likely end up arguing with her over something else and I wanted to save my energy for the more important battle yet to come.

The restaurant was half deserted on a Tuesday night, but the multiple television screens showing basketball and hockey games made the atmosphere noisy and distracting. We ordered our drinks—a raspberry mojito for me, iced tea for her—and our dinner, and didn't say much. If Mother had an ulterior motive, she was taking her time letting me know about it.

"How's your salad?" she asked.

"It's fine," I said. It was not. It was a gross pile of half-washed iceberg and red onion covered with a greasy vinaigrette dressing. I would rather have had the fried cheese, or the nachos, or two more raspberry mojitos and a cab ride home. It's almost always a good idea to show restraint, though, and it's always a good idea not to give my mother the chance to criticize my eating habits if I can manage it. I told myself I could make up the calories at lunch tomorrow.

"You want a bite of my burger?" she asked.

"Not particularly." She'd gotten a horrible hybrid between a hamburger and a Philly cheesesteak, and just looking at it was making me slightly nauseous. Not nauseous enough to stop craving another raspberry mojito, mind you.

"How about some fries? I will never finish all of this."

"Mother, if you have something you need to tell me, you can just tell me without bribing me with leftovers off your plate."

"I was just trying to be considerate," she said. "My mistake. I apologize."

Every conversation I have ever had with my mother, even about something as quotidian as who should get to eat the last few remaining French fries from her plate, has always had a hidden barb or tripwire. She has the innate ability to turn any conversational gambit to her advantage, and throw whatever you tell her back in your face, twice as hard and twice as fast. It's a skill she developed from long years of verbal sparring with my father.

Unfortunately, I am the only one left that she can practice on. My parents got divorced when I was in law school, and my father moved to Myrtle Beach to play golf year round. My older brother, Greg, is a studious, quiet Eagle Scout and is no fun to tease. My sister, Pacey, the middle child, stopped trying to argue with Mother years ago. Mother always walks right over her, and then Pacey turns around and complains to me about it. That means I have to be the one that Mother pushes the hardest, and that means I have to be the one who pushes back.

"Well, then," I said. "I apologize, too, for assuming that you have a hidden agenda for wanting to have dinner with me."

"I don't believe in hidden agendas," she said. "If I need something from you, I will ask you. Which, as it happens, I need to do. Assuming, of course, you are willing to hear me out without making a sarcastic comment."

"Who, me?"

"That sort of sarcastic comment. Exactly."

I moved around the last couple of croutons on my salad. "If you have something you need to ask me, go ahead. If it's something that doesn't impact my work schedule, I'll be happy to help."

Mother fished a French fry out of the pile on her plate, applied a drop or two of ketchup, and popped it in her mouth. "I have an appointment at ten on Friday morning in Cape May. I hate to ask you for help with this, but I just don't think I can drive all the way down there and back by myself."

Cape May is at the southern tip of New Jersey, three hours from where I live. That would trap me in my car with my mother for six hours or so, which did not sound like an ideal way to burn a vacation day.

"Well, it depends on how you want to do it. Are you thinking about getting up early and driving down there and driving back? That would make for a long day."

"I thought we could stretch it out a little, make it easy," she said. "We could drive down Thursday, after you get off work, and stay the night at one of the hotels on the beach. Then, after we're done with my appointment, we could do some shopping or something, maybe get a spa treatment. Stay another night, and come back Saturday evening, if that works for you."

Put that way, it didn't sound horrible. It sounded like something a mother and daughter might do together. But "doing things together" had never been her long suit, unless you counted supposedly fun activities like making brownies for the Honduran resistance-fighter bake sale as "doing things together." Mother's idea of fun included things like dragging me out in my Halloween costume when I was five to walk precincts for Michael Dukakis, at night, *in Camden.*

Mother wasn't as involved in heavy-duty political activism these days, but it would be just like her to drag me to Cape May and stick me in a rancid community center to give estate tax advice to the elderly. She wasn't telling me everything, and I wanted to know all the details before I signed up for whatever it was.

"If you want to do something like that," I said, "we can try to schedule it and go someplace nice. Not that Cape May isn't nice, but it's the middle of March. Not the best time to go."

"Unfortunately, this is not the sort of thing I can reschedule."

"Why not? I mean, come on, this is short notice. If you want to do Cape May, let's do it right. We can rent a house and pick a time that Greg and Pacey and her kids can come."

"I am not trying to plan a family vacation, Wendy. I have an appointment and I need a ride down there. If you think you can convince your brother and sister to take time off for a family vacation, let me know how that works out for you."

"You haven't said what kind of appointment this is," I said. "And I don't know why you want me to go, or what ulterior motive you might have."

"For God's sake, Wendy. I don't understand why you insist on treating me like a conniving harridan every time I ask you for a little favor."

"Experience?"

The waitress came over just then and refilled Mother's glass of iced tea, and Mother made a production out of squeezing the lemon and adding sweetener before she took a long sip.

"When have I ever asked you to do something like this?" she asked.

"You don't ask me," I said. "You ask Pacey, and she does whatever you want."

"I already asked your sister, if you must know. I asked her and she said no."

"She did what?" Pacey was thirty-two, a little old to finally grow a spine, but I supposed it had to happen eventually.

"She told me that her children have a birthday party to go to. Some horrible commercialized thing at the mall. She said she couldn't disappoint them. I told her you couldn't live your whole life worried about whether you were disappointing your children, which set her off for some reason."

"I can't imagine why," I said.

"So then I asked your brother."

I was drinking a sip of water just then, and I nearly did a spit-take.

"Problem, dear?"

"Nearly choked on an ice cube," I said. "You asked Greg? But he's always super-busy." Greg is a surgeon at the Children's Hospital of Philadelphia and has more demands on his time than I feel comfortable thinking about.

"Long story short, he has two different cardiac surgeries to perform on Friday; I think one of them is for a homeless child or something. And, no, before you ask, I don't have anyone else I can ask to take me. I don't want to take a car service, and I don't want to drive all that way alone. I have no one in this world I can ask to do this except for you, and now I'm asking you. Will you do this for me?"

The natural, logical, and reasonable thing to do at this point would have been for me to say yes.

"No," I said.

"Why not?" she asked.

"You are not giving me enough information to make a decision at this point. If I knew why you were asking me, or why we were going, or what we were going to do when we got there, I would be able to say yes. Until you explain to me just what the deal is, I can't agree to it."

Mother sighed. It was one of those artful, well-mannered sighs that you'd expect to hear from an ancient bat at a country-club luncheon, complaining that the tea wasn't hot enough or that her cucumber sandwich had been cut into little triangles instead of the other way. It was a sigh teetering on the balance between total exasperation and fourth-generation old-money emotional repression—or, to put it another way, between aggressive and passive-aggressive. It was a warning signal, and a familiar one.

"Fifty years ago, I was young and foolish, and I made someone a foolish promise," she said. "The time has come for me to redeem my word. I can't tell you any more than that, not here, not in a tacky little strip-mall chain restaurant."

"Why not?"

"It's a long story and a private one. If you're that curious, I can explain it on the drive down."

I reminded myself to thank her, one day, for the advanced training in negotiations tactics that she has been giving me for my whole entire life. "So you'll only tell me after I've already agreed to go. No thanks. Tell me what I need to know, or else forget about it."

I expected she would either respond with a counter-offer, or else throw my position in my face. Instead, she sat there for a long minute, as though she was probing for weaknesses. Finally, she picked up a napkin and started dabbing at her eyes.

"Please don't start that," I said.

She let out the tiniest, most artificial sob possible, said, "Excuse me," and got up from the table. She turned her back to me and stalked off in the direction of the ladies' room.

I leaned against the fake leather of the booth. I knew she wasn't really that upset. She was using her phony tears to manipulate me, and I wasn't going to let her do it. The tears were her ultimate weapon, and I was going to defuse it by not letting them get to me.

The waitress came over and took away my sad, limp salad. I had her leave the remnants of Mother's burger and fries, and ordered a cup of coffee and settled in. This was going to be a long struggle, and I was determined to win.

Chapter 3

There is a name for people who get up from the middle of a meal and run into the bathroom and pretend to cry their eyes out, and that is *blackmailer*.

It is a simple strategy. I've used it myself in mediations or in depositions, except that I skip the part where I pretend to cry. If I'm trying to negotiate, every so often I will stand up and tell the other side I need to confer with my client and leave the room. Most of the time I don't need to do any such thing. I just want the other lawyer and his client to sit there and wonder what we're talking about. Sometimes the waiting makes them nervous enough that they'll agree to concessions that they might otherwise not.

Of course, it only works if the other side doesn't catch on to what you're doing. Sometimes it turns into a contest over who can wait the other person out, and in that case, it's just a huge waste of everyone's time. The trick, as with most things, is to stay calm and not let your nerves get the better of you, and anybody can do that if they're prepared.

Mother was in the bathroom, and she wanted me to think that she was in there crying. If I played by her rules, I would go in there and try to comfort her. But I had no intention of playing by her rules. I was not going to give in to her unreasonable demand that I take a day off to chauffeur her to Cape May for a vague appointment that I didn't know anything about. It might have been the nice thing to do, and it was very much the dutiful-daughter thing to do. And if she'd been honest with me, I might have gone along with it. But she'd tried to manipulate me into doing it instead, and I wasn't willing to cooperate with her the way that Pacey would have.

Except that she hadn't been able to manipulate Pacey, had she?

I got my phone out and sent Pacey a quick text—"What's up with Mom?" I didn't get a response, which I chalked up to it being close to the time she put her kids to bed.

I sat in the booth a bit longer and thought about ordering more coffee, just to give me something to do with my hands. I had no idea how long she was prepared to draw this out. I checked the time on my phone, and it had been just long enough for her to have a nice little cry and wash up and fix her makeup, assuming that's what she was doing.

Since I had my phone out already, I checked my in-box. I had three e-mails inviting me to attend various continuing legal education seminars, and two e-mails trying to get me to buy shoes. (One was from Overstock.com, which I just deleted, but the other one was about a Nordstrom's sale that sounded intriguing but outside my price range.) The last one was a LinkedIn request from somebody named Adam Lewis.

I don't spend a lot of time on social networks, because they're a huge waste of valuable time I could be spending on important things, such as browsing Pinterest for pictures of shoes I can't afford. I maybe look at Facebook once a day, if I'm tired or bored or slightly drunk and wondering what certain guys I knew in college are up to now. But LinkedIn is at least arguably work-related, and I've gotten a couple of clients that way, so I did the responsible thing and clicked on his profile.

LinkedIn is far from an ideal dating site, but it works for me because it tells me the two things I want to know about a man—whether he has a job, and whether he's cute. I try to weigh both these factors evenly, although the second one is more important. I have no shame on LinkedIn. If the guy's profile picture is at least marginally cute, I have no problem whatsoever accepting a LinkedIn request—as long as he's got a decent job. (I try not to be prejudiced about the things that people do for a living, but I draw the line at graduate students in the humanities, freelance art designers, or "social media gurus.")

The way I figure it, it never hurts to be nice to a cute, employed guy on LinkedIn. My experience is that cute, employed guys tend to know other cute, employed guys, and being linked to one cute, employed guy helps link you up with his network. Obviously, any given cute guy may not be available, or may be gay, or may be unsuitable for all sorts of reasons, such as not liking important things like Indian food or Pedro Almodovar movies or crunchy peanut butter. But the more cute guys you connect with, the more you increase your chances of having one become interested in you, or at least that's what I kept telling myself.

Adam Lewis was a cute guy. Phenomenally cute, at least from his profile picture. Dark hair, kind eyes, just the suggestion of a smirk on his rugged features. And he was employed, too—he was an investment counselor in Freehold, a couple of hours south down the Turnpike. I mentally categorized him as a definite possibility despite the geographical proximity issue.

Having exhausted the possibilities of electronic correspondence, I switched over to *Candy Crush Saga* and settled into my booth. I finished two levels before I realized that it had, now, indeed been a long time since Mother had gone into the bathroom.

Shortly after that I realized that I needed to not drink any more coffee if I didn't want to make the gutsy call about whether or not to duck into the men's room.

It was not much longer after that when I realized that I was a thirty-year-old single woman sitting alone in a chain restaurant, sipping coffee and playing *Candy Crush Saga*.

I don't enjoy eating alone in restaurants. I would rather eat microwave lasagna over the sink than eat at a restaurant by myself, and I have. I like restaurants. I like eating better food than I could ever hope to cook for myself, and I like leaving large tips for the nice people who bring me my food and clean up after me and wash the dishes after I leave. But I detest eating by myself, especially in happy, noisy restaurants full of dating couples and families with toddlers and waiters wishing people a happy birthday.

I considered my options.

I could go and pull Mother out of the bathroom and apologize and give in to her unreasonable demand to drive her down to Cape May for her mysterious appointment.

I could sit and wait for her to pull herself together so we could talk about this, the way that reasonable people do.

I could leave and ask the bartender to call her a cab, maybe slip him a twenty and ask him to pay the cabdriver. Then I could drive home and prepare to spend the rest of my life listening to my mother complain about that time I left her alone in a restaurant.

It wouldn't be so bad to indulge her, just this once, I told myself. *Just go in the bathroom and apologize. Take her to Cape May. Maybe you can get a nice meal and a spa treatment out of it. It can't possibly be as bad as you think it will.*

That's what my inner voice was saying, but I didn't listen because sometimes your inner voice is an idiot. I finished my coffee and paid the check and sat back in the booth and made a couple of moves in *Words With Friends*. Mother came out of the bathroom just as I was playing VICTOR on a triple-word score to take the lead.

"Are you ready to go?" she asked. "You didn't pay for dinner, did you?"

"I did indeed," I said.

"How much was it?"

"If I tell you, you'll try to give me cash for it, which I'm absolutely not going to take, and then we're going to just go round and round all over again. I am tired and I would like us to stop arguing and go home."

She slipped into the booth across from me. "I just want to say one thing before we go."

"I'm not in a hurry," I said. "Would you like some coffee or something?" I had won this round, but I didn't see the point in pressing my advantage further than that.

"It is getting late, and coffee is the last thing I need right now. I've had a little time to think about how I've behaved tonight, and I wanted to tell you that I'm not proud of myself."

"It's all right," I said. "Don't worry about it."

"I should have leveled with you right from the start. I've had a very distressing day, and I thought I could count on your sister to take me down for the funeral, and when she backed out on me, I didn't know what else to do."

"I'm sorry," I said. "The what?"

"The funeral. Friday morning, in Cape May."

My back stiffened against the booth. "What are you talking about? What funeral? Who died?"

"Nobody you know, of course, or I would have told you about it already. But that's why I need to go down there, is to go to the funeral."

"Um," I said. "Er. Um." I was frustrated by my sudden inability to master the basics of the English language. *I knew it*, I thought. *Every time she calls me, it means somebody's in the hospital, or somebody's dead.*

"Are you all right, sweetheart?" Mother asked.

"You could have told me that," I said.

"I should have," she said. "And I apologize. It's just that I remembered that you aren't really much of a funeral-goer. I thought it would be best not to bring the subject up over dinner."

"I do fine at funerals," I said. It came out sounding a little more tense than I wanted it to.

"I just thought you might not be comfortable with the idea right away."

"That happened one time. I was twelve."

"I know, dear," she said. "I remember it very clearly."

"Mother, is it so much to ask to be treated like an adult? Just one time?"

"Of course not, Wendy. I would be happy to oblige you."

"That would be nice," I said. I drank the last couple of drops of coffee in my cup.

"Well, here goes. I have a funeral to go to in Cape May on Friday morning, and it would help me if you could drive me down there Thursday night. Would you be available?"

It took a moment for me to realize what she was doing. This was manipulation under another name. This was giving me the illusion of a victory without the substance. And the worst part of it all was that it was working. I'd been waiting for my mother to treat me like an adult all my life, and now she was doing it, and now it was working against me. The problem with being treated like an adult, it turns out, is that then you have to act like an adult.

"Yes," I said. "I will drive you down there. I will go with

you to this funeral, for whoever it is, because it seems to be important to you. I can take a day off without too much trouble, and I wouldn't mind taking a nice drive down the Shore."

"Thank you," she said. "I appreciate it. I know this is difficult for you."

"It's fine," I said.

"I know this won't be fun for you," she said. "But when you get to be my age, half your social life revolves around going to funerals."

"Something to look forward to," I said. "Come on. Let's go."

We gathered our purses and jackets and made our way out to my car.

Chapter 4

The next morning was brutal. I got up at the time I always tell myself I am going to start getting up, but instead of exercising and eating a healthy breakfast, I grabbed a stale cinnamon roll and a bottle of water and headed to the office. I plowed through the two wills I needed to review and managed to gulp down two cups of coffee before my clients arrived.

My clients were perfectly nice people and it wasn't their fault that they had both inherited generation-skipping trusts with significant estate-tax implications. Three generations of lawyers had worked to conserve the capital tied up in those trusts, and the wills I had drafted were designed to pass that capital down to the next as-yet-unborn generation with minimal loss. Of course, when my clients did manage to add members of that next generation, the wills would have to be redrafted to address their existence, which would result in more billable hours for my firm. (Being an estate lawyer gives you a slightly skewed view of marriage and family relationships.)

The husband was one of the vacant, uninteresting old-money drones I had spent my dating life trying to avoid. His new wife was petite and graceful, with flawless tanned skin and raven hair—in other words, everything I am not. I inherited my mother's pale-blond hair and delicate bone structure, which would have been fine if I hadn't also inherited my father's imposing height. If I were a little thinner, I could get away with being willowy and elegant, but I'm not and I haven't been willing to do the exercise and starvation needed to make that happen. Additionally, some rogue gene gave me D-cup breasts, which are more of a hindrance than anything else. Women make nasty comments behind my back about plastic surgery, and they strain my back, and they attract the wrong kind of men on top of that.

Setting aside their obvious flaws, though, these particular clients were very nice people, and they were perfectly happy with the will, and they even managed to listen closely and nod in the right places when I explained the various clauses and their tax implications. It was a pleasant enough meeting, and it ended just in time for me to grab a quick sandwich at my desk. I was in the middle of rearranging my schedule so that I could take Friday off when my sister called.

"I just had to say thank you," Pacey said.

"You are just so incredibly welcome, dear sister," I said.

"Already with the sarcasm, I see. You must have had a fun evening talking to Mother."

"A fun evening, and a busy morning." I would have complained to Pacey about the press of my work responsibilities, but I knew she would respond by telling me about everything that she had to do every day in corralling two active toddlers.

"I know you wouldn't have wanted to take Mother to this funeral. I would have done it, you understand, but it is just simply impossible."

"It's not easy for me, either," I said. I had plans to spend my evening researching safe conversational topics for the drive down.

"I know, but I appreciate it like you would not believe. Benjy and Simon have been looking forward to this party for weeks. They ask me about it every ten minutes. I ought to drop them off at the U.N. sometime and let them do some negotiating." Pacey had a graduate degree in foreign policy and used to have a good job with the German consulate in New York. She married a Swiss diplomat named Henri, and they bought a home in rural New Jersey. When Pacey found out she was pregnant with twins, Henri left the diplomatic corps and got a job with one of the big Swiss banks. It was supposed to be a more stable job for him, but he ended up spending almost all his time shuttling back and forth to Geneva. That left Pacey alone at home, tending to two three-year-old boys, who were capable of bouncing off the walls even in good moods. I thought of them as Biter and Smiter, although I would never say that out loud where Pacey could hear me. Of course, I bribed the twins with Hershey's Miniatures every time I visited, so it was possible I was not seeing them at their best.

"Well, you go to your birthday party, and I'll go to my funeral, and we'll see who has the better time. Anyway, so just what exactly did she tell you about this funeral? Because she didn't tell me squat."

"She didn't tell me anything, either," Pacey said. "I don't even know the person's name, whoever it was. I got the impression it was somebody that she had known from high school or something, going back at least that far. Maybe it was a college roommate, but that's just a guess. All she would say is that it was nobody I knew."

"She said she would e-mail me the link to the obituary. I guess that would explain at least some of it. She also threatened to tell me the story about whoever-it-was on the way down, and I can't tell you how excited I am about that."

"I do feel bad about dumping Mother on you for a whole weekend. How did she talk you into that, anyway?" she asked.

"She cheated. She treated me like an adult."

"You fell for the reverse psychology bit? Wendy, you should know better."

"Says the child who never says no to anything Mother asks," I replied.

"I'm the middle child. I need the attention. Anyway, I can't imagine what it would be like to have Benjy and Simon in the car all the way to Cape May, and then get them dressed up for the funeral of somebody I'd never even heard of. God knows how they would react. You'd have one of them asking a million questions, and the other one would be screaming and crying, and then they'd change roles halfway through. No thank you. And they'd both want to see the body, of course, and there's no telling how they'll react to that."

"Is this conversation going where I think it might be going?" I asked. "Because I don't like the way I think this is going."

"All I am saying is that if you put any kid in an unusual situation that they're not prepared for, they're going to react in an unpredictable way. You probably know more about that than I do, of course."

"Quit it, Pacey. That was a long time ago, and it only happened once, and I can't believe you are teasing me about it."

"You have to admit," she said, "that it was memorable. Most people are touchy around dead bodies, but most people don't react the way you did."

"I ran screaming out of one funeral, one time, when I was twelve, and nobody in this family has ever let me live it down," I said. "It's not fair. You did all kinds of stuff when you were twelve that you got away with, and nobody ever holds it over your head. If it hadn't been Great-Granddaddy Borden's funeral, no one would even have noticed at the time." Over twenty-four hundred people showed up for that funeral, which goes to show you that there isn't a better way to ensure a big crowd at your funeral than to have an estate worth over a billion dollars.

"I noticed. Mother noticed. If I remember correctly, the *Philadelphia Inquirer* noticed. It's just a good thing YouTube hadn't been invented yet."

"I don't want to talk about this. I wouldn't have freaked, except he looked so different in that box, all dressed up. It gave me the creeps. But I'm a grown-up now. I will not run out of the church hyperventilating just because I see a dead body." Or I hoped not.

"Do you know if there are cameras in the church?" she asked. "Maybe a live feed? Because if there's any way to record it, maybe we can put you on YouTube after all."

"Pacey, you are my sister, and I love you, but there are times when I want to punch you in the face."

Pacey chuckled at that, an evil sound. "Enjoy your weekend."

The law office where I work used to be a model of diversity, which is one of the two reasons I enjoyed working there. (The other reason is that there is a movie theater in the same complex, and sometimes they let me mooch a bag of free popcorn.) When I started, there were two other female lawyers, and three female paralegals. The lawyer who recruited me cashed out and took early retirement right after her youngest kid got out of college. The other female lawyer got a job in Philly and I haven't seen her since. The two remaining partners laid off all the paralegals as a cost-cutting move last year. I am the only woman left in the office, except for the receptionist we share with a firm in another suite on the same floor. This is a roundabout way to explain that I have the women's bathroom all to myself now. It's one of the few perks.

I mention this to say that when I got the e-mail from my mother, I was in the bathroom, looking at my personal e-mail on my phone. (I have a rule about looking at personal e-mail or social media on my work computer, which I break about as often as anyone else.) All Mother sent me was a link to the obituary, from the website for the local Cape May paper.

I read the first paragraph, just to get the dead man's name and to figure out where the funeral actually was, and I skipped the rest of it. Nobody believes me when I say this, but it's the truth and I think it's a perfectly plausible thing that happened, and if I were a man and said I was in the bathroom when I read it, nobody would think twice because that's something people believe that men do all the time. This is what I read, all that I read:

> BERKMAN, SHELDON, 67, of Cape May, passed away on Monday, March 12. He was a native of Cherry Hill, the son of the late Aaron Berkman and Hannah Berkman. He retired to Cape May four years ago. He served for twenty years in the United States Air Force, retiring as a technical sergeant. He served at Elmendorf, Dyess, and McGuire Air Force Bases. After retirement from active duty, he worked as a machinist in the engineering division of PF Avionics in Lakehurst. Funeral services will be held at First Presbyterian Church, Cape May, on Friday morning, March 17, at 10:00 a.m. He is survived by a sister, Bernice, and a nephew.

I stopped reading there, which was a mistake, but I didn't know it at the time. I couldn't imagine the loosest possible connection between my liberal-activist mother and a career military man. My best guess was that Pacey had been right and they had known each other at Cherry Hill High School.

What I *thought* I did with the obituary was to forward the link to my work e-mail, so I could forward it to our managing partner with a note telling him I was taking off on Friday. What I *actually* did was hit the wrong icon and posted the link to the obituary to Facebook, but I didn't realize it at the time. I switched over to Pinterest to check out a pair of dark orange heels. A few minutes after that, I got up and went back to work and forgot all about Mother and Sheldon Berkman and the funeral.

It took me until about eight o'clock that night to finally clean out my in-box. I responded to everything except for a couple of e-mails from the cute LinkedIn guy from the day before. My guess was he was looking to share some hot investment tips, but that could wait until I got back from Cape May.

All I had left to do for tomorrow was one memo for one of the partners, and it wouldn't take me long to finish. That meant I could sneak out early on Thursday afternoon and take Friday off without causing anyone unnecessary agita. Dinner was a plate of takeout Thai red curry left over from Monday night, which I washed down with one of my less successful attempts at mixology. It was a horrible concoction of lemon vodka, Sprite, and melon liqueur that looked like antifreeze and probably wasn't any better for me than drinking actual antifreeze.

The only problem I would have would be if one of my clients died in the next day or so. I try not to think about death and dying, but it pervades a lot of what I do. My job is to make sure that my clients are prepared for their inevitable deaths, or at least as prepared as they can be. My goal is for the transfer of wealth and property from one generation to the next to be as pain-free as possible. Part of "pain-free" involves "tax-free," to the extent taxes can be avoided. This irritates my mother no end, which makes it one of the other few perks of my job.

I can't do anything to stop death. What I can do is help package it—wrap it in legal language and forms, so my client can put the reality of death up on a top shelf and leave it there until the time comes. I tell myself I'm here to help the living, not bury the dead. It helps me put distance between what I do and what is waiting for all of us at the end of our lives.

I didn't know what had happened to Sheldon Berkman, Air Force veteran, retired aviation machinist, and native son of the Garden State. All I knew was he was dead and I wasn't and (after another swig or two of antifreeze cocktail) I was happy about that. I figured if he were in a closed casket and his surviving relatives weren't the type to buttonhole total strangers and ask them for tax advice at a funeral, we would get along just fine.

Chapter 5

I slept very well that night, and didn't have one nightmare about dead bodies coming to life and climbing out of their coffins and chasing me down the street. I know, intellectually, that dead bodies can't do anything to harm anyone, but I packed a silver cross in my suitcase to wear to the funeral anyway, because there's no reason not to be prepared. I had no evidence one way or another that silver crosses worked to stop the reanimated corpses of aviation mechanics, but it just might work and you never know. I got everything else I thought I needed into the suitcase and bumped it down the stairs and into the modest trunk of my Audi. I wanted to be able to get down to Cape May early enough to get dinner and a couple of drinks and prepare for the ordeal that Friday promised to be.

I had a five-minute commute, which enabled me to coordinate the demands of a high-powered legal practice with my incipient drinking problem. Admittedly, sometimes it's a fifteen-minute commute, depending on how long the line is at Starbucks on any given morning. But I never had any problems with getting in early and staying late and racking up enough billable hours to do my share to help keep the firm afloat. I had a headache, and maybe was dehydrated, but enough coffee would take care of both of those things.

I was about halfway through my memo—a truly fascinating bit of legal arcana involving a creative attempt to undermine a prenuptial agreement—when Tim Curlin stuck his head in my door. "I need to see you for a moment, Wendy," he said. "In my office."

"Of course," I said, because that is what you say to the senior partner of your firm when you are a lowly associate trying to make partner, and he is in charge of compensation and bonuses. I grabbed a legal pad and a pen and followed him to his office.

Curlin was one of those bald guys with a strong build and

a quiet voice. Like all the partners, he had one of the window offices, with a panoramic view of the Watchung Mountains outside the city. His office was decorated with baseball paraphernalia, none of which meant anything to me. "Please have a seat," he said. "If you don't mind, close the door behind you."

I did mind, but didn't say so. Curlin was acting very polite and solicitous, which is not the way that he treated associates. It was, however, the way he treated attorneys who were on the other side of an important negotiation. That was not an encouraging thought. I tried to hold my legal pad in an assertive way.

"Can I get you anything?" he asked. "Coffee?"

"I'm fine, sir. What did you need me for?"

"Ms. Jarrett, I shouldn't have to explain to you just how much this firm prizes its reputation for discretion."

"Of course not, sir," I said. I tried to suppress the panic I was feeling. Was this about the Underwood contract? I'd screwed the pooch on that one, sure enough, but that had been over a year ago. I'd fixed the problem with the *inter vivos* transfer in the Cooper estate plan, and I thought I'd been yelled at enough for that screw-up as it was.

"This applies equally to our professional pursuits as well as our personal lives. Both must be above reproach at all times."

That meant it wasn't work-related, which was helpful but didn't give me any clue as to what he was talking about. My personal life, such as it was, was technically "above reproach," but that was mostly because I was too broke to lead the life of debauchery I aspired to.

What was going on?

"What you do with your time is your business," Curlin said. "Unless it impacts the business of this firm, or our clients, or their interests. Then it becomes my business."

"I am not aware of any problems along those lines, sir," I said. "Certainly not recently." I couldn't think of much in my past that would worry Curlin at this point. Were those photos I'd let that adjunct professor at Drexel take of me when I was an undergrad at Temple out on the Internet? Or had someone told him the story of that continuing legal education conference in Bermuda two years ago?

"I am not aware of any problems along those lines, either," he said. "All I know for certain is that our receptionist has taken twelve phone calls from various media outlets this morning, all of them either asking to speak to you or for information about you. The majority, I am told, have come from Gawker Media."

That should have been reassuring. It was not. It was one thing to have to address something that I had done at some point. I was confident I hadn't done anything quite so awful as to attract media attention of any sort, much less from Gawker. That made their sudden inexplicable interest in me a total mystery. I don't like mysteries. They make me itch. I tried my best to look comfortable, but all I wanted to do was to run into my office and slam the door and not come out until I understood what was going on.

"There must be some mistake then," I said. "I can't imagine any reason that anybody at Gawker Media would have the least bit of interest in me." Well, I could *imagine* a reason or two, but nothing that bore any relation to reality. I am a boring person and I have a dull life and I didn't like the way this conversation was going.

"I have no interest in having this firm's good name dragged through the online scandal sheets," Curlin said. "I hope you share that concern."

"I share that concern fervently," I said.

"Then we agree. You were planning on taking a long weekend, if I remember correctly?"

"Nothing exciting, I'm afraid. I have to drive my mom to Cape May tonight for a funeral tomorrow morning," I said.

"Is there anything urgent that you're working on today?"

"I was trying to draft that memo you wanted about that case in Kentucky and how it related to the Massey pre-nup."

"Nothing urgent, then. That's fine. You are, from this moment, on unofficial paid administrative leave. This will last until Monday morning, or whenever you are able to straighten this situation out, whichever comes first. Anyone who calls will be told that you aren't available."

I did not like the way that any of that sounded.

"Is this going to impact my bonus situation?" I asked. The firm always announced bonuses for associates in early April.

"I certainly hope not," Curlin said. "Think of this as a test. If you manage to figure out what in the name of General Washington is going on, and defuse the situation, there's no reason why your compensation package should be affected at all. If you don't manage to do that, well, we'll discuss that next month. Understood?"

"Yes, sir. I'll do my best." Since I still didn't know *what* was going on, I couldn't make any promises about what I could do or couldn't do.

"So it's settled. Turn off your computer and make tracks out of here. I hope to see you on Monday."

"Thank you, sir."

I was not one hundred percent certain how I got out of Curlin's office and over to the parking garage to get in my car and back home again. I know I was hyperventilating at least part of the way down the elevator. I am not normally subject to tremors, so I must not have had any trouble driving, except for maybe a stray scream or two.

I tossed my purse and my keys on the table and dashed into the kitchen. I needed a cold drink and I had a half-empty bottle of lemon vodka chilling in the freezer. The other option was an unopened bottle of acai berry juice, purchased a couple of months ago as part of a health and wellness regimen that hadn't been quite as regimented as maybe it should have been. I decided to pour a big glass of the acai berry juice with just the littlest tiniest drop or two of vodka, for balance. It tasted foul, and I got a big blue splash of acai berry stain on my silk blouse. I gulped it down anyway, and then poured a glass of ice water as a chaser.

When I was breathing normally and not talking to myself, I sat down at my computer and clicked on my browser. I took a quick glance at my personal e-mail account first, and recoiled when it reported that I had seventy-seven unread e-mails. That was not a good sign. That was a very bad sign. I took a two-week vacation on a cruise ship last summer and hadn't come back to seventy-seven unread e-mails. Reading them all seemed like a lot of work to handle all at once. I opened up a new tab and pulled up Facebook, on the theory that social networking might provide the facts I was looking for in a digestible format.

I found that I had eighty new friend requests and twenty-eight new messages. The number of notifications looked more like an area code for a rural part of the country.

This is not good, I told myself. *This is all kinds of not good. Something I did, somehow, went viral, and I can't control it.*

Find the facts. That was my mantra at work. *Find the facts.* Once you had the facts, you could figure out what to do with them.

Not good not good not good.

Find the facts. Something has happened. You don't know what it is.

Start with your last Facebook post. That should give you a clue.

That sounded reasonable enough. I didn't remember what I had posted last on Facebook—likely a check-in at some bar or other—but I couldn't imagine that anyone cared about it. Still, it made sense to check. I ignored the part of my mind that was busy panicking and clicked on my name.

About fifty or so of my closest friends and acquaintances had put a link in my Facebook timeline to a story in a blog called *Curtains,* which was a morbid offshoot of the Gawker Media empire. The story was entitled, "Get the Hankies Out: This Obituary Is the Most Maudlin Thing Ever."

This is about Sheldon Berkman, I thought. *Has to be. I don't know anyone else who's died this week.* But that didn't make sense. Sheldon Berkman didn't appear to be the least bit interesting. His obituary had been so boring that I hadn't bothered to finish it.

Maybe that was a mistake.

I clicked on the link from the Gawker article and read the obituary all the way through, for the first time:

BERKMAN, SHELDON, 67, of Cape May, passed away on Monday, March 12. He was a native of Cherry Hill, the son of the late Aaron Berkman and Hannah Berkman. He retired to Cape May four years ago. He served for twenty years in the United States Air Force, retiring as a technical sergeant. He served at Elmendorf, Dyess, and McGuire Air Force Bases. After retirement from active duty, he worked as a machinist in the engineering division of PF Avionics in Lakehurst. Funeral services will be held at First Presbyterian Church, Cape May, on Friday morning, March 17, at 10:00 a.m. He is survived by a sister, Bernice, and a nephew. He was a resident of the Victorian Cottages active senior residence, which will hold a reception in his honor following the service.

Throughout his life, he expressed his love and devotion for Emily Thornhill, his one true love. Although she left him and married another, he held on to his undying love and respect for her, refusing all other romantic entreaties. He kept a picture of her on his wall, and talked often to his friends and relatives of just how much her love had meant to him. Although his life was lonely and sometimes sad, the memory of his beloved carried him through his many trials.

Sheldon often said that he would love Emily until he died, and it was his one wish that his dear Emily attend his funeral after he passed away. "I know that she doesn't love me as I love her," he once said. "That has been a sad and painful part of my life. I only hope that when I pass on from this vale of tears, that she will remember me and want to come to my funeral, to honor the love that we once felt for each other, so long ago."

In lieu of flowers, the family requests that

donations be sent to the American Society for Model Aircraft.

Maybe I should have screamed. Maybe I should have cried. But all I did when I finished reading poor Sheldon's final message was laugh—a high, desperate cackle that was part relief and part manic ecstasy. *Oh, Sheldon*, I thought. Poor, sad, deluded Sheldon, whose biggest mistake in life, so far as I could tell, was to fall in love with my mother.

Chapter 6

The *Curtains* article wasn't much more than a recap of the obituary, with a bit of snarky commentary about wanting to give poor sad Sheldon a big hug and a bowl of tomato soup, were it not for the inconvenient fact of his recent demise. The problem was in the comments section. Compared to the deep, swirling pit of semisolid waste that is the comments section of most Internet sites, it wasn't all that bad. It would have been unobjectionable if it hadn't been about me.

One person had asked the obvious question about who Emily Thornhill was, and that led to questions about whether she was still around, and if it could be ascertained as to whether she would attend the funeral. Mother had kept her maiden name, and she'd had a long career with the Camden County Democratic apparatus, so it wasn't that hard to find her basic information on Google. Someone had cross-referenced her name against my name (Gwendolyn Gail Jarrett, "Wendy" unless you want me to hurt you) and had come up with Grandfather Thornhill's obituary from seven years ago from the *Inquirer*. If the research had ended there, it wouldn't have been a problem, but someone had posted links to my LinkedIn and Facebook profiles in the comments. That made it easy for whoever-it-was at Gawker to come up with the bright idea of calling me at work and endangering my future employment.

The rest of the comments were a series of cutting and snarky insults about my personal life and romantic prospects. People who waste their lives commenting on websites are about as sharp as a sack of marbles.

I spent the next hour or so wading through my e-mail and Facebook in-boxes, which mostly involved deleting crap from people I didn't know and telling the people I did know to mind their own business. I got halfway through before I gave it up as a bad job. The one positive I saw was that there didn't seem to be any inquiries from legitimate media outlets, which—as I devoutly hoped—meant that there likely wouldn't be any TV cameras at the funeral. The other good news was that it didn't look as though anyone had thought to contact my brother or my sister about the story. Greg was too busy to care, anyway, and Pacey didn't use social media for anything except posting pictures of her twins and whatever thing they had destroyed most recently.

I wondered for a moment if any enterprising soul at Gawker Media or one of its competitors had thought to contact Mother directly, and then said a brief prayer on behalf of anyone who would be so foolish as to try.

I spent the better part of the afternoon wading through social media sludge as best I could until I determined that there wasn't anything I needed to do but wait for the entire mess to blow over. I took a hot shower, put on comfortable clothes, and tried as best I could to steel myself for the long car ride down to Cape May.

"You did bring a nice dress?" my mother asked.

We were stuck in traffic on a bumpy two-lane highway leading south out of Princeton. I was driving with the top up against the late-March chill. It would be a long ride, and I wasn't in a big hurry to hear the long and sad story about how my mother had stepped on Sheldon Berkman's black little heart. I was in even less of a mood to hear her carp about my shortcomings, fashion-related or otherwise.

"I have an adequate wardrobe for funerals," I said.

"I imagine that you do. Is that what you would call an occupational hazard?"

"Not at all. I want my clients to live long, productive lives, so they can change their wills every other year or so and I can bill them for it."

"I see," she said. "Dead clients pay no bills."

"Ideally, they don't pay taxes, either."

"Don't remind me, dear. All I wanted was to make sure that you didn't wear that dress you wore to your cousin Alicia's wedding."

That had been a black chiffon number with a deep neckline and a bow placed strategically to keep it decent. I will admit that it was form-fitting, but I was dressing to impress my date. Rodrigo was the assistant director of the Argentinian mission to the U.N. and was the heir to a large mining fortune. He had long, flowing black hair, an exquisite accent, and soft, supple hands. He tried to show me the basic steps of the tango, and after the reception, I showed him some moves of my own. It was a very romantic evening, and a very romantic morning after that, and it all would have worked out perfectly if he hadn't turned out to be a sexist cretin who didn't think that women should be allowed to practice law.

"I have a very nice, conservative outfit," I told my mother. "It's a very dark charcoal suit. Perfect for funerals."

"Let's hope we just have one, then."

"That would not be my preferred way to spend the weekend, no."

"I never thought about this," she said, "but you didn't have any other weekend plans, did you? I do hope I'm not impeding your social schedule."

This was her way of asking me if I was dating anyone. I figured I would get static from her on this topic during the trip, but I had at least hoped that she would have waited until we were on the other side of Trenton.

"Why do we have to do this?" I asked. "Why can't we have a conversation like nice, normal people?"

"Several reasons. I want to know certain things about your life that, for some reason, you are determined not to tell me about. Asking questions is a good way of finding this information out."

The car ahead of me finally made the left turn it had been signaling for the last half mile, and I hit the accelerator. "You could just wait for me to tell you."

"And die of curiosity? No, thank you," she said.

"I thought we had this whole discussion just the other day, about how I was a grown-up now and you were going to start treating me like one."

"Part of being a grown-up is engaging in grown-up activities, which includes romantic relationships. I am just inquiring as to your progress in that area. It's not a criticism, sweetheart."

"It is too a criticism," I said. "You're not asking me about my career, or my accomplishments, or my goals. You're asking if I'm seeing anybody, and if I am going to get married anytime soon. And I refuse to be lectured to on the primacy of bourgeois values by the co-chairperson of the Bryn Mawr Social Justice Forum, Class of 1967."

"The Sixties were *not* a revolt against bourgeois values. Unless you count war, racism, and sexism as bourgeois values."

"I was thinking more about short hair and personal hygiene." I couldn't let Mother push my buttons without pushing some of hers right back, and revisionist Sixties history was a huge issue for her.

"I will not sit here and let you call me a hippie. You weren't there and you didn't know and I took showers frequently. Anyway, most of us did end up getting married and settling down, you know, even the hippies."

"I have a very good job. I am self-supporting. My romantic life"—*or serious lack thereof*, I added silently—"is my own personal business. If and when I get engaged, I will let you know."

"A very feminist outlook," she said. "I congratulate you. I just would appreciate the occasional update, you know, as an interested party."

"There's not much to say."

The last guy I had anything to do with was named Clyde Witherspoon. I had met him in a bar on New Year's Eve, and neither of us had anyone to kiss. Clyde was an accountant who worked on the south side of the courthouse square in Morristown. He was pleasant enough, and lonely enough to be nice to me. He spent the night at my place after one too many vodka tonics on a snowy Saturday night in late January. We were supposed to go to a cabin in the Poconos over Valentine's Day weekend. But right before, he snuck off to what he said was a Super Bowl party over in Wayne but turned out to be a drunken romp with a naked Hooters girl.

So Clyde dumped me, *right before Valentine's Day,* and took the Hooters girl (whose name was Hyllton, hand to

God) to the adorable little cabin in the Poconos that we'd picked out together. He not only had the gall to take a picture of them together, standing on the balcony of said adorable little cabin, but the complete lack of common sense to post said picture on Facebook without paying any attention to the privacy settings.

I was proud of my reaction. I didn't complain. I didn't drown myself in alcohol, or at least not any more than usual. I didn't draft up a fake insurance claim form showing that Clyde had received medical treatment for an STD and e-mail it to Hyllton the Hooters slut. I just waited until he made an appearance at the Starbucks that we both frequented. Then I ordered a venti iced vanilla latte and poured it down his back. Slowly. Then I walked two blocks to the Dunkin' Donuts, got a large box of Munchkins, and took them back to my office and ate them all, one by one.

That was not, shall we say, a typical dating episode for me, but it wasn't something I cared to chat about with my mother on a leisurely drive to a funeral.

"I could help you, you know," she said. "Maybe not so much in Morristown. If you'd at least consider moving back to Cherry Hill, it would be much easier."

"I am not moving back to South Jersey. That's non-negotiable," I said.

"What about Washington? I still know a lot of people on the Hill. It wouldn't be that hard for you to find a good job somewhere. There might be a pay cut, of course."

"Not today, not tomorrow, not ever." It was bad enough that my mother wanted to run my romantic life without her running my career as well.

"I am trying to be helpful, dear. But I don't know what it is that you *want*."

"I want a husband, Mom. Don't get me wrong about that. But I want the relationship to happen... I don't know what the word is. Organically, if that makes sense. I want it to be something that happens because it was supposed to happen, not because it was something that you or anyone else made happen. I'm looking for something natural, something spontaneous. A relationship that happens because it's meant to happen, not because somebody did something to make it happen."

"Darling," she said, "I love you dearly, but that is the stupidest thing I have ever heard."

"I'm really not interested in your opinion on my dating strategy."

"Strategy is the key word. Or lack thereof, in your case. If you just latch on to the first man you come across, you might find yourself making a serious mistake."

We'd come to the end of the rural highway, and I pulled the car onto I-295 for the long haul south. "Do tell," I said.

"I was wondering when you were going to ask. It was the fall of 1962, and I was a junior in prep school."

Chapter 7

The first time I saw Sheldon Berkman was at a swim meet at Cherry Hill High, in the fall of 1962. He and your Uncle Frank were both seniors; they were on the swim team together. I was a junior, but I wasn't enrolled in Cherry Hill High that year. Mother caught me smoking a Lucky Strike under the bleachers of the football stadium, and she had me transferred to a girls' prep school in Philadelphia. The express intent was to give me a better education, but it ended up putting me in the company of some very wicked young ladies with depraved thoughts, at least by the standards of the times. Not that any of us got to act on most of those depraved thoughts, which was quite frustrating.

I didn't want to go to this swim meet, but Mother was determined to have a nice family outing, so I went. There I was, stuck in this loud, wet building that stank of chlorine, watching doughy, pasty boys going back and forth in the pool, and not one of them worth thinking any depraved thoughts about. Frank was on the relay team, which was the last event of the meet, so I had to stay through the bitter end.

And that's where I saw Sheldon Berkman for the first time. He wasn't tall, and he wasn't all that good-looking, and you could tell he would be bald before he was thirty, but he wasn't like any of the other boys there. Most of them had these strong, ropy muscles from football or baseball. Not Sheldon. He was a swimmer, and he had a swimmer's build. You watch the Olympics, so you know what I'm talking about. Powerful shoulders. Trim build, not an ounce of fat anywhere. His chest was this V-shape that just tapered right down into his trunks. And they wore very tight trunks in those days. Not the repulsive things they wear now, but they still didn't leave much to the imagination.

And I imagined. I had such an imagination in those days. Of course, your generation doesn't have to imagine anything anymore, but that's what we had to work with and it was quite enjoyable, for a while, anyway.

Sheldon noticed me too. But he didn't have the nerve to ask me out himself, so he used Frank as a go-between. Frank made the mistake of telling me about it, and of course, I said yes. So the next weekend I was home, we went out. Sheldon had this decrepit old Chrysler, and he took me to the Cherry Hill Mall to see *Mutiny on the Bounty*. We sat there in that darkened theater, and the whole time we were there, listening to Marlon Brando's phony English accent, he never tried one time to put his hand on me. It was terribly disappointing. I think he was nervous dating a prep-school girl; either that, or he didn't have a lot of experience around girls of any sort. Or Frank put the fear of God into him. I never did find out, not that it mattered.

We went on a couple of dates after that, and never moved past holding hands, so I decided to take action. The next time I was home was over Thanksgiving. My best friend at prep school was named Deanna Ellis—now, she was a hippie, that one. She went to Berkeley and ended up in a commune in Oregon. Anyway, I told her how frustrating the whole thing was getting to be with Sheldon. Her parents lived in Merion Township, and they had this huge house, very secluded. Her parents were taking the family to Hilton Head for Thanksgiving. She gave me the directions and a spare key.

So, the day after Thanksgiving, I told Sheldon that I wanted to go out for pizza. I talked him into driving over into Philly to a dive on Broad Street. We had a couple of slices and a Coke, and it was all very innocent and boring. We walked out of the pizza place, and I kissed him, and he kissed me back, which is what I wanted, of course, because that let me steal his car keys right out of his pocket. I told you, the girls I went to school with were not a good lot, and that's a skill I'd picked up. I got in the driver's seat. Sheldon's car was a lot like he was—not particularly attractive, but very powerful under the hood, if you know what I mean. Anyway, he got in the car. He didn't ask any questions, not even when I didn't head back to New Jersey right away. We had a nice, quiet drive, all the way to Lower Merion.

I didn't say anything when we got there. I just got out of

the car and tossed him his keys back. Then I unlocked the front door and checked to make sure that the house was empty—no maids or anything, I mean. I didn't one time think about what would happen if he drove away, because I knew he wouldn't. I was never a swimsuit model or anything like that, but I had a tight skirt and a good figure and there wasn't any way that Sheldon Berkman wasn't following me into that house.

He didn't keep me waiting long. I heard him slam the passenger door shut, and then I saw him walk up the steps and shut the front door behind him.

"Nice house," he said.

"It's my friend's. She says nice things about the couch in the rec room." In fact, the couch in the rec room had been a big factor in Sandra's parents sending her to an all-girls' school, but I didn't feel the need to explain that at the moment. I wasn't feeling anything but a weightless anticipation.

"Is that a fact," he said.

"It folds out into a bed. Come on, let me show you."

"Stop it," I said. "Just stop it. Now. Please. I am begging you."

"Please don't tell me you're going to get all prudish on me, Wendy. That's not like you."

"This is making me extremely uncomfortable," I said. "I mean, for God's sake, Mother, I don't need the play-by-play, that's all. I get it. You let Sheldon Berkman get in your pants over Thanksgiving weekend in 1962. Stipulated. That doesn't explain why you're dragging me down to Cape May for his funeral fifty years later."

"If you want an explanation, then let me finish the story."

"Finish the story, by all means," I said. "I just don't want to hear the sordid details."

"The sordid details make the story interesting."

I knew my mother had a sexual past, obviously. I knew Sheldon had been in love with her. On an intellectual level, I could understand that they'd had a physical relationship. But all I could hear in my head was *squick squick squick squick squick*. "Mother. Please. Just give it a rest. For the love of God."

She sighed one of those signature Emily Thornhill sighs, this one signaling exasperation with a thin overlay of parental affection. "All right then. Where was I?"

That should have been the end of it, as far as I was concerned. I didn't think that the relationship would go anywhere. Sheldon wasn't my idea of long-term boyfriend material, never mind husband material. And the worst part of it was that he wasn't discreet. He bragged to his friends about it, and of course that got back to my brother, and he popped Sheldon in the eye. I hoped it was worth it for him.

My parents were out of their minds over the whole thing, of course. It wasn't anything personal towards Sheldon, you understand. They were just being horrible old-money snobs about the whole thing, just because Sheldon's father owned a janitorial services company. They thought Grandfather Borden would disapprove. Of course, he disapproved of everything, so I don't know why they bothered. Anyway, it didn't matter. My parents told me I couldn't see him again. They thought that would solve the problem, but of course it just made Sheldon that much more attractive to me. Forbidden fruit, you understand.

Today, you would sit your children down and talk with them and explain to them why you didn't approve of who they were dating, the way we did when you wanted to take that smarmy Carruthers boy to your prom. Keep your eyes on the road, dear.

Of course, that would never happen in my generation, because it would have been awkward. So my parents decided to drag us all down to Daytona Beach over Christmas break. The idea was that I was supposed to find another boy to drool over and forget about Sheldon. It didn't work, of course. I spent the whole time writing love letters to Sheldon. I have no idea if he got them, but I hope he did, because they were steaming hot.

So my parents took things to the next level. They told me

they were sending me to a finishing school in Montreal to learn French. I locked myself in my room and cried for three days. When I came out, they told me that they'd had a change of heart, and I could keep going to school in Philadelphia, but I had to promise not to see Sheldon again. I said yes, of course, but I kept seeing Sheldon behind their backs anyway.

Of course, nothing good ever lasts. Sheldon graduated from high school and got a job at the soup factory in Camden. I spent the summer in Europe and went back to prep school, looking for someone who was better husband material. Our relationship had collapsed naturally, without hurting anybody.

I turned eighteen in October of 1963. My parents threw me a surprise party at our house. They'd hired caterers, of course, and it just so happened that the caterer was a friend of Sheldon's parents, and he let Sheldon work as one of the servers. And in the middle of the party, as bold as you please, Sheldon managed to sneak us both into a closet, and he told me his plan.

He explained that since I was eighteen now, it was legal for us to get married. His caterer friend owned a vacation house in Cape May, and knew a minister at one of the churches down there. Sheldon had talked to the minister, and he had agreed to marry us, if we could make it down there. Sheldon's plan was that we would leave the party, drive straight down to Cape May, get married as quick as we could, and have a honeymoon at the vacation house.

I remember standing there in that closet, listening as he told me how much he loved me, and how much he wanted us to spend the rest of our lives together. I never knew that I loved Sheldon. I liked him, of course, and even though I know you don't want to hear about the sex, it was fantastic. I had told him I loved him a hundred times, but I had never really felt passion for him before. But it was the first time I had ever felt anything that deeply, that completely. I told him I would run away with him, and it felt right. It felt perfect. We left the party and drove down to Cape May. We sent our parents a postcard so they wouldn't worry.

"So why didn't you go through with it?" I asked.

"Oh, but we did."

"You are kidding," I said.

"Oh, no."

"In the last thirty years," I said, "I have never once been told that you were married before. It's absolutely unbelievable that you are telling me this now, after not saying a single word about it before."

"It wasn't any of your business before, and anyway, it all happened long before you were born. And if you had asked me, I would have told you."

I felt as though a large chunk of my past had suddenly come loose, the way that cargo comes loose in an airplane hold and crashes through the bulkheads and causes a crash. I had to calm myself down and concentrate on my driving. If I didn't know a basic fact like my mother having been married before, what else didn't I know?

"Please at least tell me you didn't have kids," I said. "I mean, I don't have any older half brothers or sisters out there, do I?" The thought made me feel strange and disoriented, like I had suddenly realized that I had a third arm that I hadn't noticed before.

"No, and thank goodness for that. Pregnancy would have made things much more difficult, and things were already difficult enough. Mother and Father turned up the same day they got the postcard in the mail. They were furious, but once Sheldon showed them the wedding license, there wasn't anything they could do after that."

"Grandmother Borden must have been angry enough to roast you over a slow fire," I said. The entire Borden family was known for its longevity and its irritability, which meant that it produced a remarkable proportion of miserable old bats. Grandmother Borden had been a typical example; she'd had her final stroke while screaming at a Puerto Rican aide at her nursing home because she hadn't made the bed with hospital corners.

"Well, I'm sure she would have liked to. Fortunately, Father got her calmed down by the time that we came back, and she just found other ways to take her revenge out on me. But they put a brave face on it; they had to. So we went back to Cherry Hill, and my parents even threw us a reception. It was paltry compared to the bash that they threw when your Aunt Paula got married, but I didn't care."

"I want to make sure I understand this. What I have been told, my entire life, is that you and Dad met in college."

"Did your father tell you that?"

"Yes."

"He told you lots of things, sweetheart, but not all of them were true. That one was only half true. Yes, he was at Penn when I was at Bryn Mawr, but I never once gave him a second look. His face was spotty, and his hair was greasy, and he was dating this obnoxious twit who ended up married to an even more obnoxious twit who is now a federal circuit court judge—a Reagan appointee, of course. I didn't date your father until years later, after college, after we'd both had a chance to grow up a little."

"I want to make sure I understand what you're telling me. This man, Sheldon Berkman, whose funeral we're going to, he was your ex-husband, and you never once told me or anyone else about him until just now."

"You never asked, dear."

"I read the obituary you sent. It said he had been pining for you all these years. I thought he was still hung up on his high school sweetheart. But he wasn't, was he? He really was rejected by the one true love of his life."

Mother threw back her head and laughed. It was a truly appalling sound, a cross between a cackle and the last ding-dong of doom echoing against the last worthless rock. "Good Lord above, Wendy," she said, when she finally came up for air. "You're not seriously telling me you *believed* everything in that obituary, are you?"

Chapter 8

I pulled the car over at the service station on the Atlantic City Expressway, ostensibly to get coffee and gas but mostly to give myself a break from listening to my mother. My mother, who had until now been perfectly willing to let me think that she hadn't ever been married to anybody other than my father.

I tried hard to remember what I'd been told about how my parents had started dating. I knew it had something to do with the McGovern campaign, but the details were hazy. They'd gotten married in 1974, ten years before I was born. I never once suspected that there had been someone else for either of them.

They hadn't lied to me, exactly. They just hadn't told me everything. And I couldn't blame them. If I ever have children, I won't tell them one thing about any of the guys I have dated. Hearing the story of my mother and Sheldon Berkman was incredibly weird, though, like wearing someone else's eyeglasses, or waking up in the wrong apartment wearing somebody else's T-shirt. Not that I have done that last part. At least not recently.

It did explain why Mother wanted to go to Sheldon's funeral, unless it didn't. She'd been married to Sheldon, at least briefly. He'd won her, at least for a while, and lost her, and wanted her back. If he hadn't been lying about it, of course. But that just explained why he wanted her there. It didn't explain why she felt she had to be there—or why she felt she had to shanghai me into driving down here with her.

As horrible as it sounds, I was absurdly relieved that Sheldon had died. As awkward as it was going to be to go to his funeral, I couldn't imagine how awkward it would be to meet him in person. It was the one positive aspect, I thought, that had come from the whole experience, although it couldn't have seemed that way to poor Sheldon, of course.

There was more to the story, and I knew I would hear the rest of it. We were still an hour away from Cape May, and I had the choice of either listening to her tell the story of how their marriage fell apart or having her quiz me more about my love life. I knew which I preferred.

I pulled the car back onto the expressway. I'd decided on espresso and a biscotti to fortify myself against the rigors of the final leg of the drive. I took a sip of hot coffee and initiated the next section of the conversation. "So what was it about the obituary that was a big lie?" I asked.

"The bit about refusing all romantic entreaties, dear, for one thing."

"Oh, no," I said. "He didn't cheat on you, did he? The rat."

"Not at first. We were too busy at first—I was still in school, and he had a job. We hardly had time to see each other, and what time we did have, we didn't waste. The problem was that he needed to get an education, but he didn't know what he wanted to do. He said he wanted to get an engineering degree, but he didn't have the math aptitude for it."

"You could have had your grandfather get him a job, though, right?"

I glanced over at her as I said this, and she looked mildly embarrassed. "Your great-grandfather was a rich and powerful man, and rich and powerful men, in that era, were paternalistic like you would not believe. Your great-grandfather could have given him a job, of course. But he decided that a couple of years in uniform would be just what Sheldon needed—to toughen him up. So he convinced Sheldon that the best way for him to start his career was to enlist in the Air Force. The idea was that Sheldon would be assigned to McGuire Air Force Base after he got out of basic training, so as to be close to both our parents."

"Who thought that was a good idea?" I asked.

"Grandfather Borden did, and Sheldon's parents did, and my parents did," she said, not bothering to hide the acid in her voice. "I thought it was a stupid plan, and I said so, and nobody listened to me. But I wasn't the one holding the purse strings. So Sheldon went to basic training in San

Antonio, and I stayed behind and finished up my last semester of prep school. They let me fly down to Texas for his graduation—it was like a second honeymoon, almost. I thought we were going to go back to New Jersey and be happy together, but we reckoned without the whimsical ways of the United States Air Force. Instead of sending him to McGuire, like we thought they would, the bastards sent him to Elmendorf.”

“I saw that in the obituary, but I didn't look up where it was.”

“Elmendorf is in Alaska, dear. Just outside Anchorage. Cold, lonely, and far away.”

I tried to picture Mother in snowshoes and a parka, and wasn't coming up with anything. Then I tried picturing me following someone to Alaska, and I started shivering. “So what did you do?” I asked. “You didn't just go with him, did you?”

“Of course not. I was not about to leave my family, and ruin any opportunity I had to get an education, just to live in on-base housing in the Arctic. It was simply unreasonable, and I told Sheldon so. He understood. It was a tough situation, he said, but as long as we loved each other, we could work it out.”

“But it didn't work out,” I said. I knew, from the obituary, that there had not been a happy ending, at least not for poor Sheldon. I hadn't thought at the time that the relationship had been sad for Mother, although obviously it must have been.

“I wanted it to,” she said. “I did. But I wanted an education more. I hated to do it, but I went to your great-grandfather and asked him to pull some strings. He made a couple of phone calls and managed to get me into Bryn Mawr. I worked hard and studied and wrote Sheldon a letter every day. I thought I was being wholesome and virtuous for my husband, who was, after all, serving our country in a lonely, faraway outpost.”

“That sounds very noble of you.”

”I do not need your sarcasm, young lady. I thought I was being noble. It turns out, as it so often does, that what I thought was nobility was actually foolishness. It turned out that Elmendorf, although a far-away outpost, was not as lonely as it appeared. Sheldon, the rat, wasn't there three weeks before he started cheating on me. And it wasn't three months before he filed for divorce. No letter, no explanation, no anything, just divorce papers that an Air Force lawyer drew up for him." The bitterness in her voice had an edge to it that fifty years hadn't dulled.

"You are kidding," I said. I didn't have a worse breakup story than that one, and I'd been dumped by more guys than Taylor Swift and Adele put together. I felt real sympathy for my mother for the first time in years. "I hope you made him pay for that."

"I did, quite literally. I sent them back, unsigned, postage due. In a box with two cinder blocks."

"Nicely done."

"I wrote on them, with spray paint. One of them said ROT, and the other one was supposed to say IN HELL, but it got a little runny. Still. It got the point across to the little bum."

"What did he do?"

"I got a letter back from him a week later. He tried to tell me, if you can believe it, that it was a mistake. He said he'd asked for the lawyer to put the paperwork together, but the lawyer went ahead and sent it to me accidentally. As if I would believe anything that foolish. He admitted he was having an affair, and he said that he wanted a divorce—he just hadn't meant to tell me that abruptly and heartlessly."

"Who was the girl?" I asked.

"Oh, I never bothered to find out. It didn't seem worth it. The issue wasn't even the girl, whoever she was. Sheldon thought that my family was keeping me away from him—which was totally irrational; there was no way I was ever going to Alaska with him or anyone else. And he thought that once he left the Air Force, my family would be running his life forever."

"Well, when you put it that way, it makes sense."

"If he had been able to get a decent education and a decent job, we could have made our own way and thumbed our noses at our families. It didn't work out that way. I've always regretted that. It would have been nice to have that independence."

I decided not to comment on this particular point, having gotten through undergrad at Temple as a recipient of the Arthur S. Borden Endowed Scholarship. Independence is nice and all, but dependence has its good points, too.

"Don't get me wrong," she said. "I love your father; still do, despite everything. I am glad we had the chance to be together and have a family together. I just wonder, sometimes, how things would have been if I had stayed with Sheldon. He must have thought that, too, when he was drafting that wretched obituary. To think that we were both thinking that, at the same time, but neither of us acted on it. And now it's too late."

"I'm sorry, Mom," I said, and I meant it.

"Is that the exit for the Parkway up there?" she asked.

"Yes," I said.

"I don't know why you didn't take the Parkway the whole way."

"Less traffic coming down 295, now that the construction has worked itself out. Not as many toll booths, either."

"How much farther?"

"We'll be there in twenty minutes. Just in time for dinner."

"That's fine," she said.

We rode in silence all the way to the last exit, which led to the little peninsula of Cape May. A chill March wind was blowing in off the Delaware Bay. Most of the bed-and-breakfast places were still closed down for the season. We'd gotten two rooms in a touristy beach hotel, which I was surprised to find came attached to a respectable-sized liquor store.

"I see you looking at the inventory," Mother said. "Don't think that I don't."

"It's an unusual setup," I said, because it would have been impolite to explain just how much I needed something cold and sweet and alcoholic just then. It had been a long, emotionally draining day and if there was a better cure than a cocktail, I could not imagine what it might be.

"It is convenient. But it can wait until after the funeral. We're going to walk in and out of that church like Kennedy widows, if you know what I mean. Dry-eyed and stoic and stone-cold sober."

"So, does that mean no wine with dinner?" I asked.

"I don't think," she said, "that we need to do anything quite so radical."

Chapter 9

We had a quiet dinner in the hotel's restaurant and went straight to our respective rooms for the evening. I hadn't brought a big bag, but I still took my time unpacking. I got all my makeup out and lined it up in a row on the bathroom counter. I shook the wrinkles out of my suit and hung it up so it would be ready to go in the morning. I set the alarm on the little clock-radio, and set an alarm on my phone, and called downstairs for a wake-up call. I knew that I would never hear the end of criticism from my mother if I made her late for the funeral, especially if it was because I had been up too late the night before.

I wasn't planning on getting drunk. I'd had a glass of chardonnay with dinner, and it had tasted wonderful, and all I wanted was one more tiny little drop. I didn't need alcohol to help me sleep, or that's what I told myself to keep me from feeling that I had a problem and needed help. Of course, they don't sell chardonnay by the drop, but it wasn't my fault.

I waited until I was reasonably sure that Mother had gone to sleep—she was in the adjoining room—and walked softly down the corridor to the elevator. I would get a small glass of wine, sip it carefully, and head straight to bed. That was my plan, and it was a good one. Except that they say that the best-laid plans of mice and men often go awry, and they say that no plan survives first contact with the enemy, and they say these things for a reason.

The woman sliding onto the barstool next to me had jet-black hair, which she wore in chopped-off bangs. She had a silver skull-and-crossbones pendant on her necklace, which didn't do anything for her dead-white skin. She was wearing a black, shapeless jacket over a tight black T-shirt. I ignored her, and I thought I was doing a good job of it.

"Well, hello there," she said.

I looked up.

"Hi," I said. I am normally a friendly drinker when I'm in a bar, but all I wanted to do just then was finish the last yummy dregs of my wineglass and head back to bed.

"You don't recognize me, do you," she said.

"I'm sorry," I said.

She looked doubtful for a moment. "Just checking—you are Wendy Jarrett, right? From Temple?"

Take away the Goth necklace and the glossy black fingernail polish, add a little weight and a Villanova hoodie, and she could have been maybe familiar, maybe someone I'd seen in a bar once. Or in a lot of bars.

"It's the hair, isn't it," she said. "You'd recognize me if I were wearing my natural color."

I took a close look at her face, and imagined it wreathed in loose red ringlets. "You're not Vanessa Sullivan, are you?"

"The same," she said.

"You used to drink Long Island iced teas," I said.

"Well, that hasn't changed, at least."

I drank the last bit of my wine and signaled the bartender, who was sulking in the corner of the bar, playing *Peggle* on his phone. "Two Long Island iced teas," I ordered.

"Much obliged," she said. "It's been a thirsty day. So what else do you remember?"

"You used to date Bad Boy Tommy Killebrew," I said.

"That name," she said. "Oh, my God, you said that name. Of all the men I dated in college, you had to bring up Bad Boy Tommy Killebrew."

"You asked me what I remembered, and I only remembered it because you dated him more than once. You must have seen something in him that nobody else did." My experience of dating Bad Boy Tommy Killebrew was limited to fending off some overly aggressive groping in the alley behind a Race Street bar.

"You know what he's doing now? You'll never guess."

"He's either in jail, or he's an orthodontist in New Rochelle," I said.

"He's doing drug and alcohol counseling."

The bartender dropped off the Long Island iced teas. "Unbelievable," I said, as I took my first sip.

"He's doing drug and alcohol counseling for Eric Clapton's rehab center in Antigua."

"Seriously?"

"And he's married to a Japanese ex-porn star," Vanessa said. "Before you start booking a flight down there to visit, I mean."

"Perish the thought," I said, although just saying that didn't, in fact, stop me from thinking about Bad Boy Tommy Killebrew, shirtless on a Caribbean beach. "So what are you up to?" I asked, in a desperate attempt to change the subject.

"Freelancing," she said.

I knew I'd put my foot in it. The one question that people of my generation learn not to ask each other is where they're working, because so many of us aren't working, or at least not doing anything important. "I hope that's turning out well for you," I said, and I meant it.

"It's kind of dodgy right at the moment," she said.

"Sorry about that."

"Oh, don't be. You seem to be doing very well, though."

"I scrape by," I said, taking a long sip of my drink.

"You do better than that," Vanessa said. "You have a nice job doing estate planning for a mid-sized law firm in North Jersey. You have a downtown condo and a red convertible. You're single and unattached, and you spent a week last November at a luxury resort in the Dominican Republic. You're part of one of the five richest families in Philadelphia, with a good-sized trust fund that vests when you turn thirty-five. And tomorrow, you and your mother are going to get up early and go to the funeral of one Sheldon Berkman."

I put my glass down on the bar, resisting the impulse to see how well it would fit jammed into Vanessa's eye socket. "I could never make up my mind whether you were just a bitch, or a whore pretending to be a bitch. Now I know."

"Oh, that's a great comeback," she said. "I am going to have to write that one down. Do you mind if I use it? I can think of *so* many people that statement applies to."

"The trust fund thing is bullshit, anyway. My older brother had his fund vest, and he said that he had to pay out almost all of it in taxes."

"That must be a nice problem to have. Next you're going to tell me how much your student loans are. Can't be that much worse than mine."

"If you came all this way to work out your class resentment issues, you wasted your trip," I said.

"You mean you still haven't figured it out?" she said. "I thought you were smarter than that, dearie."

"The only thing that makes sense is that you're freelancing for Gawker, in which case, go to hell. You've already caused me enough agita."

Vanessa drained the last of her Long Island iced tea. "This is what happened," she said. "Hand to God."

"Which God?"

"Another good comeback. I am totally writing that one down. All right, look. When I got out of school, I got a job with the *Inquirer* writing obituaries. I got to be good at it. I was an assistant editor when I got downsized. And don't tell me how sorry you are about that, because it could happen to you tomorrow, and I would not shed one solitary tear for you."

I wasn't about to explain how close she'd come to putting my own job in jeopardy. "There's a market for freelance obituaries?" I asked. "No wonder you're bumming drinks off near-strangers in bars."

Vanessa snorted. "Don't you condescend to me. And no, there isn't. I've been spending the last four years copy editing the worst crap imaginable. Software manuals. Sales brochures. God-awful self-published vampire erotica novels."

"Poor you."

"So a couple of years ago, because I was bored, I started this Tumblr account where I linked to interesting or unusual obituaries. A mutual friend saw your Facebook post and sent me the link to the late Mr. Berkman's obit, and I did a squib about it on Kinja, which is the freelance portal that Gawker Media uses. It got promoted on *Curtains,* which is all I expected to happen. Somehow, it got cross-posted to the main Gawker site, which gets an insane amount of traffic, and then it went viral from there."

"So you started this," I said. "You're the one who helped

this go viral. You're the one who blew up my in-box. What are you going to do for an encore, steal my car?"

"Why do you assume this is about you? I had no idea you were involved, not until the commenters brought up your Facebook page. It was a coincidence I even knew you, sweetie. If this has inconvenienced you a trifle, well, I wish I could say I was sorry, but I can't. This is my big break. For the last five years, I've been working my heart out for a chance to be noticed by somebody. If it can't be a respectable print publication, at least it's Gawker, and they get a ton of eyeballs. And they're willing to pay me to write up the next phase of the story."

"What next phase of the story? *There's no story.*"

"You know that's not true. Tomorrow is the funeral. Will the mystery woman show up to pay her respects? The entire Gawker Media readership is curious. I'm going to be the one to tell them, and you're going to help me."

I took a short, quick sip of my drink, just for the pleasure of slamming the glass down on the bar. "In your dreams, Vanessa. If you think I am going to help you with your little scheme, then you're more pathetic than I remember you being, and I remember you were dating Herman Howard at one point."

"Howard Herman."

"Same difference. He was a little creep, and it sounds like he's rubbed off on you."

"Just hear me out, before you say anything you can't take back," she said.

"I have nothing to say. This is a small, quiet family funeral. There's no way in this world that you can get a story anybody will want to read out of this. It's not a romance, and it's not a mystery, it's just a dead guy and the people that he used to know."

"That's what you think, is it?"

"If there's anything interesting, you aren't going to find it out from me."

Vanessa folded her hands together and cracked her knuckles. It was a horrible sound in the quiet bar. "You think you have it all figured out, don't you," she said. "Your mother is not exactly the most popular person in the world, you know. And neither are you."

"You can make all the empty threats you want, Vanessa. My mother won't do an interview with you. I am sure the hell not going to. You've got no leverage."

"Then why are you sitting here talking to me?"

"Good point. Good night. Nice seeing you. Say hi to Bad Boy Tommy Killebrew for me." I slid off the barstool and headed for the door.

"I don't want you to do anything," she said.

"Then you won't be disappointed."

"You don't understand. All I want is one picture of your mom walking into the church. Maybe one of her walking out, if that's a better picture, depending on the angle. It's a very picturesque church, so it'll be hard to take a bad picture, really."

"So you're a wannabe paparazzi, too. Good luck with that."

"All I want you to do is to not make my life more difficult. Don't sneak your mother in or out of the church. Don't have her put her hands in front of her face, or wear a veil. Don't warn her that I'm going to be there. Just keep your mouth shut about me, and I'll keep my mouth shut about her."

"I'm leaving."

"You don't have to decide now. Just think about it. All I want is one good picture."

All I wanted was for Vanessa to develop a horrible, painful, flesh-eating virus, but that's not something you can say out loud without sounding hateful. I stalked my way out of the bar and up to my room, where I fell into bed like a dead thing.

Chapter 10

I am not the kind of person who writes snarky reviews of bad hotels for websites, but the coffee machine in my room produced the worst Goddamned coffee I had ever tasted in my whole entire life. I shouldn't call it coffee, even. It was coffee-flavored sludge. Having said that, it was hot and fortified with caffeine and I was in no position to complain. I forced just enough of it down to make continued existence look attractive, and then ran a hot shower to facilitate blood flow to get the caffeine moving through my system. I got dressed and squeezed into my shiniest and least-comfortable pair of black heels. I was just starting the first layer of makeup when my mother started hammering on the connecting door to her room. I opened the door just a crack.

"Is there any chance that you're even close to being ready?" she said. "I ask purely for technical reasons."

"Almost done," I said. "And it's a good two hours until the funeral. No reason to rush just yet."

"Do I smell coffee?"

"If you want to stretch the definition to include it," I said. "It's ice-cold by now anyway."

"If you can't open the door and let me in, the absolute minimum you could do would be to get me a straw and stick it through the crack in the door and let me drink some coffee that way."

I opened the door and gave her my best early-morning glare, and then let her in. She perched on the edge of the one sorry chair in the room, and I got her a paper cup of the remnants of the horrible coffee. She made a face—anyone would have—and downed half the cup anyway. "Ye gods, that's foul. It's like a mouse gave birth and died in the coffee maker."

"We've got time," I said. "We can go to Wawa and get decent coffee beforehand. If you're close to being ready to go." I looked at her in the mirror as I applied lipstick. She had a nubbly black wool jacket on over her dress, and she looked diminished and sad against the wide lapels and the dark fabric.

"I feel awful. I couldn't sleep, and I left my Ambien at home. I need coffee more than I need oxygen."

"If you give me a minute to put my makeup on, I can go downstairs and scrounge you some." I was working on a variation of my normal workaday makeup palette, with more pink in the blush to make me look halfway animate, and a slightly paler shade of lipstick. The combination made me look young and innocent, which was nice enough, except that I was going for quiet and unobtrusive. *Close enough*, I figured.

"I don't know how Jackie and Ethel did it," Mother said. "They must have been tranquilized to the gills."

"If you're not feeling up to it, we can skip the funeral. Pay our respects at the gravesite later, or something." Not to mention that not showing up at the church would frustrate the hell out of Vanessa's little scheme.

"I have to go. I promised Sheldon I would."

"When did you do that?" I asked. "Like, right before he started cheating on you?"

"No. It was the last time I saw him. He came home, on leave. This must have been the summer of 1972, right around the time I was dating your father. The Air Force was getting ready to send Sheldon to their base at Da Nang to service bombers—this was right before Operation Linebacker, if that means anything to you. Sheldon had been in Alaska all through the war, up to that point, and the poor man was terrified of having to go to Vietnam."

"He thought he was about to die, and he wanted you to go to his funeral? That's not romantic."

"It wasn't, not at all. It was sad and desperate. But he'd come all the way to Washington to find me, and he looked so handsome in his uniform. So of course I said yes, and since I promised him, of course I'm going to keep my promise. It'll be a short service, and then I can come back and try and get some rest."

I felt a small tear welling up in the corner of my eye, and blotted it away before it could ruin my makeup. I pinned an onyx-and-silver brooch to the lapel of my suit. *Kennedy widows*, I told myself. If Mother wasn't going to show the emotion she felt for Sheldon at the funeral, I wasn't going to let the sadness and sympathy I felt show through, either. "I'm all set," I said. "Let's see whether that Wawa has decent coffee or not."

The church was a largish pile of light-colored stone on a quiet street lined with Victorian houses. Most Jersey Shore towns are hodgepodges of different architectural styles— Cape Cod cottages and high-rise condos and cheesy mid-century motels, all on the same block. Cape May had the tackier features of most Shore towns, like trashy surf shops and miniature golf courses, but all the Victorian gingerbread made it look more like a New England town than it had any right to.

I didn't take a good look at the houses, though, because I was trying to figure out where Vanessa was hiding. I figured she was staying in one of the bed-and-breakfasts across the street and watching the door of the church with a telephoto lens. Either that, or she was hiding in a parked car, getting ready to pop out for a close-up. If I had been smart, I realized, I would have followed her last night, so I would know where she was staying and what kind of car she was driving. All I could do now was try to figure out how to make sure Vanessa didn't get the shot she wanted. I didn't have a real strategy other than standing between Mother and where I thought Vanessa might be lurking.

"We can try to go in a back door," I said.

"Why would we do that?" Mother asked. "Besides, we have to meet the nephew out front."

"Whose nephew?"

"Sheldon's nephew. What's-his-name. Alan or Aaron or something."

"Just the one nephew?" I asked.

"I imagine so. He's the one that called and told me about Sheldon in the first place, otherwise I never would have known that he died. He sent me the link to the obituary that I sent you. I think he said that he was all the family Sheldon had left. It would be nice to not have to deal with a lot of family. God, I hope I'm the only ex-wife that shows up."

I hadn't thought about who else would be at the funeral. To the extent that I thought about it, I would have preferred to sit in a large anonymous crowd, or else a quiet service with just me and Mother and a minister and a couple of other silent mourners.

"So, what, he just saw your name in the obituary and figured out who you were and gave you a call?" I asked.

"The nephew is the executor of the will, and Sheldon had left him my contact information, as sad as that sounds."

"How do we know what he looks like?"

"He said he'd find us. Maybe that's him, over there."

He was tall. That was the first thing that I noticed. He was tall, and he was wearing a black suit. He had big, chunky shoulders and long, loose limbs, like a swimmer. His hair was jet-black with a short cut that made him look confident and calm. And he was walking towards us like that was where he wanted to be and I was who he wanted to be with.

"Ms. Thornhill?" he asked.

"Yes?" she asked.

"Hi," he said. "I'm Adam Lewis. We spoke on the phone. And I hope this is Wendy."

He shook my mother's hand delicately, but when he took my hand his grip was strong and warm. "Hi," I said, or at least that's what I think I said. I was trying to take in all the details—the crispness of the knot in his charcoal tie, the chiseled features of his face, and the friendly tone of his voice as he said my name. "Wendy," he'd said. *Wendy Wendy Wendy Wendy Wendy. He knows my name. The cute guy knows my name.*

"I'm so glad you both could make it."

"Our pleasure," Mother said.

"I especially wanted to talk to you, Wendy. I wasn't sure if you were coming or not, but I'm so glad to see that you did."

"Oh," I said.

Here is a cute guy, I thought, *obviously smart and*

articulate, showing interest in you specifically, and you can't say anything more intelligent than the barest monosyllable. Shape up, girl.

"Yeah," he said. "I had sent you an e-mail on LinkedIn, but you hadn't responded, and I wasn't sure if you'd read it or not. We can talk afterwards, if you have a few minutes."

"Sure," I said. "I'd be happy to talk about whatever." I congratulated myself for managing to get a full sentence out of my fool mouth. *This is the cute guy from LinkedIn*, I thought. *The financial advisor from Freehold.* He had looked cute enough on LinkedIn, and he was looking much cuter in person.

"We have a few minutes, as it turns out," he said. "Since the other mourners aren't here yet."

"Well," Mother said. "If you young people don't mind, I'm going to go inside and sign the guestbook. Excuse me." She turned and climbed up the stairs into the church. Or at least that's what I infer that she did, because I was not paying her the least bit of attention. If I had been, I would have done something different than what I did, which was to keep standing there and gawping at the cute guy who was showing an interest in me.

"Who is that?" he asked. He was pointing behind me, across the street. I turned to check it out, and there was Vanessa, struggling to force her way through an ornamental hedge. She was carrying a large camera with a telephoto lens and had an unmistakable look of triumph on her face.

"Excuse me," I said. "I'll be right back." I made my way across the street as best I could, slowed slightly by my impending sense of failure and my uncomfortable shoes.

Vanessa was brushing leaves off her clothes. "That was a great shot," she said. "Fabulous. I thought you were going to help her up the stairs and block my angle, but you just stood there on the sidewalk. And here I thought we were going to have to go to the mattresses."

"Leave," I said. "Now." I was having trouble with anything longer than one-syllable words just then.

"You're looking kind of red, sweetie. Have you had your blood pressure checked?"

"Go!"

"I mean, you have health insurance, right? What's that like?"

I am sure that I was red in the face. If Vanessa had taken my picture just then, there might have been steam coming out of my ears. I was living every stupid, tired cliché there was about being angry. I tried to keep my voice level and sane. "I have a funeral to go to," I said. "Leave me and my mother alone."

"Of course, sweetheart. Go. Enjoy your funeral. And thanks so much for all the help. Your mom looked fabulous."

"I'm serious."

"So am I. Love the black on her, especially with the hat. It doesn't look quite so good on you, though. Maybe you need brighter makeup or something. I can send you an e-mail with some tips, if you like."

"Vanessa, for God's sake. Don't make me hurt you."

"So who is that nice boy you were talking to? He's *cute*. Is he single? Employed? Can you get me his phone number?"

I walked back across the street. Adam was waiting for me on the sidewalk.

"You didn't just hit that woman, did you?"

"Oh, no." Stepping on someone's instep as hard as you can doesn't quite count as hitting them, even if you are wearing high heels.

"Because it looked like she just collapsed, or something."

"I think she's disoriented," I said. "She'll be fine. Look, she's dusting herself off."

"If you say so," he said. "You should go inside and find your mom, and make sure you get a good seat. The buses will be here in a minute or two."

"Buses?" I asked.

WREATHED

Chapter 11

The senior housing community where Sheldon Berkman had spent his last days had sent two buses full of old people to the funeral, and they were late. Adam the cute nephew stayed outside to make sure that the other mourners got there safely, and I went inside to check on Mother. She was making a study of the stained-glass windows, which I'm sure were well done and artistic in their way but not something that I would spend two seconds looking at under normal circumstances.

"What exactly were you two doing out there?" she asked.

"Nothing special," I lied. "Some more people are coming, but they were delayed."

"It's not as though he's in a hurry, I don't suppose. He's not even here—well, the body isn't here. Cremated, you know."

"Oh. Where is he?" I asked, trying to disguise my relief at not having to be in the same room with a dead embalmed body. Not that I have a problem with that.

"I don't know. The nephew said they were shipping the urn to Alaska; they were going to have a bush pilot scatter his ashes over Mount McKinley."

"That sounds reasonable," I said. It was one less thing to worry about, anyway.

We took our seats in the second row of the church. I would rather have sat in the back, but Adam the cute nephew had reserved seats for us, and it would have been rude to sit elsewhere, or so I was told. The bused-in mourners were just starting to file in as we sat down, so I took advantage of the opportunity and pulled up the LinkedIn app on my phone. Sure enough, I had three messages waiting from Adam, all of them asking if I was coming and if I had a minute or two after the funeral to discuss the will.

I was oddly relieved by Adam's apparent interest in my legal acumen. As cute as he was, I didn't quite think I was comfortable with him explicitly hitting on me at his uncle's funeral. Afterward, though, maybe over a nice tasty bottle of chardonnay, that would be acceptable.

I flipped over to his LinkedIn profile, and scrolled all the way down to check out the important information. *Marital Status: Single*. I did a discreet little fist-pump, and ignored the withering look I got from Mother. *Birthday* was eight months before mine, which was nice. *Job Experience* looked stable enough. *Education* wasn't too shabby, either. He had a B.A. from Syracuse in economics, and an M.B.A. in finance from Maryland. Not Ivy League, but I wasn't in a position to be picky about such things, and anyway, every Ivy League guy I ever dated was either too full of himself to be decent boyfriend material or had an awful hidden perversion like wanting me to do their laundry or stay home to raise their children. *Interests* including restoring old houses, which meant that maybe I could invite him over to unstick my sticky pantry door...

"Ow!" I said.

"Put that thing away," Mother said. "They're about to start."

"You could have just said, without poking me with your elbow."

"Remember. *Kennedy widows*."

I silenced my phone and put it in my handbag. Maybe Jackie Kennedy didn't spend the funeral procession glancing at her iPhone, but that was mostly because they didn't have them then. Anyway. I stiffened my posture and tried to look as serene and dignified as I could.

And then Adam the cute nephew sat down next to me.

The service was blessedly short. There were a couple of hymns, and a couple of prayers, and a long, painful delay when an old guy with a walker came clomping down the aisle so he could read the Twenty-Third Psalm. During the last prayer, the minister asked us to hold hands, and Adam the cute nephew took mine again. I would be lying if I said I felt electricity in his touch, but then I would be lying if I said I didn't feel anything at all. It wasn't so much an electrical connection as the feeling that you get when a key fits in a lock and turns and all the tumblers move at once. It felt right to hold his hand, and it felt wrong to let go.

Mother kept up her Kennedyesque sangfroid all through the funeral, sitting there placidly, not reacting to anything. When the last prayer was over, she picked up her handbag and made her way to the side door of the church. I shot an apologetic glance back at Adam, one that I hoped said *Sorry, gotta go, duty calls*, and started to take off after her.

"Wait," he whispered.

"Can't."

"Here," he said, and handed me a folded piece of paper. "If you have time."

I stuck the paper in the side pocket of my purse and hurried after Mother, who was already halfway out the door. I managed a coquettish wave as I left.

"I can't do this," Mother said. She had her hand on the passenger door of my car, which was locked, because I was fumbling in my purse to find the clicker.

"Give me a second," I said. "We'll be out of here in no time."

"You don't understand. I can't just get in the car and ride away, not right this second. I need a moment."

"Are you OK?" I asked. "Do you think you're going to be sick?"

"I'll be fine," she said. "I just need a little time. Maybe we could walk for a while."

"Down towards the beach?" I asked. "Maybe some salt air would help."

Mother didn't say anything, so I knew something was wrong. You couldn't normally say something as facile as salt air being a cure for sickness without her mocking you for it. We walked the two blocks towards the ocean together, slowly, her because of the burden of sadness and regret that she carried, and me because my black heels were starting to rub blisters on my big toes.

We found an empty bench along the ocean promenade

and sat down. The March wind was blowing stiff and cold from behind us. We sat there quietly for what seemed like a long time. Mother had her hands folded in her lap, looking little different than she had during the service. Two or three dedicated joggers passed by, but otherwise the promenade and the beach and the whole of Delaware Bay were ours alone.

I wanted to comfort her, or at least help her somehow, but I didn't know what to do except to give her time and space. If there was an explosion coming—and I'd seen her explode often enough to have a wary idea of when one was coming—I didn't want to be the one to set it off. Then again, it was almost as likely that her fragile composure would just collapse into a soggy heap.

At length, she got a tissue out of her bag and started to dry her eyes. "Do you think the bars are open yet?" she asked.

"It'll be a little while yet. But the liquor store should be open."

"I need a drink. I need twelve, but let's not get ahead of ourselves. You don't have a flask, do you?"

"Sorry," I said.

"Just as well. I don't want to worry any more about your drinking than I already do."

I rolled my eyes at that, but I guessed that her criticizing me was a sign that she was feeling better. I rubbed my hands together, trying to keep warm.

"Sorry, sweetheart," she said. "I don't want to give you a hard time. And I am grateful that you came with me. It would have been very difficult, otherwise."

"You're welcome," I said, as a pair of joggers swept by.

"I love you. You know that, don't you?"

"I do, Mom. I love you, too."

"I love you, but you are young and I am old. And I got a reminder today just how old I am. No thanks to Sheldon, the little wretch. It was a mean thing for him to do, to die here. Cruel. And to schedule his funeral for the church where we were married, to drag me down here, to dig up so many memories. It's sadistic, almost."

"Oh." I hadn't realized it was the same church. "But some of them were good memories, though, weren't they? Maybe he wanted you to remember the good memories and forget the bad ones."

"You don't understand," she said.

"Maybe I don't."

"You don't understand because you're young. Your good memories are all ahead of you. You don't have anything bad to look back on, and everything good to look forward to."

"I'm not going to argue with you, Mother. Are you feeling any better?"

"I am feeling a little better, but not well enough. What I feel is *old*. Old and miserable and useless."

"You're not useless," I said. "And there's no need to beat yourself up this way. I can understand you being sad, or depressed, or angry, but you don't have any reason to do that." *And you don't need to take whatever it is that you're feeling out on me*, I didn't say.

"I have the best reason of all," she said. *"It is the blight man was born for / It is Margaret you mourn for."*

"I'm sorry, who?" It sounded like poetry, whatever it was, but I couldn't place it.

She sighed deeply, which I interpreted as *all that expensive education, gone to waste*. "It's not important. Whoever she was, she was young, like you, and she'd never come face to face with her own mortality. It's a burden, and today it's a little heavier than most days."

"It's the nature of funerals. I see it all the time when people come in to the office to sign their wills. They think, psychologically, that signing their wills means that they're going to die. Which they are, anyway."

"Mortality isn't about death. It's more important than that. Physical death comes to us all, yes. But it's different when you lose somebody you were passionate about, even if it was fifty years ago, even if it turned out badly. You get to experience that deep, heartfelt passion just a few times in your life. When you're in its grasp, when it's taking you out to sea, wild and uncontrolled, it's like doing something incredibly fast and incredibly thrilling and incredibly dangerous, all at the same time. That's what being alive truly is. You can't know your own mortality until you have that feeling, and lose it, and understand that you'll never get it back. Mortality is a terrible thing, Wendy. A terrible, terrible thing."

I put my arm around her and we sat like that on the bench for a long moment. I didn't look at her face, because I knew she didn't want me to see her cry, and I didn't want her to look at me and see me tearing up, either. We watched the wind ruffle the ocean, the breakers rolling in on the beach, and the occasional dog walker or fitness enthusiast passing by. The March wind was no crueler than the rest of the world.

At length, Mother took a long, ragged breath. "I've been sitting too long," she said. "I need to get up and walk. Alone, if you don't mind. You could wait here if you like, or go find a cup of coffee if you'd rather."

"I'll wait here," I said. "Let me know when you're ready to go back to the car."

I waited until she was a decent distance away before I dug Adam's note out of my purse. It read:

The Victorian Cottages
An Active Adult Community
Memorial Luncheon in honor of our Neighbor
SHELDON BERKMAN
1:30 pm, Friday
All Are Welcome

Chapter 12

I was late getting to Sheldon's senior apartment complex, but I figured that since everyone from there was so late getting to the funeral nobody would mind if I was late for lunch. It took me longer than I thought to convince Mother to get back in the car, but once I did, it was easy enough to drop her at the hotel. I suppose I could have worked harder to convince Mother to go with me to the reception, but she said that she would be happy with a room-service sandwich and a quart of gin, and I took her at her word.

Under normal circumstances, I would have developed a game plan—worked out ahead of time what I would wear and what to say. But there wasn't time for that, and this was the day of his uncle's funeral and he probably was depressed about that. "Playing it cool" and "letting him come to you" are not my usual style, but this wasn't a usual type of situation and, anyway, he would gravitate towards me because I would be the only person his age there.

They had started the lunch on time but I was just ten minutes late and there were mounds of food in the communal dining area. After a fairly stressful morning, my body was screaming out for calories, so I got a plate full of homemade pierogi and meatballs and fruit salad. I saw Adam at the center of one of the long tables in the room, surrounded by a crowd of old bats who were plying him with noodle kugel and sympathy. I sent him what I desperately hoped was a sultry nod, and his face lit up, just for a second, before he realized that he wouldn't be able to ditch his well-wishers right away. I took my plate to one of the smaller round tables over by the side, figuring he would come over and join me when he could.

I had not so much as eaten one delicious Central European dumpling before three incredibly old, wrinkly men sat down next to me. "So you're Emily's daughter," one of them said. They all had giant mugs of coffee that read *Victorian Cottages of Cape May.*

"I'm sorry," I said. "We haven't met."

"I'm Ed," he replied. Ed was bald with thick glasses and a thick sprouting of ear hair. He had been the one to read the Psalm at the funeral. "This is Hans and Paulie."

Hans had a mat of thick iron-gray hair and a sweater that looked as though it had walked off the set of *The Cosby Show* and was currently trying to swallow him whole. Paulie was short and thin, with an alarmingly large nose and a lime-green T-shirt with an unprintable pun about beaches.

"We were at the funeral. You probably didn't see us because we were in the back," Paulie said.

"I suppose not," I said. "My name's Wendy. I was up front with my mother."

"Wendy," Hans said. "That's a nice name. You know Peter Pan?"

I shot Hans a withering glance, which I hoped was Emily Thornhill–quality, or close enough. It shut him up, which was all I was after.

"Hans thinks he's a comedian," Paulie said.

"That was her, right?" Ed asked. "That was Emily? Sheldon's Emily? Sitting up front with you?"

"That was my mother, yes, and her name is Emily, and she used to be married to Sheldon, fifty years ago."

"Fifty years ago," Paulie said, "I was in Puerto Rico on shore leave. Aboard the USS *Sea Owl*. That's a submarine, you know, or it was before they scrapped it. It was left over from World War Two."

"Just like you," Hans said.

"Who, me? I was just a kid back then. Wet behind the ears."

"He's only telling you about his submarine," Hans said, "because it was long and hard and full of seamen."

"Stop it, both of you," Ed said. "We're being rude to our guest. Let me apologize for these two. They got old, but they never matured, if you know what I mean."

"It's all right," I said. "So, you were Sheldon's friends? What was he like? I never met him."

"He was an obsessive," Paulie said, as he took a big slurp of coffee. "Big-time."

"He was a model-airplane guy," Hans said. "That's all he liked doing. Ruined his eyesight, just about. But he knew his shit. He could tell you about every turbine and every strut on every plane the Air Force had, and drive you crazy doing it."

"That, and talking about your mom," Ed said. "He loved her, very much. Still did, after all those years. Sheldon talked about her all the time, so it's kind of like we know her, too."

"He talked about her way too much, if you ask me," Paulie said. "I mean, they hadn't seen each other since the Nixon Administration. You think you'd give it up after a while. But not Sheldon."

Ed reached over and patted my knee, just enough to make it seem avuncular and not enough to make me want to swat him. "We don't want you to think he was unhappy all the time, because he wasn't. But there were days he was so miserable that you couldn't talk to him. And there were other days he was so miserable that he couldn't get out of bed, all because he was still sad and blue because he was still in love with your mom."

"You have to understand, though," I explained. "She never knew that. She thought he had gone on with his life, the same way she went on with her life after they divorced."

"Oh, we're not blaming your mom," Hans said.

"It was a nice thing she did, coming to the funeral," Paulie said. "Even though she didn't talk to anybody, or come to the wake. It was what Sheldon would have wanted, the big dummy. You make sure you tell her that, now."

"She knows," I said. "It was important for her to come."

"Well, we're spoiling your lunch," Ed said. "We just wanted you to tell your mom that we appreciated her coming, on behalf of Sheldon, and that he loved her, right up until the end."

"I will," I said, and they left me alone with a plate of cold Eastern European delicacies and a big lump in my throat. *Poor Sheldon.*

It did not take me long to notice that none of the women at the wake—and it was about eighty-percent women there, if not more—were interested in coming over and saying hello to me. Those that looked in my direction were giving me a fishy stare, if not the evil eye. God knows what Sheldon had been telling these women about my mother, but I would bet money it was different from what he'd been telling his male friends. For all I knew, he'd been leveraging his supposed romantic depression into getting nookie from every gray-haired biddy in sight, and more power to him if he had. Whatever the reason, they were making a point of ignoring me, while they were hovering around Adam like fruit flies on a Carmen Miranda headdress.

He didn't look like he was enjoying it all that much. He had more food piled in front of him than any reasonable person could ever hope to eat, and there was a large plate of pastry and brownies close at hand. I didn't have any place else to go, so I just sat and watched him nibble at his food for a while. He still had his dark suit on, but he'd loosened his tie, and it looked charming on him.

I eventually had the bright idea to get up and cross in front of him on my way to where the coffee urn was. I went with less coffee than I would normally drink and more creamer, because I didn't need the jitters and strong coffee is contraindicated with too much Eastern European dumplings. I took my time stirring and adding sugar, and sure enough, Adam came over before I was done.

"Sorry," he said. "I meant to come over earlier, but I had a hard time just convincing them that I was capable of pouring my own coffee."

"They're just trying to be nice," I said. Adam took his coffee black, which I thought was a very positive sign. Generally speaking, the more junk a man puts in his coffee, the fussier he is about other stuff. Guys who drink nutmeg and cardamom soy milk lattes are the same guys who will give you grief for having a Maroon Five CD in your car or not knowing what Pokémon are.

"The problem is that they're succeeding. How's your mom?"

"She's been better. Today was kind of hard for her."

"I can see that," he said. "It hasn't been easy for me, either, but I can see how it would be worse for her. Speaking of things that aren't easy, um, I wonder if I could ask you for a favor?"

"Sure," I said, trying to sound bright and animated. I guessed that he was going to use the opportunity to ask me for free legal advice, and hoped that he wasn't going to ask me to help him change the oil in his car.

"I have to finish cleaning out Uncle Sheldon's room before I go," he said.

"Oh."

"Don't worry. I'm not asking you to move boxes or anything like that."

"Oh. Good. Not that, you know, I have anything against moving boxes, you know. In principle. I'm just sort of overdressed at the moment. With the heels and everything." *Shut up, woman,* I told myself. *You're babbling again.*

"The apartments here are furnished, so there's no furniture to move, thankfully. I got all of the heavy stuff loaded last night. There are just a few personal things left—most of them are fragile. And there is something I think your mother might like to have."

I couldn't imagine what Sheldon might still have that my mother might want. My best guess was that she would want to forget that today ever happened. But it wouldn't hurt to check out whatever it was Adam wanted me to look at, and I wasn't going to turn down a chance to spend time with him.

"I'd be happy to help," I said.

"Thanks. If you'll excuse me, there's a whole bunch of little old ladies that will be real disappointed if they don't get another chance to give me indigestion. I'll meet you out by my U-Haul in ten minutes, if that's OK."

It wasn't the most romantic invitation I'd ever gotten in my life, but these days a girl can't afford to be that choosy. "See you there."

Chapter 13

If I hadn't known which apartment was Sheldon's by the U-Haul truck parked out front, I would have known it from the wreath on his door. It was a big heavy thing, with white roses and some other orange flowers that weren't roses. (I do not know the name of those flowers, because my parents spent a lot more time making sure I knew about the importance of the prime interest rate and the composition of the New Jersey delegation to Congress than they did the names of flowers.) The door was locked, which ruled out any solo snooping, not that I would ever do such a thing. I pulled a paper napkin out of my purse and wiped off part of the back bumper of the U-Haul, took a seat, and applied myself to *Candy Crush Saga*.

It only took Adam a couple more minutes to shed his well-wishers and make his way over to his uncle's room. I heard him open the driver's side door of the truck and I switched my phone off and went around to join him. He was taking off his jacket and I got a better look at his shoulders, which were solid enough that you could bounce a hubcap off them. I decided I was letting him carry all the heavy boxes.

Adam slipped his tie off and tossed it on the passenger's seat. "God, that feels so much better," he said. "It's the one thing I had in common with Uncle Sheldon. He hated ties, too. He always said the Air Force was the best employer in the world because they wouldn't make a man wear a tie if he didn't want to."

"Not a slave to fashion, I see."

"I tell my clients that there are lots of financial advisors out there that wear very nice silk ties that they bought with their clients' hard-earned money."

"Does that work?" I asked.

"Up until the point they see me drive away in my Jaguar." He rubbed the bridge of his nose with his knuckle. "God, that sounded pretentious, didn't it? Sorry. "

"Not at all," I said. "As long as you can afford it, you

should be able to drive whatever you want."

"Believe me, I'm not trying to impress you," he said. "I've had the car for ten years, and it was ten years old when I bought it. It's starting to rust, too."

"OK," I said, which is what I say when men start talking to me about cars. I like *my* car, because it is pretty and shiny and I picked it out myself, but I have rather less interest in anyone else's car, and if he had started talking about gear ratios or transmissions just then, I would have howled.

"But the real problem with the Jaguar is that you can't load very much in it. Hence the U-Haul. Shall we?" He beckoned towards the door with the wreath on it.

Adam had done a good job of cleaning out Sheldon's things, to the point that you couldn't tell that anyone had ever lived in his apartment. The only items of any personal value left were three or four large Air Force recruiting posters up on the wall, complete with heroic airmen looking up as though they were tracking the progress of enemy planes in flight.

"I haven't figured out how best to pack those," Adam said. "I suppose I ought to have them boxed up or something, but I didn't bring any boxes that size, and I don't want to drive all the way back up the Parkway to find ones that fit."

"Do you have any blankets?" I asked. "Wrap them up in those for the time being and they should protect the glass well enough."

"Gotcha," he said, and went back to rummage around in the truck. He emerged with wool Hudson Bay blankets, just like the ones I'd seen in Great-Grandfather Borden's mansion in Philadelphia. I guessed Sheldon had acquired them in Alaska. I helped Adam wrap up the frames and he carried them out and stowed them in the truck. Adam followed instructions beautifully. I like that in a man.

"Is there anything else you need help with?" I asked.

"I have some glassware to pack in the kitchen, but that'll just take a minute," Adam replied. "While I'm doing that, the stuff for your mother is in the bedroom—just poke around, you'll find it."

All that was left in the bedroom was a bed, a nightstand, and an IKEA bookcase on the far wall. (If you are an IKEA fan, it was, one of the larger EXPEDIT units, with square bays.) The bed had plain dark-blue sheets and another one of those Hudson's Bay blankets. The sheets looked clean and the bed was made, as though Sheldon had just left overnight and expected that he would be coming back.

There weren't any books in the bookcase, which was a disappointment. I am not a huge snoop but when you go to someone's house, the fastest way to tell what kind of person they are is to look at the titles of the books they have bought. Instead, the bookcases were full of model airplanes. A couple of them were sleek fighter jets, but most of them were huge ungainly things with multiple engines. The old guys at the luncheon had been right; Sheldon had been obsessive about model planes. Except for a matte-black stealth bomber on the top shelf, they were all painted with incredibly small and detailed designs. A white FedEx box sat on top of the bookshelf, which I guessed held more planes that Adam was shipping somewhere else.

Some of the planes had pictures of women prominently displayed. I checked them carefully to see if one of them sported my mother's name, but none of them did. Could Sheldon have left one of the planes for Mother as a memento? It would not have been anything I would have chosen to give her, but then I had spent my childhood listening to lectures from her about the military-industrial complex. I was looking at a particularly detailed bomber plane when Adam came into the bedroom.

"They're nice, aren't they?" he said. "You can tell he spent a lot of time on them. His favorite was the B-52 you're looking at."

"I guess everyone needs a hobby," I said. Mine is thinking up ideas for disgusting cocktails and then drinking them, but I didn't feel the need to tell Adam that at the moment.

"Did you find the letters? They're in the drawer on the nightstand. I cleared out everything else, but I left them there just in case you or your mom wanted them."

"No, I hadn't." I am not that much of a snoop.

He motioned towards the nightstand (a black HEMNES piece). "Check it out."

I sat down on the edge of the bed and opened the drawer. I found eight or so yellowing letters, wrapped in a bit of old Christmas ribbon. I glanced at the first. It was dated December 28, 1962. I recognized Mother's angular handwriting.

"She told me about these," I said. "She wrote them after they started... dating, when her parents took her to Florida for Christmas vacation."

I glanced at the top letter. *I love you*, she had written. *I ache for you, for the feel of your tender hands in delicate places. I want to wrap myself up in your strong arms and once again...* well, it went on from there. I felt that same squicky feeling I had felt on the drive down. You're just not supposed to think about your mother having those kinds of thoughts and feelings, even though it's the only reason any of us are ever born.

Paper that old should be crinkly and stiff, I thought, but this wasn't. These letters had been folded and unfolded, read and reread. I had no idea how many times Sheldon had picked up each of these letters, taking the time to underline every single one of the passages that read "I love you" in red ink.

"I just glanced at them, you know," Adam said. "They are kind of... I guess *passionate* is the right word."

"They're alive," I said. "Or they were alive to him."

"I never thought about Uncle Sheldon being passionate. I mean, he was just this guy who would show up every other Christmas and give me weird presents." Adam sat down next to me, the two of us together on the bed. "It feels wrong, somehow, to think of him of being young, and in love."

I glanced at Adam, sitting next to me, in a friendly way, not even very intimate. But I heard a sadness in his voice, and it wasn't just grief for his departed uncle. I didn't know anything about Adam, but it sounded to me as though he was lonely. If so, it was the one thing we had in common—a void in our lives, a lack of not just togetherness but passion. And there we were, sitting together, with an opportunity to reach towards each other, and neither of us wanting to make the first move.

"Of course, I bet you feel the same way," he said.

"Oh, I do," I said. I hoped that my voice had just the right husky intensity.

"I mean, you don't think about your mom that way, I bet."

"I'm not thinking about her at all, just now." He turned his head, just a little. It would be no effort at all just to kiss him, I thought, just to press my lips against his, just to unbutton that first button on his shirt. "What are you thinking about?" I asked.

"Well, a couple of things," he said.

I was thinking of a couple of things, too. I was thinking that my mother was right, that having a passionate desire in your heart was what living was all about. I was thinking about Adam's body, warm and naked against mine. I was thinking about his hands caressing me, exploring me, right there on that bed.

"I'm thinking I have to get to the FedEx store in Sea Isle City before it closes," he said.

"Oh," I said, because you can't say things like *that is the single absolute least romantic thing I have ever heard anyone say in my whole entire life up until right this minute.*

"I mean, I want to make sure the urn gets to Alaska in one piece. I can't just leave it in a drop box."

When I heard that word, that short little word *urn,* a billion little hormone molecules that had been racing around my bloodstream died a quick, short, sudden death. "*Urn,*" I said, "as in ashes?"

"Well, yeah. I meant to drop it off before the funeral, but I was running late and I didn't have time. The closest FedEx location is in Sea Isle City, and I need to finish getting packed here and drive it up there before they close."

I touched the little silver cross pendant I was wearing. I felt the muscles of my chest tighten, just a bit, and then relax.

I breathed in and breathed out, and did it again, and then again. *I am in a room with a corpse*, I told myself, *but it's not a problem. It's just a pile of ashes encased in an urn wrapped up in a FedEx box. It can't hurt me in any way. And I will not run from the room like a scared little girl and embarrass myself in front of the cute guy. I will not I will not I will not.*

"Are you OK?" he asked. "Can I get you some water?"

"I'm fine," I lied. "I just heard that the box had already been shipped, that's all. I didn't think your uncle was in there. I was a little surprised."

"Well, he's not getting out of the box, if that's what you're worried about."

"I'm not worried." I'd made it through an entire funeral without having one bit of twitchy anxiety. I wasn't going to let a FedEx box bother me, no matter what was in it.

"That's good," he said. "I didn't think you were the type to be touchy about dead bodies. I mean, here you are, sitting on the bed where Uncle Sheldon died."

Adam had left the bedroom door open, which was a good thing, because I would have done horrible damage to the door frame if he hadn't. The front door was closed, but it was unlocked and it had a lever on it instead of a doorknob. I was able to fling it open, and I was just aware enough to keep from falling into the open maw of the U-Haul truck. I lost a bit of forward momentum in the process, which kept me from running full-tilt across the highway and onto the beach and into the deep blue water of Delaware Bay. As it was, I made a sharp right turn and collided with an elderly gentleman. He had a bristly white mustache and he was wearing a black suit.

He managed to both hold himself up and keep me from falling to the pavement. "Steady there, miss," he said. "Steady. Nobody's going to hurt you. Just calm down."

I stood there, bent over, with my hands on my knees, trying to control my breathing enough so that I knew I wouldn't die, because if I died I wouldn't be able to kill that idiot Adam for letting me sit on a dead man's bed like that.

"That's right," the old man said. "Breathe. It'll be just fine, you'll see."

"Thanks," I said, and took in another gulp of air. "I'll be OK as soon as I have a chance to calm down. I just had a little scare, that's all."

"I understand perfectly," he said. "By the way, your name wouldn't happen to be Gwendolyn Jarrett, would it? Emily Thornhill's daughter?"

Chapter 14

The old man's name was Daniel Miller, and he was a partner in a three-man law firm that handled real estate issues in Cape May Court House, a mile or two up the Parkway from Cape May proper. He hadn't been looking for me at all, he assured me, but he was very pleased to see me nonetheless.

"Why is that?" I asked.

"Your mother," he said, "is next on my list. After young Adam here. I take it that he's the young man over there."

Adam was making his way toward us, warily, the way a cautious person might approach an injured woodland creature. "Are you OK?" he asked, from a safe distance.

I could not kill him at that moment, because that would leave a witness, and Mr. Miller seemed like a nice old man who didn't deserve to die because he was an innocent bystander.

"I am going to live a nice, long, happy, and fulfilling life," I said, "no thanks to you."

"I am sorry. I mean, I had no idea you would react that way."

"You mean the completely normal way that anyone would react to finding out she was sitting on the bed where someone died?"

"I said I was sorry," he said.

"Excuse me," Mr. Miller said. "I have no wish to intervene in this highly entertaining and stimulating discussion you two are having, but I do have sensitive matters to discuss with the both of you, and it would be a courtesy to us all to take care of this inside. Yes?"

We all went back in Sheldon's apartment. Adam took a moment to determine just who Mr. Miller was and why he was there, and then he rummaged around in Sheldon's refrigerator, emerging with a large bottle of cranberry juice. I drank mine out of a "Strategic Air Command" coffee cup that Adam had retrieved from one of the boxes in the U-Haul. Mr. Miller took a courteous sip of his juice and then withdrew two envelopes from a battered black leather briefcase. "I apologize if this is a bit unusual," he said. "But I had strict instructions from my client, Mr. Berkman."

"So what is this?" Adam asked. "A last letter? Final instructions?"

"Nothing so exotic, I'm afraid," Mr. Miller said. "It is just an ordinary codicil to Mr. Berkman's will, with one specific bequest, based on one specific condition. What I am hoping to get from the two of you—or from Ms. Thornhill, if she's available—is confirmation that the condition has, in fact, been met."

"I don't understand," Adam said.

"A codicil is an amendment to a will," I explained.

"I know that," he said. "I went to college, you know."

"You said you didn't understand. I was trying to explain. To be helpful."

"You're not being helpful," Adam said. "You're being annoying."

"Can we get back to the subject at hand?" Mr. Miller asked.

"Sorry," I said, more to Mr. Miller than to Adam. I didn't intend to let Adam off the hook for scaring me just yet.

"What I was trying to say is that I didn't know there was a codicil, much less one that was conditional," Adam said. "I'm the executor of the will. It seems to me that I should have been informed of this codicil beforehand."

"I have to apologize to you both," Mr. Miller said. "First, to you, Mr. Lewis. Your uncle drafted this codicil nine months ago. He gave it to me, and specifically asked me *not* to deliver the codicil to you before his death. I advised him against doing so, but he was very clear in his mind about what he wanted. I am sorry to spring this on you at such a sad time. Having said that, if I had followed my instructions to the letter, it might have been worse."

"What instructions were those?" I asked.

"Well, this is a place where I must apologize again, this time to you and your mother, Ms. Jarrett. My specific instructions were to attend the funeral and deliver these envelopes, after I had documented the condition that triggered the codicil. Unfortunately, I had a family emergency and wasn't able to make it to the church on time."

"Is everything OK?" Adam asked.

"Perfectly fine," Mr. Miller said. "Unfortunately, my inability to attend the funeral personally means that I was unable to determine whether or not the condition was actually met."

"What does that mean?" I asked. "Was the codicil tied to the funeral in some way?" That would be a very odd thing to have in a codicil, but people had come up with stranger things.

"At this point," Mr. Miller said, "I would prefer not to answer any questions until both of you have had the chance to review the document in question."

I can take a hint as well as anyone. I ripped open the envelope and scanned the codicil. The key sentence read: *I do hereby bequeath the property known as 228 Idaho Avenue in Cape May, New Jersey, in fee simple to my former wife, Emily Thornhill, and her heirs and assigns, on the condition that she attend the funeral and/or memorial service held after my death.*

"You understand my concern," Mr. Miller said. "If I had been able to attend the funeral, I would have been able to personally verify Ms. Thornhill's attendance at the funeral. As it is, I must rely on the good faith of both parties to confirm that the condition has, in fact, been met."

"Give me a second," I said, and pulled out my cell phone. I opened Safari, pulled up the voice prompt, and said "Gawker Curtains blog." It took a second, but I was able to pull up the *Curtains* site, and sure enough, the story about Sheldon's funeral was right there. "Mystery Woman Shows Up at Funeral of Cape May Man with Maudlin Obituary." Vanessa's picture, as she had said, was tremendous.

I handed the phone to Mr. Miller. "That's my mother," I said, "walking up the stairs to the church. The photo appears in a blog post, dated today. I can get an affidavit from the photographer if it's strictly necessary." I decided not to mention that I dearly hoped that it wouldn't be necessary.

"It's not necessary," Adam said. "We both know your mother was at the funeral. We all sat together. That's not what I'm worried about. What I want to know is what kind of property it is that we're talking about, and when my uncle bought it."

"I can look that up, too," I said, and opened up the Zillow real estate app. The property at that address had been bought nine months ago for below market value—which still made it a princely sum, considering what market value was for property in New Jersey shore towns. "It's listed as a fixer-upper," I said. "Do you know if he was trying to flip the house, Mr. Miller?"

Mr. Miller folded his hands. "Ms. Jarrett, I hope I do not have to remind you of the strictures of the attorney-client relationship with respect to confidentiality."

"Of course not," I said. Flipping a house seemed an odd thing to want to keep secret, but why else would someone who was already living in a retirement home take out a huge mortgage on a dilapidated house that they didn't need?

"So," Adam said, "nine months ago, my Uncle Sheldon bought this house. And now he's giving it to Wendy's mother, just because she went to his funeral?"

"Without revealing anything confidential, having her come to his funeral meant a lot to him," Mr. Miller said.

"Would you mind?" Adam asked, gesturing in the direction of my iPhone. I handed it to him so he could check out the Zillow listing. "This explains some of the charges on his Home Depot card. I couldn't figure out what that was all about."

"So he was trying to fix it up, then," I said.

"It's my fault. I told him about all the money I made flipping houses before the recession, and he must have figured he could do it, too. I just can't believe that he borrowed that much money for a house down here, and then he goes and gives it away to his ex-wife from fifty years ago. That makes zero sense."

"Again, allow me to apologize, Mr. Lewis," Mr. Miller said. "If there is any way I can be of assistance to you, let me know."

"Thanks," Adam said.

"I have one more item for each of you." Mr. Miller dug two key rings out of his briefcase. "The first one is for Mr. Lewis; it's the safe deposit box—the deed for the house is in there, and some other personal items, I believe."

"What about the key to the house?" Adam asked.

"There are two keys," Mr. Miller explained. "One is in the safe deposit box, that's yours. The other is for Ms. Thornhill, and I have that one here." He handed me the other key.

"Wait a second," Adam said. "You can't just give her the key to the house like that. It's not hers."

"Those were your uncle's express wishes, I'm afraid." Mr. Miller said. "Ideally, I would have put the keys in her hand at the funeral, and given her directions to the house."

Adam sat straight up in his chair. "That's ridiculous. The codicil doesn't give her the right to just take the house. I mean, I'm the executor. I would have to make the transfer. Get her name in the chain of title."

"That's all true," I said. "The house doesn't pass to my mother until you complete the title transfer. But it doesn't hurt anything for her to have the key, just to look around."

"As long as she was just looking around, I don't think that would be a problem," Adam said. "But this whole thing is nuts. I mean, totally squirrely. I never figured Uncle Sheldon for this kind of melodrama."

"Well, we all have our little secrets," Mr. Miller said. "I know I've said it already, several times, but I really do apologize. Unless either of you have any questions, I should be going."

It took Mr. Miller a while to straighten up, and to repack his black briefcase. We tried to thank him, but he waved us off and headed out the door.

I sat at the kitchen table, waiting for Adam to finish washing out the cups we'd been drinking from and load them back in the truck. It was a nice moment, quiet, almost domestic.

"Do you need me to help with the airplane models?" I asked. "It looks like that's all you have left to pack."

"They're too fragile to throw in the back of the U-Haul. I am going to ask the facility to hold on to them for a few days. They don't have anybody ready to move in, and now I am going to have to come back here anyway to get into the safe deposit box and look at the mortgage and figure out what is going on here."

"Not to speak ill of the dead," I said, "but that was an awful thing for your uncle to do, springing a surprise like that on the day of his funeral. In a way, it's a good thing that the lawyer couldn't make it." My best guess is that my mother would have chewed out poor Mr. Miller something awful if he had been bold enough to serve her with legal papers at the funeral.

"You do this for a living, right?" Adam asked. "Did you ever come across something this weird?"

"Ambushing people at a funeral? That's a new one on me. You do get clients who ask for odd things in their wills. Most of it's not that unusual—deciding who gets what family heirlooms, or who has to take care of which pet, that sort of thing. Sometimes people give their money to strangers, or set up gifts to unusual charities. But I frown on putting that in your will, from a legal perspective. If you have something different or unique you want to do, you're almost always better off doing it while you're alive rather than trying to control things from beyond the grave."

"Or from beyond the FedEx box, as it were."

"Ha," I said. I still wasn't ready to forgive him for that.

"Seriously, though. I had no intent to scare you that way. I mean, I never would have said anything if I thought you would run off like that." He had the most devastating twinkle in his eyes when he said that, as though the idea of me running through a seaside retirement community in sheer panic was one of the funniest things he had ever encountered.

Of course, I hadn't been that frightened of sitting on a dead man's bed. That wasn't why I took off running in my best heels, pell-mell towards Delaware Bay. I had been seriously freaked out about having an explicit sexual fantasy on that bed, one that could have come reasonably close to being an actual sexual experience, or at least it might have if Adam hadn't been so damn unromantic about the whole thing. I couldn't very well *tell* him that, of course, because God knows how funny he'd think that would be.

"Let's just not talk about it, shall we?" I suggested.

"I just want to rewind a little," he said. "If you don't mind. I said I had two things to do before I left. One was dropping off the urn, and the other one was asking you if you wanted to go to dinner sometime."

"Oh," I said, reverting back to my monosyllabic ways. What *was* it about Adam that made the connection from my brain to my mouth stop working?

"I had been thinking maybe you might want to have dinner somewhere tonight, but I need to head north and you are probably going to want to eat with your mom."

"Oh. Her."

"I guess we could all go out together, but that doesn't strike me as a good idea right now."

"That's reasonable enough," I said. I needed Mother to come with me on a date like I needed a large, seeping, gaping wound in my abdomen.

"I don't mean this in a bad way, but your mom is a little intimidating."

"You haven't gotten to know her very well. She's a lot intimidating. And you're changing the subject. We were talking about dinner."

"Yes. Sorry. Are you free next week? We could meet halfway. I know a nice place in New Brunswick that would be perfect."

It had been a long day. I had to put up with my mother's craziness, and gone to a funeral, and eaten one too many dumplings at the wake, and I'd sat on a dead man's bed. Now a cute guy who was interested in me was asking me out, and the last synapse I had working in my brain right at that moment was the one that said, *say yes.*

"Sure," I said. "That would be nice."

"Good," he said, and his features relaxed into a winning smile. "Will Friday at eight be all right?"

"That would be lovely." I couldn't make the muscles in

my face move. I was simpering, and I knew it, and I couldn't stop.

"OK then. Deal?" He stuck his hand out, like we were closing a real estate deal, and I shook it.

"Deal," I said.

I held on to his hand a little longer than I needed to. He didn't try to disengage, either, but after a long moment he smiled. "Your mother is waiting for you," he said, "and my uncle is waiting for me to drop him off."

He let go of my hand and picked up the FedEx box, and we walked out of the apartment together. He got in his U-Haul, and I watched him drive off. *Every time I think he's said the least romantic thing possible*, I thought, *he comes up with something new.*

Chapter 15

I wasn't in a hurry to check in on my mother, so I drove over to see the house that Sheldon Berkman had left to her in his will. The building on Idaho Street was spacious, imposing, and horribly, aggressively pink. I had no idea whether it had been painted pink when Sheldon had bought it, or if he had painted it that way. If it was his fault, then there was an open question as to whether the Air Force needed to revise its testing procedures for color-blindness.

As bad as the pink was, it clashed with the abominable mint green porch railing and the dark green shutters. The only other color was the white faux-Victorian scrollwork under its dingy gables. Three yucky-looking wicker chairs sat on the porch. The yard was microscopic and badly tended. The house looked altogether dismal, and I decided not to bother going inside just yet—I figured I could always check it out tomorrow, if Mother was interested. I took photos with my phone and got back in the car and headed to the hotel.

I made a quick detour into the liquor store for the necessary supplies for cocktail hour. I got a bottle of vanilla vodka and two bottles of diet orange soda. The creamsicle is not the most complex of mixed drinks, but it is tasty and easy to make if you're drunk. The cashier gave me an approving look, anyway, so I figured I hadn't gone too far wrong. I am a person who has tried to mix chocolate vodka with Yoo-hoo, so I am perhaps abnormally sensitive to what cashiers at liquor stores think. (I am, seriously, *not* endorsing mixing chocolate vodka with Yoo-hoo here. The resulting concoction is most vile, although it will get you drunk fairly effectively, and I had a very detailed and intricate dream that night about Willy Wonka.)

I got back to the hotel room and took my shoes off, which was the single best thing I had done all day. I wriggled my way out of the somber dress and slipped into blue jeans and a nice comfy black hooded sweatshirt that said TEMPLE on it. I figured the responsible thing to do was to check on

Mother and make sure that she hadn't jumped out the window or that she wasn't drunk-dialing old boyfriends or something. I put my ear up to the connecting door and listened for a short moment, just so I could tell what she was up to. I heard something that sounded like snoring, which I interpreted as a positive sign. Taking a nap couldn't do anything but good for her at this point.

I ducked out of the room and filled my ice bucket, and then settled on the balcony with a liquid refreshment. All I had to drink from was one of the little plastic glasses they put in your room, but that wasn't an insurmountable barrier for the truly determined drinker. It was still chilly outside, but the sun was shining and I was warm in my sweatshirt.

I had business to take care of before the serious drinking started. I sent a quick e-mail to my boss in Morristown, telling him that I had resolved the situation with Gawker. I said that all they'd wanted was information on my mother's ex-husband, which was accurate enough, and that I'd be back to work on Monday. I tried to respond to the Facebook messages I had been neglecting. I played WHISTLE on a double-word score in *Words With Friends* to take a commanding lead over the sexist pig I had been playing. After that, I looked at the ocean for a long while.

A wise man once said that human beings were programmed to like boundary conditions—places like tree houses, mountain cabins, or transgressive gay bars. Boundary conditions exist in places where you can stay in one element and look at another different and fascinating element for as long as you wanted. That's why people like beach towns like Cape May; you can sit and look at the ocean, or go in the ocean and look back at the land, whatever's more fun.

If that's true, then maybe that's why people go to funerals. Funerals are the boundary condition between life and afterlife. Sheldon Berkman had crossed the boundary between living in a tacky, seaside retirement community and trying to flip an old Victorian house to being a pile of ashes in a fancy urn in a U-Haul truck on its way to the FedEx office in Sea Isle City. I didn't think much of that particular trip, and wasn't thrilled about having to make it myself one day.

Another wise man said that you should get busy living, or get busy dying. Of course, that was just something Morgan Freeman said in a movie once, but he had a point. I was stuck where I was, and I knew it. I was living a static, lonely life in a nondescript town in North Jersey, handling the paperwork for other people's deaths. It was slow and safe, and it was paying off my student loan drip by drip, but it wasn't making me happy and I didn't know what to do about it, other than to take another nice long frosty smooth sip of creamsicle.

I need a man, I thought, not for the first time.

But it couldn't be just any man. I wanted someone stable and devoted. I wanted someone smart and honest. I wanted someone devastatingly handsome but not narcissistic.

But more than that, I wanted someone with a deep romantic streak. Someone who would fall madly in love with me and do great things to earn my love in return. Someone charming, affectionate, and sweet. Someone who would be the great love of my life for today and for all time.

Was that person Adam Lewis?

He was cute. I would give him that. He was drop-dead gorgeous, honestly. Just the right age. Single. Employed. Interested in me, as far as I could tell. All of these things were positive marks in his favor. The one thing wrong with him was the most important thing that could be wrong with him, that he didn't seem like the type to sweep a woman off her feet. I mean, who asks a girl to help him clean out his dead uncle's apartment for a first date?

The good news was that he was single and he seemed to be unattached. But there was every reason to think that he was single for a reason. Maybe he didn't have a romantic bone in his body. Maybe he was an insensitive lout who liked to poke fun at people's personal weaknesses. Maybe he was bad at sex, although I would have to find that out on my own.

On paper, he seemed like the perfect guy. But there was no way he could be the perfect guy, because the perfect guy doesn't exist.

Maybe you should stop looking for him, then, I thought.

I poured myself another creamsicle and watched the ocean slam into the beach for the next hour.

Mother came out onto her balcony before five. She was wearing a shapeless gray wool poncho as protection against the chill wind, and she had a martini glass in her hand. "How long have you been sitting out here drinking?" she asked.

"Not long enough."

"What revolting concoction is that? It looks orange."

"Vanilla soda and diet orange vodka," I said. "No, wait, the other way around."

"Oh, dear. Will you be up for having dinner?"

"I had enough food at the wake to sink the *Queen Mary*," I said. "I could eat a little something, though, as long as you don't ask me to drive you anywhere."

"That is why God gave us room service," she said.

"Is that where you got the martini glass?"

"I packed it in my suitcase," she said. "In case of emergency."

I saluted her with my sad little plastic cup. "You are my hero," I said.

"Of course, dear. How was the reception?"

"Interesting. It was at the retirement home complex. Many, many, many pierogies."

"What on earth possessed you to go there? It sounds dreadful."

"They were very nice pierogies. Tasty. Filling. And there was fruit salad. I liked the fruit salad. I should have asked for the recipe, if I ever decide to learn how to cook. And there were pierogies. Did I say that?"

"You made that very clear, dear."

"It's important, when you are as drunk as I am, to try to be as clear as you can." I got that out very slowly, over-enunciating each word, which I do when I've gone well over my limit.

"I understand. But what made you decide to go?" she asked.

"Motivation. Adam asked me to go, so I went."

"Oh, the nephew. Is that his name? Charming young

man. He asked you to go to the wake with him?"

"Exactly positively."

"So did you screw him?" she asked.

I stared at her, which was hard because there suddenly seemed to be more than one of her. "How many of those martinis have you had?" I asked.

"Don't answer a question with a question, darling. It's common."

"You can't ask me that. Not when I'm this drunk. It's a violation of the Geneva Constitution. You could go to jail."

"I am not judging you, sweetie. It's a common reaction. Funerals make us want sex. It's part of our genetic programming. It's how we express our love for life."

"Oh."

"So? Did you go out and love life?"

"None of your business, Mother." I said it very slowly to be sure I was enunciating.

"I thought he was *exceptionally* good-looking," she said. "And he seemed every inch the eligible bachelor. It's a shame you didn't at least try."

"He had an errand to run," I explained. I was not about to tell her what kind of errand. "He did ask me out, and I said yes, even though he was not being the least bit romantic."

"Why on earth were you waiting on him to feel romantic?" she asked. "Let me tell you something about romance. When you're dealing with a very attractive man with whom you want to have sex, it pays to be direct. Some men wouldn't know a signal if it hit them over the head with a gin bottle. Just come out and say you want to have sex with him. He will appreciate it. If he's any good at it at all, so will you."

"I cannot believe I am having this conversation," I said.

"Then you clearly haven't had enough to drink."

I poured myself another creamsicle and raised my plastic glass over the railing separating my balcony from hers. "Cheers," I said, as she clinked it with her martini glass, minus the satisfying *clink* sound. We sat there for a long time, watching the shadows grow longer. Room service showed up with club sandwiches just as it was getting too cold to sit outside. Mother took her sandwich off to her room, and I don't recall anything about the rest of the night other than that I was so drunk and tired when I went to bed that I woke up the next morning with a mayonnaise smear on my forehead.

Chapter 16

That next morning found me sitting in my car again in front of the pink house on Idaho Street, with a hangover that would incapacitate Charlie Sheen.

"Are you sure that's the right house?" Mother asked. "It looks decidedly odd."

"That's what it said in the codicil. It's 228 Idaho Street. Unless it's a misprint."

"More like a practical joke. I would say it was a white elephant if it were not that wretched shade of pink. What do you suppose Sheldon expected me to *do* with this thing?"

"You could always rent it out. If you were ambitious you could start your own bed-and-breakfast."

"Don't you dare disturb my hard-earned retirement, Gwendolyn Rose."

"Wouldn't dream of it. Of course, you could move down here full-time."

"And deprive your sister of free babysitting? I wouldn't dream of it." She peered through my window, as though she was trying to see something exceptional in the house that just wasn't there. "Do you think it's all right to go inside?" she asked.

"We have the key. You can go in if you want. But Adam thinks Sheldon was in the middle of a reconstruction project when he died. It might not be safe. There could be holes in the flooring, or a gas leak, or disco wallpaper. You should have a home inspector check it out first."

The house, like the rest of the world, looked worse in the glare of the harsh morning sunlight. I had dark glasses on, but everything in the world that was sunlit was bringing me intense pain. I would be lucky to get out of the car, much less navigate the steps up to the front porch without throwing up.

"Is it legal?" she asked. "Do I really own this thing?"

"Not yet."

"What does that mean?"

"Mother, I am far too hung over to give you legal advice

right at the moment," I said.

"How middle-class of you."

"Hangovers are middle-class? Since when?"

"Since forever," she explained. "Poor people can't afford to have hangovers because they have to go to work the next day. Rich people have enough money that they can just say they're indisposed. You have to be middle-class to have a hangover."

"What are we?"

"We are old money, dear. We have hangovers, but don't complain about them. That would be déclassé."

"We wouldn't want to be déclassé, then, would we? Anyway, before I could even tell you anything helpful, I would need to look at all the legal paperwork—the will and the mortgage and the title certificate—to make sure everything was in order. But you clearly met the condition in the codicil by attending the funeral. You should inherit the house, unless Adam contests the will or the codicil."

"I can't help feeling as though Sheldon is trying to influence my life from beyond the veil. He's manipulated me into something, but I don't know why."

"It's just a house, Mother. It's real estate, like on a Monopoly board. If you don't like the house, you can sell it. Or you can let the bank take it back; it must be mortgaged from here to next Wednesday."

"Something is wrong about that house," she said. "I can't put my finger on it. I don't know what the problem is, but I don't like it, and I'm not sure I want any part of it. What do you think we should do?"

"I remember, very distinctly, somebody, not that long ago, promising me a spa day if I drove them down to Cape May."

"Then what are we doing sitting around looking at an ugly house?" Mother asked. "Onward and forward."

Mother thought all the local spas had tacky names, so we left Cape May and headed towards Atlantic City, where we checked in to the Elizabeth Arden spa at Harrah's. I got a hot stone massage from a stout Polish exchange student named

Magda that would have brought a plaster saint back to life. That was followed up with just enough time in the sauna to leach all the alcohol residue from my body but not enough time to make me sick, and a facial that unclogged pores I didn't even know that I had. Mother got the deep-tissue massage, which must have worked because she was so relaxed that she slept in the car all the way back north.

I got a text from my sister Pacey as we were pulling into Princeton; she wanted to see if we would have dinner at her house. I love Pacey. She is an exceptionally smart person, and she has had a tough time with her twins, and I admire her deeply, but she cannot cook. I don't blame her, because I cannot cook, either. The difference is that I am generally able to feed myself without giving myself food poisoning or starting small fires, and you can't always say that about Pacey. But I needed to talk to someone else about the events of the last few days badly enough to brave whatever badly cooked meal she had planned. Then I thought about it more, and sent her a text suggesting Chinese delivery.

Pacey and her husband lived in a large development that wasn't quite finished yet; there were several houses in varying stages of construction on her street. They had moved there from New York, where her husband Henri still worked, just before their twins were born. Henri took the train into the city most days, but he had to be in Europe for meetings every so often, and I think he was in Zurich just then.

Pacey had been working at the Swiss consulate in New York when they met. Pacey had a master's degree in foreign policy from GWU and spoke four languages fluently. She'd put her career on indefinite hold to ride herd on three-year-olds in a nondescript suburb. I honestly didn't know what to think of that, and I am not sure that she did, either.

Mother woke up as I pulled into the driveway of Pacey's house. She was blinking like an owl. "Please tell me your sister is not planning to give us all salmonella infections," she said.

"Averted," I assured her. "General Tso's and lo mein are on their way."

"Egg rolls?" she asked.

"I can't promise you egg rolls. Fortune cookies, I can promise."

"Let us go inside, then, and meet our fates."

My nephews spent dinner dunking dinosaur chicken nuggets in sweet-and-sour sauce, throwing rice at each other, and asking Mother if she would do Legos with them after dinner. They were annoying little pests about it, if you ask me, but when someone that cute says, "Gwandmama, can you pwease play Legos with me?" then you play Legos with them. Pacey insisted that Benjy and Simon wash their hands first, which seemed like an excellent idea to me, but they whined about it for what seemed like forever but was probably only twenty minutes. Finally, they complied with the parental order and started playing with the Legos, punctuated by healthy cries of "BAM" and "POW." I had no idea what Mother was making of it all. I decided to help Pacey wash the dishes.

"What I don't understand," Pacey said, "is why Mother was acting so cagey about the whole funeral thing. Who was it that died, anyway? She wouldn't tell me."

"Sheldon Berkman," I said. "I got to hear the whole story on the way down. It's amazing. They were dating in high school, and then when he graduated, they eloped to Cape May. She hadn't even finished high school yet."

"Oh, him," she said. "I thought he was in Alaska or something."

"You knew about Sheldon?" I asked. "Holy shit, Pacey. You knew Mother was married before, and you didn't tell me?" I could hear my voice go shrill with outrage and jealousy. Why would she tell Pacey about Sheldon and not me?

"You didn't know about that already? I thought Daddy would have told you about Sheldon. You know how he loves undermining her when he thinks he can get away with it."

"I never heard Word One about this guy until Thursday night. Why did Dad tell you and not me?" *That's not fair*, I thought, but our parents had drilled "life isn't fair" into all of us, like an evil mantra.

"Special circumstances," she said.

"Spill."

"No."

In the background, we could hear Mother imploring Benjy to take the Darth Vader Lego piece out of his mouth.

"Spill or I give your kids double cotton candy when I take them to the zoo next time."

"You wouldn't *dare.*"

"Spill."

"Never," she said.

"One day, not so far from now, you and your husband will be in the same country at the same time, and you are going to want me to babysit, and I am going to feed your clever, adorable children as much sugar as I can cram down their little throats, and you won't be able to stop me, and they will keep you up *all night long.*"

"*Quid pro quo?*"

"If you insist," I said.

"Fine. Sophomore year at UVa, I was dating this guy named Wade Prescott IV. Very bright, very sexy, and unfortunately, very Southern. He drove up to Philadelphia, totally without me knowing about it, and walked up to Daddy at his office and asked for my hand in marriage. He had it all planned out. He was going to ask me to get married in Virginia Beach over spring break, just the two of us and a preacher."

"Wade Prescott who? Why am I just hearing about this now?" I started wondering what else Pacey knew that I didn't. "So what happened?"

"Oh, I dumped him. That was an easy decision. If he had approached me about the idea of eloping, well, it might have gone over better. But he went behind my back to Daddy. Bad move on his part. It worked out for the best, though. I think that he ended up getting married to a Tri-Delt from Richmond. Anyway, the important part was that it got Daddy all worried and upset enough to drive down to Charlottesville to talk me out of it. It was a wasted trip, of course, but he told me the Sheldon Berkman story. What he knew about it, of course, which was rather a lot."

"He was trying to talk you out of eloping?"

"Right. Wasted effort, like I said. Daddy wanted me to graduate, and I wanted to graduate, so we were in agreement about the basics. All that happened was that I didn't have to take Mother seriously anymore when she started criticizing me for having indiscriminate sex with cute boys. Speaking of which, how's your sex life?"

"None of your business."

"*Quid pro quo*. When you walked in the house, you were glowing. Don't deny it."

"Spa treatment. I got a facial. That's it."

Pacey put the last of the plates in the dishwasher. "Mother said to ask you about the nephew, whoever that is."

"Sheldon's nephew. We met at the funeral. He's the executor of the will."

"Is he cute?"

"That isn't relevant."

"*Quid pro quo*, dear sister. Spill."

I rolled my eyes. I could hear Simon squealing, and Mother telling him not to stick another light saber up his nose. "He's cute. Very very cute. I like him. But I don't know."

Pacey put a sippy cup in the dishwasher. "What don't you know?"

"I don't know how I feel about him. Yes, he's cute. Yes, I like him. Yes, I could see myself getting naked with him sometime in the not-too-distant future. But everything I feel about him is kind of shallow."

"Nothing wrong with *that*. You deserve a little fun every once in a while, sis. Take him to Barbados, drink some rum punch, and frolic on the beach."

"That's the problem," I explained. "If he suggested that, I would go. Tomorrow. Well, maybe not tomorrow, but sometime. But that would be a romantic thing for him to do, and he's not the least bit romantic, and it's bothering me."

"You just met him," Pacey said. "Give him time."

"It's important to me. If he's not able to be romantic, I'm maybe better off looking for someone else."

Pacey slammed the door of the dishwasher shut and

pushed the buttons to set it running. "You are going about this totally backward," she said. "When are you going to see him again?"

"Friday. Dinner in New Brunswick. He lives in Freehold and it's halfway. The practical approach, you see. Not very romantic."

"At least he's moving fast, though. Well, you had the facial. That's a good start. What's your schedule look like the rest of the week?"

"Work. I have some catching up to do, I expect."

"Can you take Friday off?"

"Why would I need to?" I asked.

"Wendy," she said. "Wendy, Wendy, Wendy. You need your hair done, for a start. Mani-pedi. That's an absolute *requirement*. Leg wax, if you have time."

"Pacey, for God's sake. I am not getting my legs waxed. I had it done once and it hurt like fire."

"It's meant to. You ought to think about the Brazilian while we're at it."

"Pacey!" I yelled.

Just then, Benjy came running in to the kitchen. "You two! Cut that out!" he cried. "*Right this second!*"

Pacey stared at her son. Then she started laughing so hard that she couldn't stand up, and sank to her knees. Benjy came over and gave her a big hug.

"Does Mommy say that to you and your brother?" she asked.

"All the time," Benjy said.

"They repeat everything," Pacey said. "Which is why I am going to spell it out for you. B-R-A-Z-I-L-I-A-N."

"It's not funny," I said.

"Benjy, is Aunt Wendy funny?"

"Yes," he said.

"See? There you go. Proof. Go play, sweetie. Show Grandmama your stuffed tiger."

"You are out of your mind," I told Pacey, after Benjy had toddled off.

"You realize, I am only suggesting that you get one because I don't have time to get one myself. And because I think Henri would make fun of me. But the closest thing I am getting to a date this week—more like this month— is living vicariously through you. So listen to your big sister. Get the mani-pedi, even if you don't get the Brazilian."

"But why?" I asked. "He already likes me. Why go to the extra effort?"

"Because, my dear, romance is the socialized expression of frustrated sexual desire. Repeat that, please."

"Romance is the socialized expression of frustrated sexual desire," I said.

"So how does that apply in your situation?"

"If I want to heighten the romance," I reasoned, "I have to heighten his sexual desire. Hence the hairstyle, and the nails, and a nice outfit and heels."

Pacey smiled a knowing, evil smile. "Absolutely correct. And then, you have to *frustrate* him. You want romance? Then make him *work* for it."

Chapter 17

A late-season cold front ran through northern New Jersey late that night. I got up at about eleven o'clock on Sunday morning to find that the world had turned to slush overnight. I despise cold weather and have been known to indulge the occasional elaborate fantasy about moving someplace where the frosty breath of winter doesn't reach, like Venezuela or Nairobi or the surface of the sun. I microwaved a bowl of oatmeal, loaded it down with brown sugar and raisins, and tried to think warm thoughts.

I spent a few ineffectual hours trying to sift through all the social media nonsense that had accumulated over the last few days. I gave up the project as a bad job after the sugar rush from breakfast wore off. The good news was that the post-funeral Gawker piece was very brief, didn't mention me by name, and didn't say anything one way or another about my mother outside the fact that she showed up. My guess was that Vanessa had tried to savage me in print out of revenge for knocking her Long Island iced tea–drinking ass down at the funeral, but that cooler heads in the Gawker editorial department had prevailed. To celebrate, I broke out a French bread pizza from the freezer and put it in the oven, and managed to eat it without burning the inside of my mouth. Things were looking up.

I was putting my plate in the dishwasher when it occurred to me that I'd been so busy looking at my personal social media nightmare that I hadn't bothered to look at Adam's Facebook page. He hadn't sent me a friend request, and I didn't want to send him one, because that would make me look needy or worse. But he had quite a few pictures that he'd made public, enough for me to get a good idea about how he liked to spend his time. A few of the pictures showed him working on a house, including one of him with his shirt off, standing on a partly shingled roof. I bookmarked it for later review. Some other pictures showed him somewhere on the Shore, fishing. I was equivocal about this aspect of his life, because I like eating fresh fish but have no real idea how to cook fish, and absolutely no desire in my life to clean fish or to have fish scales in my sink.

For the last six months, the only pictures of Adam on Facebook were either selfies or shots taken by one of his friends. Going back farther than that, though, someone else started appearing with him in the pictures. Her name was Marie Lawrence, and she was short and thin and brunette and adorable, and I hated her on sight. Marie and Adam had taken trips together—Southern California last summer, Stowe before that, Aruba over Thanksgiving, and what looked like three weeks in Australia two years ago.

I clicked on her name, which said that she was "in a relationship" with someone named Trey, and was living in West Hartford, which made her much less of a threat than I initially worried she was. Still, she was very cute, and had obviously had an extensive long-term relationship with Adam. I wondered what had happened. Had he done something to drive her away? Maybe she was his type and I wasn't. Or maybe he had decided that she wasn't his type, and that tall, awkward, buxom blondes were. Or so I hoped.

I didn't get back online until right before I went to bed, which is to say after I had downed two shot glasses of Frangelico and cinnamon vodka, which I christened the "Coffee Cake," if anyone wants to put it on their cocktail menu. It was quite tasty—too tasty, actually, because I would have liked another one, or six, but I had to go to work the next day and it was probably a good idea to start thinking about dialing back the alcohol intake.

I had two e-mails that I couldn't delete out of hand. One was from my mother; there was a picture attached to it. I opened the file and it was, of all things, a Polaroid picture of the house on Idaho Street. The house was painted a subtle shade of aqua in the picture, but the pitched roof and scrollwork hadn't changed in the intervening years. A young girl stood in front of the house in the picture, with a fetching smile on her face.

The message read, "I knew I recognized this house. It's

where we spent our honeymoon, back in 1963. It seems that rat Sheldon bought it to give to me for some bizarre reason. What's the best way to get rid of it at this point?"

I took another look at the picture. It seemed impossible that the happy girl with the sunshine in her hair and the wide smile on her face had grown up to be my mother, but she clearly was. I wrote her a note back that agreed with her that the whole thing was odd, and I'd figure out the best way for her to dump the house once I got the chance to look at the paperwork. If the house was worth less on the resale market than it was mortgaged for, the easiest thing to do would be to have Mother sign a quitclaim deed turning the house back over to the estate. It would take me just a second to draft that up, but there didn't seem to be a reason to hurry. It never hurts to have all the information in place before you make a decision.

The other e-mail was from Pacey, and it just had a link to a Pinterest board she had made for me. I checked it out, and I was immediately impressed by the amount of time that she had spent to make it for me. Everything after that was horrifying beyond words. About half of the board was given over to maps to places that she thought I should go before the big date. The largest of the maps was for a local establishment devoted to the forcible removal of unwanted genital hair, which, hand to God, was called "The Pretty Kitty." I made a note to start my own Pinterest board of different ways I could get my revenge on Pacey for butting into my personal hygiene like that.

The one picture that looked intriguing was a pair of suede heels in a very fetching dark-red hue. The heels were higher than I would have liked, and the shoes were open-toed, which I could have done without. But they were on sale and Pacey had included a coupon code to get them online, shipped free tomorrow. And the shoes went with a nice sleeveless Ralph Lauren dress Pacey had found. I looked around a bit and found a knockoff with a slightly lower neckline at Forever 21, so I ordered that, too. Pacey had suggestions about a matching bra and panties set. What she had picked out was a bit risqué—especially if I had followed her other suggestion—but I decided I could always dash out at lunchtime and go to Victoria's Secret and pick out something nice if I felt the need.

I was in the middle of making an online appointment for Friday afternoon with Pacey's hairdresser when I started wondering what I was doing. I hadn't questioned Pacey when she said that romance was nothing more than the expression of frustrated sexual desire. It sounded reasonable on the surface, but it wasn't the whole story.

I wanted romance in my life, which meant that I wanted Adam to behave towards me in a romantic way. But what did that mean? Flowers? Flowers would be nice. A nice bottle of chardonnay? *Yes, please.*

But that was a very mercenary outlook. I didn't want Adam to just give me stuff for the sake of giving me stuff. He didn't have to give me anything. Not that I wouldn't *take* a nice bottle of chardonnay, because I am human and fallible and I really, really like chardonnay, especially the old French vintages that I don't get to drink very often because I am trying to pay off student loans. But my neighborhood is well-stocked with liquor stores. I don't need to be in a relationship to get alcohol or chocolate or flowers if that's what I want.

What I wanted was for Adam to look at me as though I were the most important thing in his life.

And, yes, that was a function of frustrated sexual desire, and yes, one way to encourage that was to get my hair done and get a manicure. And since the shoes I had just bought were open-toed, that meant that I had to get a pedicure, too.

But was that the best way to go about it?

I went over to the counter and found my purse and dug out the yellowing packet of letters I had taken from Sheldon's apartment. I hadn't shown them to Mother the day of the funeral, and I completely forgot about them after that. I picked a letter from the middle and read it carefully, the way Sheldon had through all those lonely nights. *I love you*, the letter said, each time underlined in red. *I want you. I want to feel your hands entwined in mine. I want to feel the sweet slickness of your tongue in my mouth. I want to feel your kisses, hot and desperate on my neck. I want to feel the hard muscles of your chest pressing against me, my hands exploring, searching, finding. I want everything you are and everything you can be.*

That's what I wanted, and if a day at the salon could help me get it, then that's where I needed to be. I put the letters in a safe place in my desk, and went back to the computer to look at the shirtless picture of Adam for a few minutes before I went to bed. It took me longer than usual to go to sleep.

Chapter 18

The restaurant that Adam picked out for our date was a converted warehouse that backed up against Route 18. I am not saying this because I am picky, because I am not. I would happily have met Adam at the meanest dive or the fanciest bistro in Central Jersey, so long as they served alcohol. The problem with this particular place was that it did not have a parking lot. I drove past the building twice looking for one before I figured out that there was complimentary valet parking. Then it was a matter of finding a valet, and there didn't seem to be any of them around. I was late, and headed past the fashionable side of being late, and I didn't want to take the chance that Adam might think that I'd stood him up. I pulled the car over to the next block and found a convenient parking garage.

It was late March, and winter was still hanging on like an unwanted houseguest. The weather had been vile and miserable all week, and there was still slush on the sidewalks. It was drizzling and cold and I could feel my hands turning blue. I managed to make my way down the slick sidewalk in my brand-new heels without a mishap, although I cursed myself for picking out the ones with the open toes.

I took my coat off just before I opened the door to the restaurant. I didn't know if Adam was waiting for me at the bar, or if he had gotten us a table already. I wanted him to see me resplendent in my new dress before he saw anything else, and it was worth putting up with the chill for that. The dress had been designed for someone a bit shorter than me, but that meant that I got to show a little leg, which was all to the good. It was an arresting shade of garnet that just matched my shoes.

It had taken all day, and cost me in terms of vacation time and in next month's credit card bill, but I looked fabulous. My hair had been unleashed from its usual conservative, professional style. I felt confidence radiating through me. When I walked into that restaurant, I felt self-assured and dynamic, like I was being carried along on the crest of a giant wave.

I wanted to make heads turn. I wanted every man in there to stare at me, and if I made their girlfriends and wives a bit jealous in the process, so much the better. I was in a nice restaurant, getting ready to have a nice dinner with a handsome man and everything would be perfect. Everything would be romantic.

That feeling lasted for six seconds. Maybe eight. I was making heads turn up and down the bar, but not Adam's. He was sitting at the bar, sipping a Coors Light and watching a basketball game. He had on an old disreputable-looking pair of jeans and a blaze-orange hoodie with SYRACUSE written on it in bright blue letters. He wore a battered orange pair of sneakers. He looked like a bum. He looked like a barfly. He looked like every drooling frat-house lout I'd ever turned down for a date in college. And worst of all, he wasn't looking at me.

"Hi there," I said, in the driest, most ironic Emily Thornhill manner I could summon.

Adam put down his beer and turned to look at me. It would be wrong to say that his jaw dropped, because it happened in about three distinct phases—the initial shock, which turned to abject terror, which turned to what I hoped was a sudden realization that he had miscalculated on the tenor of this evening very, very badly. He said "Oh," which is about all you can say when your mouth is hanging open that far.

"It's nice to see you," I said, turning up the frost level in my voice. "If you like, you may tell me that it's nice for you to see me, as well."

"Nice to see you," he said, as he managed to get his mouth back in working order. "Very nice to see you, at that. That's quite the dress you're wearing."

"Just a little something I threw on. You appear to have done much the same." I saw a fine spray of drops of white paint on the left shoulder of his hoodie.

He unfolded himself from the barstool. "We have casual

Friday at work," he said. "I meant to change, honest I did, but I heard on the radio that Route 18 was all backed up, so I didn't have time to go home before I left."

I wanted to look nice, I thought. *I wanted to look desirable, and magical. I wanted to see myself reflected in your eyes, and now I don't know what I'm seeing.*

I should have walked out on him right then, just to see if he would chase me, but I didn't want to go back in the cold and I was hungry anyway. "Do we have a table?" I asked.

"Right this way."

I followed him upstairs to the dining room. I didn't think I was turning many heads, and if anyone was looking, they were wondering how the schlub in the orange hoodie had ever gotten any woman to go out with him, much less someone in an amazing dress and stunning heels and perfect makeup.

It took me about twelve seconds after we sat down to order a glass of chardonnay. One drink wouldn't impair my driving, and I needed the moral support if I was going to get through the evening. Adam got another Coors Light, which was mildly distressing but ultimately not that important. I would have been much more annoyed if he was drinking chocolate martinis or herbal tea or something awful like that. Coors Light was plebeian and tasteless and horrible, but it wasn't evidence of anything other than terrible taste in alcohol. As long as he had decent taste in women, I could work around that.

"Did you have any trouble finding the place?" he asked. "I thought I sent you decent directions."

"No trouble," I said.

"You probably have GPS, though. I use it all the time myself. Couldn't find anything without it."

"No, I don't," I told him. "I don't have to drive all that much, living in Morristown. Just occasionally, on the weekends, and I use my phone if I ever get lost."

"Apple Maps or Google Maps?" he asked.

"I don't pay a lot of attention to it," I said. "I have whatever map is on there, and maybe two games, and e-mail and text." I have a little more on there than that, of course, but I desperately did not want to be drawn into a long conversation about smartphone apps. The waiter brought over our drinks just then, and I took a big yummy gulp of chardonnay. *Careful, girl,* I told myself.

"Well, you do the social media stuff," he said.

"I do Facebook, a little. Maybe too much, or at least that's what I'm thinking after this last week."

"I mention this," he said, "because I had a long talk with your friend Vanessa."

I know how my mother would have handled this tidbit of information. She would have gone all icy outside, with a core of burning hot hate kept packed down inside. I can do the second part but have trouble with the first. *"What did you say?"* I asked Adam.

"Your friend Vanessa," he repeated, and there was a mischievous smirk on his face. "She had a few things to say about you. Most of it was stuff she got from your Facebook timeline, as far as I could tell."

"She is *not* my friend. She's not your friend, either. She's a leech on the backside of society."

"Was she the one taking those pictures at the funeral? The ones that showed up on that blog?"

"That was her, hiding in the bushes like a coward. Like a rat. Like a cowardly rat."

Adam took a sip of his beer. "She said you assaulted her."

"Apparently not hard enough. What did she tell you?"

"She said you were stuck up because you have relatives who have lots of money, but you don't have any to speak of."

Lying bitch, I thought. "You didn't believe that, did you?" I asked.

"Well, no. But she was right about one thing."

"What was that?" I very much wanted this conversation to not be about Vanessa at this point.

"She also said you had posted some amazing swimsuit pictures from your vacation in the Caribbean." There was that smirk again, and this time it was more devilish. "She was right about that. That aqua-looking one was spectacular. The purple one was nice, too, but that's not your color."

"Thank you. I think." I decided not to say anything about the shirtless one of him I had seen online.

"Are you thinking appetizer?" he asked.

"I'm thinking not." I had been hungry, but I was going to have heartburn for the next three days thinking of ways to get back at Vanessa.

"I don't know if you looked me up on any of this social media stuff," he said. "It's OK if you did, I mean. It's weird that these days, you know a lot about a person before you ever go out with them, and it takes away a lot of the mystery of getting to know someone. It's not that romantic, I guess."

I took another long fortifying gulp of chardonnay. "Some people say romance is dead," I said. It was an easy conversational setup, a chance for him to recover his dating fortunes.

"I mean, you might have seen some of the stuff about me and Marie in my timeline."

I did not want to hear one word in that sentence. "No. I didn't," I lied. "And it isn't productive for either of us to talk about other people. We're here, and it's a nice restaurant, and a nice evening, and maybe we should just relax and find something else interesting to talk about."

"I wasn't trying to talk about me and Marie, honest I wasn't. I am not bringing her up to talk about her, necessarily. But there's something about me that you probably want to know, and that you definitely deserve to know."

"Whatever it is, you don't have to tell me anything." I devoutly hoped that he'd change the subject, fast. There are things more depressing than being on a date and hearing someone else talk about their last toxic relationship, and those things involve pain and suffering and complex medical treatment and insurance companies and hospital food.

"I want to tell you, because I think you might have an expectation about me that I may have a hard time meeting. Unless you'd rather order dinner now, so I can leave you in suspense."

"You might as well go ahead and tell me. If it's something terrible, I can leave now, without ordering anything. That way you're not out thirty bucks for a grilled pork chop and a glass of wine."

"All right. Here goes. I dated Marie for three years. She wanted to get married. I knew that. She had a *Brides* magazine subscription, OK? All I had to do was ask her."

"Did you?"

"I was going to. I had the ring. I wanted to get married. But I couldn't just take her out to a nice restaurant and ask her. She wanted her own special engagement moment. I'd go on her Facebook page, and there were all these links to all these YouTube videos of people getting engaged, and doing all these impossible stunts. I am not an imaginative person. I am not going to skydive and land on the boardwalk in Point Pleasant and kneel in front of somebody and give them an engagement ring. Other people can think up stuff like that, and that's fine for them, but it's not something I can do. So I asked for help."

"That seems like the sensible thing to do," I said. "Except, wait. You didn't go on social media and ask for help, did you?"

"Oh. That would have been a worse idea than what I actually did, so I guess that's something. Anyway, no. I asked my cousin Grace. She's a wedding planner out in Toms River. She said I should propose at the New York Botanical Garden—she'd had a few clients do that, and it always worked."

"That sounds romantic enough."

"I thought about it. I went around and looked at different options. But it seemed like a really obvious thing to do, and I didn't know how to set it up so she wouldn't be suspicious. So I decided to improve on the idea—take the basic concept and do something memorable. Something she wouldn't forget."

"Please tell me you didn't make her climb a tree," I said.

"That would have been cheaper, and maybe more effective. What I actually did was hire a string quartet. The idea was that I would lead her into this woodland area, and then when we walked by, they would start playing this Beethoven song, and I would get down on my knees and ask her to marry me."

"That sounds romantic," I said, trying hard to underreact. If a man half as cute as Adam had whisked me away to the Botanical Garden and proposed to me *with a freaking string quartet in the background*, I would have blown a circuit right on the spot. "So what went wrong?"

"Somebody else had done the same thing, the week before, on *The Bachelorette*. It was out in California, but it was the same idea, with the beautiful garden and the string quartet. She thought I had stolen the idea from the TV show. I tried telling her that I didn't watch *The Bachelorette*, which, I mean, was totally the case, but she didn't believe me. She thought I had gotten the idea from my secretary or something."

"Well, that's just ridiculous," I said. "You proposed. It was romantic. Why be persnickety about the details?"

"If she had just been persnickety about it, as you say, I could have dealt with that. She was not persnickety. She was furious. She wouldn't even look at the ring. Then she took off running for the exit. I tried everything. I tried to explain. I tried to get her to drink something cold to calm her down. I drove her back to New Jersey and tried to get her to go out to dinner with me. She wouldn't talk to me the whole evening. First thing the next morning, she piles all her stuff in her car and takes off for Connecticut. I never saw her again."

"Bitch," I said, and I meant it. If that was how his last relationship had gone, no wonder he wasn't trying to be romantic. He was probably subconsciously sabotaging himself with his clothing selection and wasn't even aware of it. "That was a crummy thing to do, Adam. I'm so sorry she treated you that way. You didn't deserve it."

"I did, though."

"That's not true," I said.

"She sent me a note, later. She explained why she acted that way. She told me that when I proposed, I wasn't authentic. I wasn't being my true self. I was just pretending to be romantic and borrowing somebody else's ideas. If I truly had romantic feelings towards her, I would have been able to come up with something beautiful and unique and special. And since I didn't, she felt she had to dump me on the spot."

I let my mouth fall open in shock. "Oh, my God. You didn't *believe* that line of bullshit, did you?" I wanted to drive up to Connecticut and throw rocks at this woman's car, and at her head if she wasn't too scared to come outside and face me like a woman.

"Of course I did. After all, she was right. I'm not romantic. It doesn't come naturally to me. And I'm no good at pretending otherwise."

I gave him a sad little smile. "Oh, Adam," I said. "You poor thing."

The good news, from where I sat, was that if he was willing to tell me all this depressing backstory, that meant he was being honest with me. It sounded like this Marie person had him all twisted up in knots in the relationship department, which wasn't ideal, but it was something I could work on rather than something that was hopelessly wrong with him. *All you have to do*, I thought, *is not be as much of a conniving bitch as his last girlfriend, and everything will work itself out.*

"I just figured you needed to know, that's all," he said.

"So, when she left you, what did you do?"

"I drank," he said. "A lot."

"A man after my own heart, then." I tilted my empty wineglass in his direction.

"You want another glass of wine?" he asked.

"God, yes."

Chapter 19

The date got much better after the second glass of chardonnay. Of course, lots of things get better after two glasses of chardonnay, which is why they sell it in those big bottles. Anyway, the wine took the edge off, which was all to the good. Then our dinner came, which meant that we didn't have to talk quite so much. Adam didn't say anything else about his ex, and he didn't ask about my checkered romantic history, and neither of us said anything about our jobs. It was delightful.

The problem was that the date didn't seem to be going anywhere. We liked each other, we had a mutual attraction, and we both thought that Adam's bronzed salmon was dry. It wasn't clear that we had any shared interests, though. I didn't get anywhere talking about movies with him, and he didn't get anywhere talking about sports with me. He liked skiing in Vermont and I liked snorkeling in the Caribbean. He liked Springsteen and I liked Bon Jovi and that was about the limit of our combined musical knowledge.

But it wasn't a bad first date, at least not by my standards. I was seriously thinking about a second date, if he was willing. But I wasn't that sure he would go for it. We did live a long ways apart, so it wouldn't be convenient for either of us to keep on dating. I couldn't blame him if he didn't want to ask me out again. I was hopeful that the power of the low-cut garnet-red dress would inspire him, but I was uneasy about my chances.

Adam wanted the peach cobbler, so I ordered a slice of pecan pie that I didn't want and nibbled at it. He attacked the cobbler, leaving tiny drops of ice cream on his worn orange hoodie. He wiped them off with his napkin, looking vaguely sheepish at his inability to eat neatly. "It's really good," he said. "How's yours?"

"It's fine. I'm just not hungry enough to finish it, that's all."

"You mind?" he asked. I slid him the plate, and he made

the pie disappear. I envied him his appetite, and wondered if it crossed over to other spheres of activity.

The waiter handed Adam the bill, and he fished a credit card out of his wallet to pay for dinner. "You want some coffee?" he asked.

"I should be good, thanks." I was maybe a tiny bit tipsy, but I thought I would be safe enough to drive home. There was a McDonald's on the way where I could grab a cup of coffee if I needed the stimulant.

"Where did you end up parking?" he asked.

"I'm a block or two away, in a parking garage."

"Well, why don't I drive you over there? It's cold outside, and slippery. I want to make sure you get there safely."

I thought about making the long, cold walk uphill on the icy sidewalk, by myself, after a blah first date. "I would appreciate that, thanks."

I retrieved my coat, and we waited inside in the bar until the valet brought Adam's Jaguar around. The temperature had dropped another ten degrees, and a chilly wind was blowing off the river. Adam cranked up the heater and drove around the block to the garage where I had parked my Audi.

"OK, then," he said. "Safe travels."

"Thanks. I had a good time," I said.

"I did, too." He had a slight smile on his face, and he looked absolutely fetching in the dim light. But he wasn't leaning over to kiss me, or even hold my hand. Maybe he was afraid to. Maybe he was bored. Maybe he'd had a terrible time and couldn't wait to get rid of me. Maybe he would go home and drunk-dial his ex. *Maybe I'm never going to see him again.* I felt my body go tense, like before taking a deep dive into black water.

"So do you want to go out again next weekend?" he asked.

"Please tell me you didn't say yes," Pacey said.

"I wanted to," I said. "I almost did, like a reflex. But I stopped myself in time."

I was in my car, driving north towards Morristown, and

talking to Pacey so she wouldn't call me first thing in the morning and wake me up when all I wanted to do was sleep late.

"Good work," she said.

"He's attractive. And he's smart. And I like him. And he's attractive, if I hadn't said that already. But I decided that if he wanted a second date, that he needed to work for it, and not just show up."

"That's a hundred percent right," Pacey said. "Remember, confidence is sexy. You just have to keep telling yourself that you are a desirable modern woman, not some lonely, desperate loser who can't find a man."

"Hey!" I said.

"Not trying to be insulting, dear sister, but if you project that kind of attitude, you'll never get anywhere. So where did you leave it?"

"He is supposed to make reservations somewhere," I said. "He's going to e-mail it to me, and if I approve, I'll meet him there. If he chooses the Roy Rogers at the Cheesequake rest stop, I'll know to dump him. If he chooses someplace suitably romantic and interesting, then we'll see."

"That should work. This is what you do in the meantime. Clear your mind. Don't think about him. Don't try to think about him. It'll only cause you problems. Work if you have work to do. Go see a movie if you don't. But don't spend the weekend obsessing about him. Understand?"

"Sounds reasonable," I said.

"If you're really desperate, you can come over and watch my kids and let me do some laundry in peace, and even take a nap."

"Didn't hear that," I lied. "The cell reception is breaking up."

"Fine," Pacey said. "Don't help your sister who loves you and wants you to be happy. Go relax. Enjoy being single and free and irresponsible."

"Thanks! I will."

I couldn't come up with anything really irresponsible to do, though, so I stayed home on Saturday and spent the day in my pajamas. I watched a couple of soppy romantic comedies on cable, lying on my couch with a glass of chardonnay in my hand. It was a relaxing way to spend the day, and it didn't require me to think, but it wasn't productive, and it didn't help me deal with the low-grade anxiety I was feeling. So on Sunday, I drove down to the Bridgewater Commons Mall for a good dose of retail therapy.

I didn't need anything, but that was hardly the point. I made a quick run through Macy's to see if they had updated their shoe selection, and as always, I was disappointed. I poked around Pottery Barn looking for a new entertainment center for my apartment, and I found one that I liked, but buying it would mean that I would have to get a bigger television, and that meant I would have to research a lot of technical stuff to figure out the right size and type of TV to get, and the thought of doing that gave me a headache. I got lunch at California Pizza Kitchen and planned my assault on Bloomingdale's and Lord & Taylor.

I ended up not getting anything at either store. I couldn't find anything I liked, and I couldn't justify spending the money on stuff that didn't quite fit or that wasn't right in some other way. Just about everything I wear to work is a variation on the basic theme of a navy jacket worn over a white silk blouse, which is the default Woman Lawyer Uniform, as set forth by either the fashion gods or the American Bar Association, I forget which. I must have looked at fifteen different dark-colored jackets at Bloomingdale's, but every one of them had some minor flaw—too expensive, some of them, and the cheaper ones were either too short or too long or had cheaper fabric than what I wanted. I did find a lovely gray striped skirt that I spent a long time thinking about buying. It was a Kate Spade number that fit me perfectly, and it would have gone nicely with half the jackets in my closet, but it was expensive and I couldn't decide whether it actually looked good on me or not. I spent five minutes going over the pros and cons of buying it before I put it back on the rack.

I am not a perfectionist, and I don't aspire to be one. I don't think that every single thing about a piece of clothing, or a relationship, has to be perfect. All I want is to not expend any unnecessary energy on worrying about things, or forcing things to fit that aren't ever going to fit. I want to be sure of myself and not be weighted down by uncertainty all the time. I hated the feeling of standing in a store, holding a perfectly fine skirt that I thought would improve my wardrobe, and not being able to decide one way or another whether it was worth it.

I would ten times rather order takeout and eat and be done with it than spend an hour in the kitchen wondering if I had the oven on high enough and if the sauce I was making was going to come together or not. I would rather spend hours finding the perfect case on Westlaw to cinch a legal argument than dashing off a memo that said that the arguments on both sides were equally good. I don't like not knowing where I stand. It makes me uncomfortable and out of place.

I left Bloomingdale's and walked past the Victoria's Secret store on the top level, and there I felt even more uncomfortable and out of place. I didn't need any underwear, but I had a sudden impulse to walk in and pick out some sexy, stunning lingerie for my second date with Adam. Except I didn't know if there was going to be a second date. I hoped so, but if he wasn't going to make even a minimal effort to be more romantic, I wasn't going to make the effort to pursue him. And even if there was a romantic second date, he hadn't so much as kissed me yet. Was I being presumptuous by even thinking about lingerie? Would he even care?

I walked past Victoria's Secret and out through Macy's to my car. I pulled on to 287 and merged into the fast lane. Driving therapy was a lot simpler than retail therapy, and a lot cheaper so long as I didn't get a ticket.

Monday was easier, because I had work to distract me from thinking too hard about Adam. I told myself that Pacey was right, and that all I had to do was wait for him to do something, and that I would be able to figure out what to do based on whatever it was that he did. All I had to do was bide my time, and not think about his expressive brown eyes, or his strong, warm hands, or the well-defined muscles of his chest. *Stop that, woman*, I told myself. *Calm down. Be patient. You'll hear from him soon enough.*

I was deep in the middle of reviewing the credentials of an expert witness when our receptionist stuck her head in my office.

"Are you the girl in the red dress?" she asked.

"Not today," I said.

"I have a package up front addressed to the girl in the red dress. It must be for you."

"How do you know?" I asked.

"Because I am the only other female person on this floor, and I don't have a red dress, and nobody knows to send me anything here except my husband, and it's not my birthday or anniversary, and Valentine's Day was last month, and if he sent me anything else at any other time, the world would implode in on itself and all life on Earth would come to an abrupt end."

"That's convincing."

"You, on the other hand, being young, single, and available, must have a closet full of red dresses, and suitors lined up around the block."

"Would that it was so," I sighed.

"It doesn't look like flowers," she said. "Might be fragile. You should come pick it up."

I trooped over to the front desk. Whatever it was, it was in a large box.

"Is there a card?" I asked.

"Maybe it's in the box," she said. "Hard to say."

"I can't imagine what it is," I said. It wasn't flowers, or I thought not. If it was chocolates, there was enough sugar in there to give diabetes to the entire building. "Maybe we should have it scanned for high explosives."

"I am incredibly curious as to what is in that box," the receptionist said. "I am even more curious as to when you will get it off my desk."

I lifted the box. It wasn't that heavy, which was good. It didn't rattle, which didn't mean anything. "I'll take it back to my office."

"If it's popcorn, I want some," she said.

"If it's anything edible, everybody's getting some." The box was big enough to hold a side of beef.

I walked the box back to my office, and then looked inside my desk to find an X-Acto knife. I cut away the tape and opened the top of the box. I found a card inside, right on top of a large quantity of Styrofoam packaging peanuts. It was a generic card that said "Thinking of You" in flowing blue script. It didn't say who it was from, although there wasn't anyone else other than Adam who would have sent me anything.

I knelt down on the floor and tilted the box over so that the Styrofoam peanuts spilled out into my trash can. I stopped when I saw a dark hank of hair inside. I recoiled, pulling my hand back. I banged my elbow against my desk.

It's a head, I thought. *It's a goddamned human head. Bastard sent me a human head.*

One of my fellow associates, a thick, pasty fellow named Warren Briggs, heard me struggling and came over from across the hall to check on me. "You OK there?"

Warren was a nice enough person, and I thought he probably had a giant crush on me, but he was one of the most boring people on the face of the earth, and married to boot. I thought about telling him to go away, but I needed a witness in case there was criminal evidence in the box. "Can you just check and see what's in there? I'm having a little trouble."

"Sure thing," he said. He grabbed whatever-it-was by the hair and gave it a yank. "Oh. Cute," he said.

"Cute?"

He lifted something large and brownish out of the box, spraying Styrofoam peanuts everywhere. "Looks like a giraffe," he said. "Cute. Did you order it?"

I got up from the floor to take a closer look. It was a stuffed giraffe. It was very high quality, almost lifelike. It was maybe two and a half feet tall, and had packaging material clinging to its tail.

"It was a surprise," I said.

"I seem to have made a mess," Warren said. "Let me help

pick up the peanuts."

"No," I said. "I'll get them later. I need to think for a minute, if you can leave me alone for a little bit."

"Happy to help," he said, and stepped back across the hall. He had a couple of Styrofoam peanuts clinging to the back of his pants, but I figured he would find them soon enough. I reached over and closed the door and sat back down on the floor, trying to process what was going on.

I decided to ignore the fact that Adam hadn't sent me flowers or chocolates or chardonnay or, you know, anything that you would normally send to a female person in whom you had a romantic interest. If Adam hadn't sent me anything, I would have been fine with that. If he was going to send me something, it was best that he'd sent me something romantically ambiguous. But a giant stuffed giraffe wasn't romantically ambiguous. It wasn't romantic at all. It was the complete polar opposite of romantic. A stuffed giraffe was a thing that you sent somebody when you had no idea what else to send them. If he had sent me a Hickory Farms summer sausage, well, I would be able to figure out what *that* meant in short order. But what could a stuffed giraffe *mean* other than *hey, I got you a stuffed giraffe!*

I wanted to understand Adam. It was fairly clear that I didn't. More than that, I wanted to understand myself and how I felt about him, and whether my attraction to him was just based on a surface appraisal of his good looks and energy, or whether it was based on something deeper, something substantial. The stuffed giraffe didn't help with that. It was just a large plush *thing* that would take up space in my apartment, and that had already shed a large quantity of Styrofoam peanuts across my office. If it were a clue, I didn't know what it meant. If it was a symbol, I didn't have the codebook. All I knew for certain was that I didn't have any better idea of what Adam felt about me, or what I felt about him, than I had before.

Chapter 20

Adam, to his credit, had picked a decent restaurant. It was a seafood place overlooking the Manasquan River in Point Pleasant Beach, just a few blocks from the boardwalk. It would have been packed in the summer, but it was still late March, and winter was still hanging around like somebody owed it money. We watched the boats move up and down the channel as a cold rain pelted against the window. There was candlelight, calamari, and chardonnay. Adam was wearing a sport jacket and a clean shirt and it looked like he had gotten a haircut. I had put on a nice floral dress, with a white cardigan over it. Everything was in place for a wonderful romantic evening, and I would have been perfectly happy and content if I hadn't been bored out of my skull.

I didn't want to talk about gadgets or sports. He didn't want to talk about reality television or politics. Neither of us wanted to talk about our jobs or our families, and we didn't know anyone in common that we could gossip about. We finished our appetizers and sat there and stared at each other, both of us hoping that the other person could find something for us to talk about.

"We should have gone to see a movie first," Adam said. "That way, we could talk about the movie."

"They have a movie theater at the mall in Bridgewater where they serve dinner during the movie," I said. "You go and watch the movie and eat at the same time. My sister and her husband do that when they can get a babysitter. It's more efficient that way."

"There's something to be said for efficiency, I guess."

"The problem is that sometimes the food isn't good, and sometimes the movie isn't good, and then when that happens you're kind of stuck."

"That's not good," he said. "But at least we won't have to worry about that here. The food's good. I used to eat here every weekend for a couple of months."

"Seems like a long way to drive," I said. "Unless you're

really into fresh seafood."

"A friend of mine from college inherited a couple of rental properties down here. This whole area got hit pretty hard during Sandy, and the houses he owned had some water damage, so he decided to do a full renovation. He knew I had a lot of experience, so he called me to check and see if I'd be interested in helping him get the houses fixed so he could rent them again over the summer. I would drive up on Saturday mornings, and we'd spend the day working, and then we'd come here for dinner."

"So what all did you do?" I asked. I have only an academic interest in house renovation, but I watch the occasional real estate reality TV show and it was something to talk about.

"We had to remove the flooring," he said. "That was the first step. Everything was soaked. We ripped out the carpet, which was a huge job, mostly because it stank. We put in new hardwood and kept it that way, because it would be easier to deal with if there was ever another storm. The deck was a total loss, although we kind of lucked out on it because we were able to reutilize a lot of the scrap lumber once it had all dried out. I sanded it down and used it for wainscoting on the staircase. It was a really cool effect, too."

"That's a good idea." I said.

"Yeah," he said. "Uncle Sheldon actually came up with it."

"Oh," I said.

"Yeah. It's funny, because I've been forced into doing all this nonsense with the estate. You'd think all of that would remind me of him, but it hasn't. I hadn't thought about him at all until just now, thinking about us working together on that house."

"I'm sorry about your uncle," I said.

He smiled. "It's all right."

He told me about the work that he and his friend and Uncle Sheldon had done with the kitchen, and the bathrooms, and the perils attendant to installing window air conditioning units on upstairs floors. That reminded me of the time my father had tried to install a new hot water heater by himself, and that reminded him of a cast-iron bathtub he had tried to install in a house up in Syracuse, and then our entrees arrived and we didn't have to talk much after that. The restaurant was right about the seafood being fresh, and Adam was right about it being good.

"Are you sure you don't want coffee?" Adam asked.

"Very sure," I said.

"The desserts are not really that great. Either that, or I'm not hungry."

"Me neither."

"If the weather was just a little nicer, we could go out on the boardwalk and stroll for a little while. Maybe get some ice cream or something."

"I would like that," I said. "If it wasn't for the weather. It's supposed to be nice next weekend, though."

We had a nice recovery on what had been shaping up to be an unproductive second date. I didn't have the desperate feeling I had last time, where I thought Adam was slipping away from me and that I'd never see him again. Being with him was starting to feel comfortable and right, the way it had been when we first met. I was looking forward to our next date, whatever that turned out to be.

"I was thinking more about this weekend," Adam said.

"What did you have in mind?" I asked.

"I think we should have sex."

I heard him say the words, but it took me a moment to process the fact that he had said them. He had a bland look on his face, as though he'd said that he thought we should have some coffee after all. I finally decided that he was either joking, or pretending to be joking to see how I would respond.

"You mean right here? On the table?" I asked.

"That wasn't quite what I had in mind. I'm not an exhibitionist. Unless you're an exhibitionist, in which case maybe we could start small and work our way up."

"So you were kidding me, then," I said.

"I wasn't kidding. I think we should have sex."

"Why? Because it's our second date?"

"That's not why," he said.

"Why, then?"

"Because it would be fun. Because it would be good for us. Because we can."

This was not romantic. This was not seductive. This was preposterous, and presumptive, and worst of all, it was *working*. I was starting to feel a little lightheaded, and it wasn't because of the chardonnay. I needed to slow this down a bit before I was swept away.

"Let's just suppose," I said. "Let's just suppose for one second that this was something we should be doing, which it isn't. Do you have some place in mind for us to go?"

"You remember me telling you that my friend had a beach house he rented out?" he said. "I still have the key. It's not that far from here, and I know nobody's using it. We could take your car and be there in five minutes."

That dealt with that objection, and a cozy little beach house certainly had romantic possibilities. I was now fairly certain that Adam had planned all this ahead of time, but if I confronted him about it, he'd just grin and deny doing any such thing.

"I just want to hear one good reason why you think this is a good idea," I said. "Convince me."

Adam didn't say anything. He looked at me, and there was a light in his eyes that hadn't been there before. It was almost as though he was seeing me for the first time. I felt for a moment like he was a wolf and I was a raw bloody steak.

"Because you want to," he said at last. "Don't you?"

I could think of any number of good reasons to say no, and only one good reason to say yes. It was late. I did have to drive home at some point. The weather wasn't great. I thought he was rushing things. I wasn't sure how I felt. All I had to do was sit calmly and explain very gently to Adam that tonight wasn't the best time.

"Yes," I said.

I was surprised to hear myself say it, but I had said it, and I couldn't take it back. I didn't want to take it back. I wanted to have sex with Adam. If that was a deranged, desperate thing to want right then, it didn't matter to me, not right then. I wanted to feel his touch, his warmness, his skin soft against mine. Compared to that desire, all the other reasons felt small and unimportant.

We left the restaurant and got in my car. I drove down the beach road until Adam told me where to turn and where I could park. He got out of the car first, and came around to the driver's side to take my hand. The houses were all packed together, and I didn't know which house belonged to his friend.

"It's the one on the right," he said. It was a tiny house, and not quite on the beachfront, but I wasn't in any mood to pay any attention to trifles.

Adam found the right key on the third try. We went inside and I followed him up the stairs. I gave an appreciative glance to the rough wood on the wainscoting, in case he asked me about it later. He opened the door to the master bedroom and we went inside together.

It was freezing in there. It wasn't just cold. It was penguin-exhibit cold. It was subarctic, with global warming a distant rumor.

"Well, this is not good," he said. "I mean, it could be a little warmer in here."

"It is ridiculously cold," I said. "We can't stay here."

It was a beautiful room, decorated in blue pastels with a nautical motif. You could see a corner of the Atlantic out of the window. The bed looked inviting and had a thick, warm down comforter. But it didn't have a fireplace, and therefore was uninhabitable for anyone this side of polar bears.

Adam walked over to the window air conditioning unit. "Here's the problem," he said. "This thing has probably been running all winter. Let me just turn it off. It'll be fine."

"It will not be fine. It is *never* going to be fine. You should check the bathroom for icebergs."

"It's not that bad," he said.

"Not that bad? *Not that bad*? This is unacceptable."

"Some people like having a cold room to sleep in, so they can be warm under the covers."

"Those people are fools and idiots. Is there another bedroom? Preferably one south of the Arctic Circle?"

"There's only one other bedroom, and it is set up for kids. Bunk beds. Don't worry. It'll warm up before too long."

"Can I take a moment and remind you exactly why you wanted to come here?"

He grinned that insufferable grin of his. "I remember."

"This is an activity that is usually conducted *without clothes*. I am feeling distinctly underdressed at the moment. I could use a scarf. And a parka. And a set of hand warmers."

"We could go downstairs. Get some coffee. Come back when the room is warm."

"If we do that, I can't promise I'm going to want to come back here," I said. "Don't get me wrong. I want to have sex with you, tonight. But if we wait too long, I am going to think of reasons not to do this, and there are reasons not to do this."

"OK, then," he said. "I have an idea."

"Do tell."

Adam found a wide, low armchair, which was upholstered in a green nubbly fabric. He picked it up effortlessly and carried it over to a far corner of the room. "The main vent is over here," he said. "Come here. You can feel the heat coming up from the floor. And I turned the thermostat up to seventy-nine; it should be warmed up before too much longer."

I followed him over to where he was standing. It felt marginally warmer there, like going from a glacier to a slightly smaller glacier at a lower elevation.

"What would you want to do?" I asked. "Just sit here and wait for the spring thaw?"

"You realize that we're doing this all backward, right? I mean, we haven't even kissed yet."

"So?"

"So I was thinking that we should."

He wreathed his arms around my body, encircling me. It was already feeling warmer. I gave him a long, low, wet lingering kiss.

"See, that's what I mean," he said. "We need to do things in the proper order."

"Stop talking," I said.

I straightened up a bit, and he responded just the way I wanted him to, by kissing my neck. He took his time, pressing his lips against my soft flesh, exploring with his tongue, then repeating the process. I felt my breaths get deeper and sharper as desire swept over me, wave on wave.

Adam slipped my cardigan off, and it fell to the floor. He found the zipper of my dress, lowering it just enough to find the bra underneath. He unfastened the bra with a practiced hand, and drew my body closer to his. I lowered my lips against him and kissed him again. His tongue felt smooth and warm in my mouth, like a bracing glass of wine.

I let him come up for air after a long moment. "Getting warmer?" he asked.

"Working on it."

One of his hands was caressing my back, and the other one was beginning to explore my neckline. He was careful not to expose too much of my bare flesh to the cold air, for which I would have been grateful if I wasn't so lost in the earthy smell of his cologne.

"It's body heat, you know," he said. "If you're ever stuck in a snowbank, you just huddle up with someone."

I straightened up to kiss his lips again, hoping to get him to shut up. He pressed his hand against my chest, moving it in slow, gentle circles.

"Shall we?" he said.

I glanced over at the bed, at its thick down comforter.

"It's a risk," I said. "But it's one I'm willing to take." My dress fell halfway down my body, taking my bra with it. The room was still ice-cold, but I was feeling a warmth course through me, and when he looked at me in that moment, I felt it blaze to my very fingertips.

"Let's get in bed before I get frostbite," I said.

Chapter 21

I woke up the next morning under that toasty comforter, warm, happy, sexually fulfilled, and utterly alone. Adam wasn't in bed next to me. He wasn't elsewhere in the room. I couldn't hear any telltale morning sounds coming from the bathroom. Despite all the ups and downs, it had been a wonderful evening, ending in a deeply satisfying and thrilling way. I had expected the morning to be even better, and here I was, naked and alone.

There has to be a reasonable explanation, I thought. *You don't just get up and leave someone alone in a room without a reasonable explanation, or at least a note.* I looked around the room, and indeed, there did seem to be a scrap of white paper on the coffee table. The problem was that the only way I would be able to *read* the note would be to get out from under the comforter and expose my bare body to the elements. It was warmer than it had been, but there was every possibility that it was still ice-cold out there, and I had zero interest in testing the veracity of that possibility.

OK, I thought. *He left a note.* But I couldn't figure out why he had ventured out of the bedroom this early. I considered the alarming possibility that he might be a runner—not that he had run off, mind you, but that he was one of those monomaniacs who believes that it's advisable to start your heart each morning with a brisk five-mile run. For all I knew, he was a marathoner, which would require me to either stand around assorted racecourses across the country, waiting for him to jog by, or else start running myself. I shuddered at the thought.

I snuggled deeply into the covers, trying to stay as warm as possible. I closed my eyes and tried to will myself back to sleep, but it was clear that the demands of biology were going to force me out of bed sooner rather than later. I wiggled my way down to the far end of the bed and commenced wrapping myself up in the comforter and sheets as tightly as possible. I bunched the bedding under my arms and stood up, and unsteadily made my way over to the closet, hoping against hope that someone had left a robe or a sweatshirt or some warm piece of clothing.

The closet was empty. I swore. I would have thrown things if I had things handy to throw. I swept back towards the bathroom, stooping to pick the note off the table on the way. It was ice-cold in the bathroom, but the note was scorching hot:

I have gone to get coffee. I can't want to be back, so I can get back in bed with you. There was more to it, including a line about *devouring your warm flesh* that I hoped just meant that he had spent too much time reading vampire or werewolf fiction, but it was deeply felt and enthusiastic and if he managed to show up in the next five minutes with actual coffee, with cream and sugar, I would be willing to forgive him.

When Adam didn't appear right away, I decided to jump in the shower, mostly to warm up. The water was satisfyingly hot, and the towels were thick and soft. I wrapped the largest one around myself and headed back into the bedroom, where Adam was waiting with two tall cups of coffee.

"Good morning," he said. "I had a little clothes shopping to do," indicating a large red plastic bag on the foot of the bed. "I thought you might appreciate it."

"You went clothes shopping?" I was mystified. Not that he didn't need new clothes, mind you, but it seemed like an odd thing to do, especially in a beach town that probably didn't have a lot in the way of clothes stores.

"Well, I mean, that towel looks very fetching on you and all, but you might want to wear something else for later." He pointed towards my dress, lying in a wrinkled heap on the floor.

"Coffee first," I said. He reached across the bed and handed me one of the cups.

"Two sugars," he said. "I didn't know if you took creamer or not."

I took a long, restorative sip. "It's fine." It was better than that. It was *hot*.

"You read the note," he said. It wasn't a question.

"I did. It was very nice. Romantic, even."

"It's not my strong suit, but I try."

"You did very well last night," I said. "I had a great time."

"The first of many. Hopefully."

"We'll see. For the moment, I would like to fix my hair, if you can be a little patient."

He smiled that infuriating, insufferable smile that indicated that he thought he had my number. "Not a problem."

It turned out that the red bag contained a black sweatshirt and matching sweatpants, both of which said "Jenkinson's Boardwalk." "Best I could do on short notice," Adam explained.

I thought about giving him a tongue-lashing for abandoning me in order to buy me some cheap, tacky fleece. But it was still chilly outside, and it beat freezing to death. "I appreciate it," I said.

"Of course, you don't have to wear it right now," he said. "If you don't want to."

"I think clothes are a good idea right now," I said. "Do you have any specific ideas on how we should spend the rest of the day?"

"I am just trying to take things one moment at a time," he said.

"Well, it's worked out so far."

"That it did," he said. "By the way, while I was out, I went and fetched the copies of the paperwork for the estate, like you asked before. I had meant to give them to you last night, but I forgot."

"Just as well," I said. "Real estate and romance don't mix." I slipped the sweatsuit on, and it was more than a bit baggy.

"Anyway, no need for you to go over it right now, but at some point, we're going to need to talk about the issue with the house. Did you and your mother take a look at it when you were down there?"

"We did a quick drive-by." I drank the last of my coffee,

and wished Adam had thought to grab me a scone or a muffin or something else with some calories in it. "We were in a hurry to get back. Mother did a little research, and she found out that the house in the will was the one where she and Sheldon had their honeymoon, back fifty years ago."

"I hadn't known that. I guess that's why he bought it, then. How does she feel about the house? Do you think it brings back bad memories for her?"

"I think it brings back good memories," I said. "But they're painful memories, too."

"So, if there was an arrangement we could make, where the estate took the house off her hands, would she consider it?"

"I can't speak for her, Adam. And I have a rule about not doing settlement negotiations in sweat pants. But if you made her a reasonable offer, I'm sure she'd listen."

"A reasonable offer based on what?" he asked.

"Well, based on the equity in the house. I'd have to look at the paperwork. Do you happen to have the HUD-1 where I could look at it?"

"Sure," he said. He opened up his gym bag and drew out one of those red-brown expanding file folders that lawyers call a "redwell" and everyone else calls "one of those expanding file folder thingies." Everything was arranged in file folders. I was impressed. Adam may not have been the most romantic man in the world, but there was a lot to be said for practicality, too. The HUD-1 was in its own folder, and I looked at it first.

"What kind of offer were you thinking about?" I asked.

"I hadn't decided," he said. "I want this to be fair. Say, maybe twenty-five thousand in exchange for a quitclaim deed."

"Seriously?"

"That's a pretty good haul for just showing up to a funeral, and getting rid of a house you don't want," he said.

"How did you arrive at that figure?" I asked.

"Honestly? It's based largely on the amount of money I could raise. Given the debts that the estate has accrued lately, I would be taking money out of my own pocket.

Twenty-five thousand dollars is a significant percentage of my net worth at the moment."

"Have you looked at these documents closely?" I asked. "Because if you had, you'd realize just how bad an offer that is."

The HUD-1 is the document that gets completed at any real estate closing. It is basically the summary of who contributes what money to the deal, and where the money goes. The HUD-1 for the house on Idaho Street indicated that Sheldon Berkman had purchased the property for $645,000 in June of last year. Given its size and location, it was priced about forty or fifty thousand dollars under the comparable value for homes in the area. That indicated that either Sheldon had gotten a very good deal, or that the house was in very poor condition—and given that the house was over fifty years old, I thought the latter was more likely. Whichever way it was, that type of information doesn't show up on the HUD-1.

What does show up is the amount of the mortgage. Sheldon had only borrowed $375,000 to buy the house. That meant that Sheldon made a down payment of $270,000, which likely represented every nickel he had managed to save throughout his Air Force service and his subsequent career. If the house was the sole asset left in the estate, that meant the codicil had taken that one asset away from Adam and gifted it to my mother.

I could see why Adam would be sore about this; anybody would be. It wasn't fair for him. But it wasn't reasonable for him to want my mother to trade him a quarter of a million dollars in equity for a twenty-five-thousand-dollar gratuity. Nobody would ever agree to such a lopsided deal.

Having said that, I knew Mother wasn't crazy about the house. She'd be glad to be done with the property and the long shadow that Sheldon Berkman's death had cast over her life—but not if that meant walking away from hundreds of thousands of dollars.

"It's not a terrible offer," Adam said. "Admittedly, it's not ideal. But I take over all the risk. I assume the mortgage payment, which is not insubstantial, not to mention the property taxes. I'll find a real estate agent and try to find a buyer. It's a very tidy guaranteed profit for your mother, and all she has to do is sign a piece of paper."

"She can rent the place out and make that much in one year," I pointed out. "It's not reasonable."

"You're assuming that she's entitled to the house," Adam said. "I am not convinced of that."

I should have stopped there. I should have realized that he was talking nonsense and changed the subject and taken him downstairs to get something to eat and replenish our blood sugar. You don't gain anything by arguing about important issues on an empty stomach. Maybe everything would have happened the way it did without me pressing the issue the way I did, but it still would have saved a lot of upset and hurt feelings later on, mostly mine.

"You are *wrong*," I said. "Look at the codicil. It is very clear about this. My mother went to the funeral. That was the only condition in the codicil, and the grant of the house by your uncle to her is very clear. She fulfilled the condition; therefore, she inherits the house, complete with the mortgage and the equity. You don't have any claim to it as executor, and you don't have any claim to it as the heir."

"I'm not sure about that," he said. "I don't think the codicil is necessarily valid."

"The codicil was signed properly. It was witnessed properly. The affidavits are all here. Everything appears to be in order."

"I understand all that. And I know you do this for a living, Wendy. But I don't think my uncle was in his right mind when he wrote that codicil. I don't think he meant to give all that money to your mother. I think he was delusional."

"The legal standard for whether someone is in their right mind for drafting a will is very low. Admittedly, this was an unusual bequest."

"Admittedly," he said, taking a sip of coffee.

"But it was made to someone that he knew; someone that he had a relationship with. He didn't give it to the Hell's

Angels or the Three Musketeers or the three-armed alien people from beyond the Crab Nebula. He gave it to his ex-wife. Even if he was as lovesick over her as he seemed to be, that's pretty far from being delusional."

"You don't know how much he talked about your mother, especially since he moved down to Cape May. *Delusional* is putting it mildly. As far as his financial condition goes, believe me, you don't know the half of it. The house is the only asset left in the estate, and there are all kinds of debts that are coming due, and I don't have the liquidity to deal with them effectively. This is a very messed-up situation, and it's all falling into my lap, and I cannot make it come out right unless I can make a deal with your mother about this house."

"Believe me when I tell you this," I said. "Threatening a contest of this codicil in court is not going to make things any easier for you. It is not going to make things less expensive. And, I don't know if you realize this or not, it is going to put the two of us on opposite sides of a lawsuit."

"What do you mean by that?" he asked.

"If you file a will contest, I will be the one who represents my mother in court. There are conflict-of-interest rules for attorneys in this kind of situation, and the biggest one of those says that you can't sleep with an opposing party."

"Holy shit," he said. "I hadn't thought about that."

"I am not trying to sandbag you with this information," I said. "I'm not. If I had thought this was a real possibility, I never would have gone out with you in the first place. But if you're seriously going to take my mother to court over this will, we can't see each other. It's as simple as that."

"What the hell? We can't see each other anymore? Over Uncle Sheldon's will?"

I crossed my arms over my new, itchy fleece sweatshirt. "I have to, Adam. I don't want to. But I don't have a choice. If you're going through with this will contest, we have to stop seeing each other. And we have to do it now."

"I don't have a choice about this, Wendy."

"Then neither do I."

Chapter 22

Adam didn't handle the news very well. I couldn't blame him, because I didn't handle the news very well either, but he was more obnoxious about it. I think he had expected to come back to the room and enter straight into another round between the sheets, and I'd disappointed him already. (Not that I would have been *averse* to such a thing, but a girl likes to have a coffee first sometimes.) So he was already worked up, and me breaking up with him—no matter how reluctantly—made things worse.

"There's no law that says you have to represent your mother," he argued. "She could always find another lawyer. You could recuse yourself."

"Even if I did that," I explained, "it still wouldn't matter. I am a party-at-interest in this litigation."

Adam looked puzzled. "Wait. No, you're not. You're not named in the will."

"The codicil says the house goes to Emily Thornhill *and her heirs*. I stand to inherit from her. If she decides she doesn't want the house and disclaims the inheritance, then, according to the will, the house goes to me and my brother and sister, in equal shares."

"So if your mother decided she didn't want the house, the house wouldn't automatically go back to the estate?"

"Not the way the codicil is written, no."

"That's crazy. You never knew Uncle Sheldon even existed until he died. And you end up with a third of the estate, and so do your brother and sister, who didn't even come to the funeral. And I would get nothing. That's total crap." He started pacing around the room, and almost tripped on his gym bag. "It's not fair. And don't tell me life's not fair, because I know that, but still. I mean, that's really unfair."

"I know this sucks for you, Adam. Take a deep breath. Calm down. Even if you go through with this lawsuit, which I am not recommending that you do, this is just a temporary situation. One way or another, it will be resolved, and then we will be free to do whatever we want."

"I know how I feel already," he said. "I don't need to wait. I very much don't need to wait until this nonsense with the will is cleared up, because I feel like that's going to take forever. I want to be with you. I don't want to break up with you, and I don't understand why you feel you have to break up with me."

"It's basic legal ethics," I explained. "You can't sleep with an adverse party. And as long as you insist on treating my mother like an adverse party, that means we can't be together, no matter how much we would like to be."

"It's not about ethics for me," he said. "It's about financial survival at this point. You don't know how messed up the estate is."

I tried to keep my voice calm and level and deal with this in an analytical way. "The best thing to do at this point," I said, "is for all of us to sit down, wearing proper clothes, in a conference room, and hash things out, before this goes to court and you have to convince a probate judge that your dear uncle was cuckoo for Cocoa Puffs. Once we do that, and settle this like reasonable human beings, we can pick up where we left off. Preferably in a room with a nice hot fireplace and a cushy bathrobe."

"You're unbelievable. Did you know that? You want to stop seeing me, over, basically, *money*, and then you sit there and tease me like that. Unbelievable." He stopped pacing and started running his hands through his hair. "I can't deal with this right now. I can't. On top of everything else, I can't deal with this particular form of anxiety. You want us to stop seeing each other? Fine. Let's stop. Now."

"I don't *want* to stop seeing you," I said. "I want us to be together at least long enough so we can figure out how we feel about each other. But we can't do that until we get the house issue resolved. And if we can all be reasonable, we can manage that."

"I have to leave," he said. "I can't stay in this room any longer. I need to be somewhere where I can get some fresh air and wrap my head around everything that's going on. I need to stop talking to you before I say something I can't take back."

"Maybe you should do that," I said. "Maybe we both should. Give me a minute to gather my things and I'll go downstairs with you. We both need a little time to process this, I think."

I folded up my dress and put it in the red plastic bag with the paperwork Adam had given me. We went downstairs and I tossed the bag in the back seat of my Audi. I opened the driver's side door, but I didn't get in right away.

"Are you going to leave, or what?" he asked.

"I want to stay. I wish I could. I feel terrible about this. You have to understand that."

"My Uncle Sheldon had a saying about airplanes," he said. "He said, at thirty-five thousand feet over the Arctic Ocean, the pilot of the B-52 doesn't care what you know, or what you think, or how you feel. He only cares whether you did your job or not when the airplane was on the ground."

"What does that have to do with anything?" I asked. "We're not in an airplane. Feelings matter. Your feelings matter. My feelings matter."

"But they don't matter enough," he said.

"So what did you do?" Pacey asked.

We were sitting on a bench at a playground in her development, where her sons were working up their courage for an assault on the monkey bars. I was still wearing my itchy black fleece and ridiculous high heels.

"I didn't say anything. I couldn't think of anything else to say, not even goodbye."

"But what did you do?" she asked. "Did you just get in your car and drive over here?"

"I thought I would just drive home and lock myself in with some sad movies and a bottle of wine. But there was a Dunkin' Donuts right on the highway, and I hadn't had any breakfast."

"Oh, don't tell me. You got the white chocolate latte?"

I nodded my head. "And half a dozen French crullers to go. And a bag of Munchkins for the road."

"Oh, sweetie," she said. "I didn't know you were *that* stuck on him. I guess it's a good thing there wasn't a liquor store right there, or else I would have had to come get you."

"I don't have any self-control issues with alcohol," I said. It wasn't strictly true but I said it anyway. "Donuts are another matter altogether."

"I just don't want to see you taking it to the next level and developing an expensive Viennese pastry habit," she said. "Benjy! Stop pushing your brother."

"I'm not Benjy," the child who had pushed the other one said. "I'm Simon."

"Whoever you are, quit it. What was I saying? OK, so you're stuck on this guy that you can't sleep with right now because... why was this, again?"

"Legal ethics."

"Well, that's impressive," she said. "You may have invented a brand-new way to dump a guy. I mean, I think very highly of legal ethics, but they don't often intrude in the romantic sphere."

"What do I do?" I asked. "I like him. I really do. I don't like anybody else enough to eat half a dozen French crullers over."

"And a bag of Munchkins."

"And a bag of Munchkins. I can't believe how much I have screwed this up."

"Pull yourself together, sweetie. This is Day One. Everything else will look better and brighter from here. I promise."

"Time heals all wounds?" I asked.

"Nothing of the sort," she said. "Benjy! Get that *out of your mouth*. God, I wish they had put in a different surface than these wood chips."

"You were saying?"

"You don't understand," she said. "You did exactly what I told you to do. You did it in exactly the wrong way, mind you, but you came up with exactly the right outcome, which is maximum sexual frustration."

"You don't have to tell me about sexual frustration right now," I said. "Believe me."

"You were supposed to just give him a tease, right? Instead, you gave him a taste."

"Maybe a little more than a taste." *More like a banquet.*

"You gave him a taste, and then you yanked it right out of his mouth. That's a recipe for sexual frustration."

"On both sides," I said.

"Yes. But you can cope better than he can. You'll see. All you have to do is stay away from him and control your carbohydrate intake. Sooner or later, he's going to realize what he's missing, and he'll do something terribly romantic that will melt your heart."

"I don't know about that, Pacey. You didn't see how ticked off he was at me."

"He's feeling a lot of different emotions," she said. "They will pass. Eventually, he will end up thinking about you and hormones will win out over emotion."

"And what if they don't?" I asked.

"Then you know he wasn't the right guy. If he's not willing to take that understandable frustration he's feeling right now and turn that into something romantic, then he's not worth wasting your time over. But if he's the kind of guy you want him to be, then he will. You just have to have faith that it will work out."

"'Faith is the substance of things hoped for, the evidence of things not seen,'" I quoted.

"Just be patient, sweetie. If it's supposed to work out, it will. You've done everything you can. Just wait and see how it works out. Are you thinking of staying for dinner?"

"What are you having?"

"Fish sticks and macaroni and cheese. A real gourmet meal. I'll even put panko crumbs on the macaroni if you like."

"I'll pass," I said.

"Suit yourself. Simon! We do *not* go up the slide the wrong way!"

I hugged my nephews and my sister and got back in my car and headed north towards Morristown. I knew there was a Starbucks not that far from her house, but I drove right past it. There was a Dunkin' Donuts on the other side of town, and I drove past it, too, although I took a longing look out the window. But just at the edge of town, there was another, newer Dunkin' Donuts, and this one had a drive-thru. I got another white chocolate latte and two bags of Munchkins—one for the drive home and one for in the morning. I didn't bother to dust the powdered sugar off my tacky sweatshirt.

Chapter 23

I see no reason to describe the drunken debauch that I fell into over the next thirty-six hours, except to say that I managed to get through it without calling Adam (or any other old boyfriends, for that matter), doing anything unforgivably stupid on social media, or setting fire to my apartment. By those standards, it was a complete success. I even managed to make room in my makeshift liquor cabinet by draining the last of the random bottles of brandy and gin and Kahlua. The result was a cocktail so epically awful that I christened it the "Prisoner's Dilemma," because it was a no-win situation either way: either you drank it, or you stayed sober.

Right before I fell into bed Sunday night, I set my alarm to go off an hour early. I hated to do it, but I knew I would need the extra time for my body to soak in the hot water from the shower and for my brain to soak in caffeine. I got out of bed and took three ibuprofen tablets, and after a shower and coffee and the last couple of remaining Munchkins, I felt almost sentient. I wasn't planning on doing any higher-order thinking, but I would be able to stumble my way to work and answer e-mail and smile when senior partners walked by my door, which was my average level of functioning on Monday mornings anyway. I poured myself another slug of coffee in my travel mug.

I was about halfway through putting my office back in order when my cell phone rang. It was my mother, which meant that something else horrible had happened again. I figured that it was already Monday, so whatever catastrophe she was calling about couldn't make things that much worse.

"I have a caveat," Mother said.

"About what?"

"No, I mean, I have a caveat. In my hand. A nice young man delivered it to me at breakfast."

"Who did what now?" I asked.

"He said he was a process server, and handed me this

very thick envelope, and inside, there was a caveat. Or that's what it says on the front page. I haven't bothered to look through the whole thing yet, not without legal assistance close at hand."

I dimly remembered that, in New Jersey, the document that you use to file an initial will contest was called, for some archaic reason, a caveat. "Let me guess," I said. "It says that Sheldon Berkman was off his rocker when he signed the codicil."

"If that's what they mean by 'diminished capacity,' quite possibly," she said. "What does it mean if he was crazy?"

"It means that if the court finds Sheldon was legally crazy, the codicil goes away, and you don't inherit anything."

"Would there be any disadvantages in doing that? Just having the codicil go away?"

"As it happens," I explained, "there is an offer on the table from Adam. He is willing to give you twenty-five thousand dollars if you will sign away your rights to the house."

"Where do I sign?" she asked.

"I could get something drafted and sent to you by close of business today," I said. "But if you did that, you'd be walking away from the quarter of a million dollars of equity locked up in that ugly house."

It was the first time in as long as I could remember that I had been able to say anything to my mother that left her speechless for any length of time.

"Are you still there?" I asked.

"That beautiful house," she said. "With so many precious memories. It would be such a shame to let it go. For anything less than full market value, that is."

"That's the spirit," I said.

"So what do we do?" Mother asked.

"I think it's time to see exactly what it is that you may have inherited. Sometime this weekend, I'll drive down there and take a look. If it's a wreck, or if it's burned down in the last week, you might want to consider taking the offer. But if it's in nice shape, and there's a good chance of you getting back a significant return, then we can go to court and see if we can show that Sheldon wasn't as crazy as he seemed."

"I will leave it in your capable hands, dear daughter."

"I appreciate the vote of confidence," I said.

"Why, Gwendolyn Rose," she said. "You always have my complete confidence."

"Thank you, Mother."

"As long as it's something that doesn't involve men. Ta-ta, dear."

I had a roommate in college who was a psychology student, and she was doing research on the link between depression and obesity. She said that Americans were depressed because they were obese and obese because they were depressed, and that the important thing to do to get out of the vicious cycle was to avoid standard American junk food when you get depressed. So I decided to follow her advice and walk across the courthouse square to get Thai for lunch. I got the grilled shrimp salad and some unsweetened green tea and tried to think healthy thoughts. The sun came out just as I left the restaurant, and I walked back to my office tower feeling as though I had accomplished something important. I was ready to tackle the rest of my day and not think about Adam and be productive and useful to my firm and the legal community at large.

I opened the glass doors and walked into the reception area. I noticed a young man sitting on one of the couches, but he was on his phone playing a game and didn't notice me come in. I walked towards my office, and was surprised to see Tim Curlin standing in my doorway.

"You're back," he said. "Long lunch break?"

"Not any longer than usual," I said. "What's going on?" I heard a quaver in my voice that I couldn't control. Curlin had no reason to be standing there, arms folded, blocking me from getting into my office, unless he was trying to keep me out.

"Did you talk to the young man in reception?" he asked. "He's been waiting on you."

"I wasn't expecting anyone," I said. "And he didn't talk to me, so I don't have any idea why he's here."

"He's a process server," Curlin explained.

"Then he's not a very good one, because he let me walk right past him."

"Be that as it may," Curlin said, "he's still out there. I am curious to know what your explanation is for him being there."

"Since I haven't talked to him, I'm not entirely sure," I said. "I did get a phone call earlier from my mother, and she said that she had been served in a matter related to a will contest regarding some property she had supposedly inherited. My best guess is that he's serving me with a copy of those papers as her attorney."

"That's what you think?" Curlin said. "That's what you're telling me?"

"It's the most reasonable thing I can think of," I said. "I don't know what else it could be. I'm not trying to hide anything."

"You're not trying to hide anything. Like, for example, getting sued for assaulting a photographer at a funeral."

"You're not serious," I said. I felt a hot jet of anger rush through my bloodstream. I knew I hadn't heard the last of Vanessa Sullivan, but I hadn't imagined that she would be so deranged as to sue me for stepping on her foot.

"I am *extremely* serious," Curlin said. "In my opinion, you should be, as well."

"I am extremely annoyed and irritated. This is harassment on her part. It's a nuisance-value lawsuit at best."

"So you deny the allegations in the complaint?" he said. I couldn't help noticing that he was standing in the door.

"I haven't read the complaint yet. Have you?"

"The plaintiff's attorney was a classmate of mine at Penn. He forwarded to me as a courtesy. It says that you intentionally stepped on the plaintiff's foot and that she will need surgery to repair ligament damage."

"Bullshit," I said.

"And she's asking for punitive damages on top of that."

"Unreal. Delusional, even. Well, I'll take care of it."

"I asked you to take care of this before," Curlin said. "You said that you had. You told me the situation with the media interest in your affairs had been resolved. Clearly it has not."

I felt that rush of anger again, and had to remind myself to breathe. "I am dealing with a freelance writer who has decided to conduct a very misguided vendetta against me. I can't be held responsible for her actions."

"I expect our associates to be able to resolve problems without brawling in the street. If you can't do that, then you need to find somewhere else to work."

"I stepped on her foot. That's hardly a street brawl. She's exaggerating what happened."

"And you gave her the opportunity to sue you by doing that. That doesn't speak well for your judgment," Curlin said.

Not punching Vanessa in the stomach spoke very highly of my judgment, I thought, but this was not the time to make that particular argument. "If it hadn't been that, it probably would have been something else," I said.

"And yet, you were surprised when I told you what was going on."

I knew Curlin was angry with me. I was wasting his time on something trivial, which was his pet peeve. And he was right that I shouldn't have stepped on Vanessa's foot the way I did, although at the time it seemed like the quickest way to handle the situation. I couldn't even entertain the fantasy of smacking Vanessa with something flat and heavy, because anything I did to her would likely result in another lawsuit. I would have to figure out another way to get her back, probably something sneaky and underhanded. Something she wasn't expecting.

"I'm sorry, sir," I said. "I let myself get provoked into doing something that damaged my reputation and this firm's reputation, and I shouldn't have done it. Let me do what I can to repair the situation."

"Well, you'll have plenty of time to do that," Curlin said.

"Am I fired?" I asked. I'd suspected as much, what with Curlin blocking me from getting in my office. I told myself that if Curlin was going to fire me, I wouldn't show the anger or outrage I felt in front of him. I wasn't going to whine or beg, either. If I had to leave my job, I would do it with dignity.

"All personnel decisions have to be approved unanimously by the management committee," he said. "If it was my decision, you'd be on your way home now. But I'm only one vote out of five."

"And the other partners?" I asked.

"Fortunately for you," Curlin said, "we don't have a quorum at the moment. Warren is still in Bermuda on that reinsurance merger. He gets back next Monday. He wants to defer the final decision until then."

"I see," I said. Warren Cornelius was the oldest of the partners. I had dated his grandson at one point. It hadn't gone well.

"Warren likes you personally, but he shares my concerns about your professionalism. I wouldn't count on his support."

"And the rest?"

"Yaniv and Ryan are concerned about your drinking habits. I am not overly concerned, but you didn't help yourself by dragging in here hung over this morning."

"Oh, great," I said.

"And Fielding is thinking about the bottom line. None of us are inclined to give you the benefit of the doubt here."

I knew what that meant. Firing me now meant that the firm wouldn't have to pay me a bonus, which would increase the pool for everyone else. That also meant I couldn't expect any kind of severance payment. I was going to have to scramble to find any kind of job to pay my bills until I could find a position with another firm.

"It's your decision," I said. "What do I do in the meantime?"

"You are suspended without pay," Curlin said. "Indefinitely. If we decide to terminate you, I will let you know on Monday and arrange for your things to be delivered to you."

"Then there isn't anything else to say," I said. I could think of several things I would have liked to have said, but all of them would have made things worse and wouldn't have accomplished anything other than proving that Curlin was right about my lack of professionalism.

"You have the rest of the week," he said. "If you can manage to resolve this unpleasant litigation you seem to have stepped into, let me know and we'll take that under advisement."

"Sure."

"And don't forget to see the young man in the reception area on the way out," Curlin said.

There was a ghost of a smile on his face, and I devoutly wished that there were some way I could wipe it off his smug features. I stalked my way down the hallway, snatched the complaint from the process server's hand, and made my way out the glass doors and down the elevator.

It took me five minutes to get home. I slammed the door shut and threw my pocketbook on the counter. I went into my bedroom to change clothes. The stuffed giraffe Adam had sent me was staring at me from across the room.

"Shut up," I told the giraffe. "You're not helping matters."

Chapter 24

It didn't take me long to go through Vanessa's complaint. It was remarkably frivolous, even by the low standards of the personal-injury bar. I'd never litigated a tort claim before, but it did not appear that it would take that much effort to swot up a defense. At a minimum, it was a way to keep current on my New Jersey civil practice.

The simplest thing to do was to make an immediate settlement offer. I could see if Vanessa would take nuisance value at this point. That was the quickest and easiest way to make her claim go away, and I knew that was what Curlin would want me to do. But I had no intention of offering her a thin dime. Vanessa was taking me on my home turf, and I had every intention of grinding her into the dirt.

I spent the better part of the week drafting my answer to the complaint and putting together a countersuit, along with a motion to dismiss and a slew of intrusive discovery requests. I knew Vanessa was strapped for cash, and that she probably wouldn't be able to keep paying her lawyer forever. Once he got a good look at exactly how expensive fighting me in court was going to be, he would back out and Vanessa would be forced to withdraw the lawsuit. That was my plan, and the only drawback was that it wasn't as satisfying as direct physical force would have been. You can't have everything.

I switched off between that and working on my résumé and developing a plan of attack for the likely event that I wouldn't have a job come Monday. I had a list of recruiters to call, and I was hopeful that I could get a short-term contract job somewhere doing legal scutwork. I wasn't relishing the job search, but it was a necessity. Even if I somehow managed to avoid being fired, I was going to have to find another job eventually. If all five of the partners didn't think I had a future at the firm, it was time to find another firm.

I had used up most of my reserve alcohol in last weekend's drunken stupor, and I knew that I needed to save every nickel in case I was out of work for the long term. So I didn't buy any more liquor, which was annoying but had the side effect of making me feel virtuous. Once I got a new job, I told myself, I'd get a nice bottle of wine to celebrate. But for now, I had to stay sober. It was a challenge to stop drinking so abruptly, and I didn't enjoy it, but the lack of alcohol kept me focused on what I needed to do.

I got up early on Saturday morning. I looked at the clock, rolled over, and right before I was able to get back to sleep, I remembered my promise to drive down and scope out the house on Idaho Street. I threw on my comfy Temple hoodie and a pair of jeans, loaded up a Thermos full of coffee, and went downstairs to the garage. It didn't take me long to get the Audi out on the interstate, and it took me much less time than that to get up to eighty miles an hour. I had a long day ahead of me and I didn't want to waste any time.

My game plan was simple. I had the key to the house in my pocket. I was going to drive down to Cape May as quickly as the laws of physics and good judgment would permit. When I got there, I would walk up to the porch, unlock the door, and check out whether the house was in good enough shape to put on the market any time soon.

In a perfect world, the house would be vacant, without any furniture or other clutter. All the inside walls would be freshly painted neutrals, just the way that you'd want it if you were staging it for a prospective buyer. I had no plans to lift one finger to clean out a lot of old junk, or deal with whatever else might be wrong with the house.

I didn't know what to expect, but I knew what to be worried about. I had three main concerns, all of them tied to different types of reality shows. One was that the previous resident of the house had been a hoarder, and that the house was crammed full of dead cats or worse. The second was that the house had been under intensive renovation when Sheldon died, and that there were holes in the walls and sawdust everywhere. The third was that the house was haunted. In any of these events, I would advise Mother to hand the house back to Adam as a bad investment, especially if there were teams of paranormal investigators rooting around, because you can never get rid of those guys.

If the house was in a serious state of disarray, we were both committed to dumping the headache of selling it on Adam and figuring out a way to split whatever profits remained after all the bills were taken care of. Mother was comfortable in her apartment at the senior community, and wasn't interested in a near-beach house. I wasn't all that interested in spending my precious vacation time anywhere other than the Caribbean, thank you very much. I was anxious to seal the deal in any case, so I could salvage whatever was left of my relationship with Adam.

Assuming I still wanted to.

In the last week, Adam hadn't called me or tried to call me or sent me any other large, awkward presents. I'd checked his public Facebook profile, and he hadn't done anything except go out to a Mexican restaurant in Freehold the night before. He had posted a picture of a plate of nachos. Other than that, he was running under radio silence as far as social media was concerned. I had no way of knowing whether he was still thinking about me, or if he still wanted to be with me. If he was feeling any pressure from sexual frustration, it wasn't apparent.

I had a roommate in college who once dumped a boy because he got his ear pierced. It turned out to be the right decision, because the ex-boyfriend ended up going to jail for running a meth lab and my roommate ended up marrying the lieutenant governor of Minnesota, but that's not the point of the story. My roommate had been nearly besotted with this guy, and never stopped talking about how much she cared about him and how sweet he was, but she dropped him cold over a tiny little diamond stud in his earlobe—more accurately, because he wouldn't take it out when she asked him to. (The boyfriend was majorly cute, and I thought my roommate had made a big mistake in dumping him, and I would totally have dated him if my roommate had not specifically threatened to smother me in my sleep if I had tried.)

The house on Idaho Street wasn't a small thing, like a diamond stud, but it was coming between me and Adam and

I hated that. It was a big, expensive thing, and it was tied in to my relationship with my mother, which was another big thing and one that I wasn't equipped to walk away from. It wasn't fair, and it wasn't reasonable, and it sure as hell wasn't romantic. But I still spent the entire drive down to Cape May wishing and hoping that the house on Idaho Street had caught fire, or crumbled in on itself, or had blown away in a freak tornado.

The day was clear and sunny, but it wasn't yet warm enough for me to put the top down on my convertible. I made excellent time coming down the Parkway all the way to Avalon, and then hit traffic in Cape May Court House. I was finally able to make my way across the causeway to Cape May proper, and made a quick stop by the Wawa on the north side of town and fortified myself with a hot chicken sandwich and a cold Diet Coke. If the house was a hoarder house, and if the smell made me want to throw up as soon as I walked in the door, I thought it was a good idea to have something in my stomach, just in case.

I drove down Lafayette Street through the middle of town, past the cute little antique shops and the bed-and-breakfasts and the twee art galleries. I turned left on to the beach road. It was just warm enough for people to be walking along the promenade without serious risk of frostbite, and they were out in force. Most of them seemed to be couples, walking hand in hand, enjoying the sunny day and the brisk wind whipping off the bay. I found the cross street I wanted and turned towards the house on Idaho Street.

The street was empty, and I parked right in front of the house. The landscaping needed serious work, and the right-side banister on the front steps looked to be loose. The exterior paint looked even worse up close. The pink was a wretched pastel shade, like Pepto-Bismol. The green trim looked like dead pine needles. I had to resist the urge to take the battered white wicker chairs off the porch and put them on the curb so that someone could put them away in a nice landfill somewhere where they couldn't poke anyone ever again.

The only interesting thing on the porch was the door, which was a massive thing, hand-carved, with two lovely slender stained-glass panels running down its length. They needed to be cleaned, but that would take somebody five minutes with Windex. And right in the center of the door, there was a wreath.

It was a large wreath, with white roses and orange flowers that I didn't know the name of, and a fading black ribbon. The flowers looked like they had been cut three weeks ago. This was because they had been.

I had seen this wreath once before, but it was attached to the door at Sheldon Berkman's apartment.

I felt the stereotypical cold chill skitter up my back, but I shook my head to dismiss the momentary feeling of dread. *All it means is that Adam moved the wreath from there to here*, I thought. *Nothing to worry about.* I found the house key and turned it in the lock. I heard an audible *click* that said the key had caught, and opened the door.

The foyer was narrow, and had a gorgeous long mahogany table in front of a graceful staircase. The flooring was a deep, rich red wood, gleaming in the afternoon sunlight. The side of the staircase had matching paneling, except that there were dark maroon inlays in complex geometric patterns. The banister was hand-carved from what looked to be ebony. I looked up, and there was a glittering reddish copper chandelier hanging down. Its metalwork was as intricate as the woodwork on the stairs.

I went into the parlor on the right-hand side. It was a large room, with crown molding whose pattern was echoed in the deep-red Persian rug. The furniture was clearly antique but looked comfortable and inviting. A huge brick fireplace was decked out with gleaming brass tools. On the back wall, there was an ancient upright piano which had been polished, deep and glossy. A set of sheet music sat on the piano, and I looked to see that it was an old Elvis song, "Can't Help Falling in Love with You."

The chill down my spine came back, stronger than before. I sat down on the piano bench. I noticed I was breathing hard, and I tried to relax.

It wasn't just that the inside of the house was as gorgeous as the outside wasn't. It was that everything looked bright and new and shiny. Somebody had put a hell of a lot of effort into making it that way. Based on the price that the house had sold for, and the description on the listing, it hadn't been the previous owner. If the rest of the house was like this, it was worth a million dollars. *Easy.*

Of course, the smart move wouldn't be to sell the house. The smart move would be to *keep it*, to *run it*, to rent out rooms all summer for an exorbitant, astronomical price. You could earn enough to pay the mortgage for the year in two months, if you had full occupancy, and the rest would be pure profit. It might be enough to live on, even, if you had a law practice on the side that made you a little extra money.

It could work, I thought. *It could.* All I had to do was prove that poor dead Sheldon Berkman was not as crazy as everyone else thought he was—which shouldn't be that hard—and take over the house. Mother didn't want anything to do with the house; she'd be happy to let me take it over and handle the rentals and keep up the maintenance. I could sell my condo and quit my job and move down here full-time. I could put out my shingle, too, and do wills and divorces and contract work during the quiet winter months. Once I got my student loans paid off, I could buy the house from Mother outright, or wait until after she died and buy out my siblings, whichever made more sense. I could spend my mornings walking on the beach, and my evenings watching the sun set over the bay.

All this could be yours someday, kiddo, one side of my brain said.

As long as this is what you want, the other side said.

"Too early to make any kind of decision," I said, and then I jumped because I had said that out loud without meaning to. "I must be getting nervous in my old age," I said, mostly to reassure myself. "Let's move on to the next room."

The kitchen was splendid, with gleaming white cabinets and salt-and-pepper granite countertops flecked with quartz. The big appliances were stainless-steel and showroom new.

There was a shiny silver espresso maker and a Kitchen-Aid stand mixer. At the far end of the kitchen was a breakfast area with a sturdy butcher-block table. It looked like the Crate and Barrel catalog had come to stark, glittering life. The next room was a dining room with lush, velvety green wallpaper and a handsome antique table and spindly, elegant chairs. The table was set with silver candlesticks, and I imagined how exquisite it would look by candlelight.

Of course, the make-or-break item was the state of the guest rooms upstairs, and the bathrooms. People might file in and out to gawk at the house, but if nobody wanted to stay there, we'd be better off selling it. I went up the stairs, checking the banister to see if it was loose anywhere, and it wasn't.

The first room I checked out was painted a dark blue, with stark white crown molding and a brushed-nickel chandelier by way of contrast. The bed had a soft, squishy down comforter, and all sorts of comfy throw pillows. I had to suppress a sudden desire to dive in and take a long, restful nap. The room had a fireplace as well, but the bricks were painted white, with contrasting iron tools.

There was a white display cabinet in the corner, which I went over to check out because it was the first modern piece of furniture I had seen in the house. It was glassed-in, and had three or four airplane models inside. The one at the top was the largest, and had pride of place. I took a close look, and it was a large bomber plane.

Adam said that it was a B-52, I thought. It was the same plane, the one I had seen at Sheldon's old apartment.

Well, the wreath got here some way, why not this? If Adam didn't bring it over himself, maybe one of Sheldon's friends did. No reason to worry about it.

"I thought I heard somebody," a voice said. And it wasn't my voice. It was a hard voice, harsh and stern.

I must have jumped sixteen inches in the air. I came down awkwardly, twisting myself to see where the voice was coming from. I banged my left hand on the glass of the cabinet, hard enough to hurt my hand but luckily not enough to crack the glass. I yelped loudly, partly out of pain and partly out of fear.

I could see him framed in the doorway. He was short and balding, with powerful arms and dirty hands. He was wearing a leather tool belt that bristled with sharp implements. His face was cold and still at first, but then as I looked at him, I saw his eyes widen and the corners of his mouth crinkle with happiness.

"Oh, my God," he said. "You came. You came after all."

"Who are you? What are you doing here?"

"You haven't aged a day," he said. "Do you know that? Still as beautiful as the last time I saw you."

A bright pinpoint of realization dawned in my brain.

"You are a dead man," I said.

Chapter 25

"Don't be scared," Sheldon Berkman said. "Look. Everything's all right. Calm down."

I did not calm down. I screamed. It was a high, pure note that would have cracked any wineglass in the general vicinity. With my uninjured right hand, I picked up a navy throw pillow and chunked it as hard as I could at Sheldon. My momentum carried me towards the fireplace. When Sheldon took a step backwards to dodge the pillow, I grabbed the fireplace poker and brandished it in his general direction.

Sheldon Berkman was a dead man, and he was standing between me and the stairway and the front door and my car. I tried to extract my phone from the pocket of my hoodie with my left hand, but my hand was still smarting like anything and I abandoned the effort. I couldn't think who to call anyway. The police? The local exorcist?

"Wait just a minute," he said. "I'm sorry. I thought you were someone else. I didn't mean to startle you like that. Can you put that thing down, please?"

I was not going to calm down. I wanted Sheldon to get out of my way, and if that meant running a fireplace poker through his eye socket, I could handle that. I tried to say that, but I was hyperventilating just then and it came out as a vicious hiss. I held the poker up and cocked it back, as though I was getting ready to bring it down on Sheldon's unprotected skull.

He put his arms up in what he must have thought was a nonthreatening way and took a step into the room. "Are you OK?" he asked. "Looks like you banged your hand there."

"What are you *doing* here?" I said, slowly and deliberately. It came out as a rattle, deep and throaty. "Get out of my way."

"I don't want to upset you," he said. "But I can guess who you are. You're Patricia, right? The daughter."

"No!" I shouted. I took a swipe at him with the poker, and he took a step back. "I am *not* Pacey."

"Gwendolyn, then."

"*Don't call me that.*" I edged towards the left side of the room. If I could get him to maneuver to my right, I thought I could squeeze past him and rush down the stairs. "Wendy," I yelled. "My name is Wendy. *What* are you doing here?"

"OK," he said. "OK. Look. Wendy. You need to calm down. Your face is all red. Just put that thing down, and let's talk like civilized human beings."

"Get out of my way first. And answer my question."

"I'd rather not do either one, right this second. I would also rather not get skewered by that poker. If we go downstairs, quietly, I can get you some ice for your hand."

"How do you know my name?" I asked.

"Well, you're Emily's daughter," he said. "It's obvious. You look just like she did at that age, which was the last time I saw her. I thought you were her. I didn't mean to startle you just now, but you look extraordinarily like her. And you have the same kind of temper, if you don't mind me saying so."

"You *are* a dead man. I am going to smash your head in with this fireplace poker for scaring me like that. Since you're already legally dead, I can't be tried for murder."

"That's right," he said. "You're a lawyer. I had forgotten that. Were you at the funeral? I know your mother went, but I didn't know if she was by herself or not."

"Get out of my way," I yelled. I raised the poker over my head and cocked my wrists, as though I was getting ready to hit a baseball over whatever it is that you hit a baseball over.

Sheldon opened his mouth to say something, thought better about it, and retreated down the hallway. I held on to the poker and made my way to the top of the stairs. My knees were shaking, and I took the steps slowly, one at a time. I tried to transfer the poker to my other hand, but it was too sore for me to work my fingers. The poker went clattering down the stairs. I clutched the banister with my good hand, and stomped my way down the staircase. I felt light-headed by the time I got to the bottom, and I sat down on the last stair. I was still breathing heavily and I tried to calm myself down.

I looked up to see Sheldon standing with a kitchen towel wrapped around some ice cubes. "For your hand," he said. "Are you all right? I came down the back steps. I thought you might've fallen."

"Just give me the ice," I said. I wrapped the towel around my left hand. The ice stung, but it took a bit of the pain away. "If my hand is broken, I am blaming you."

"I do want to thank you for not breaking my cabinet. Or my skull. Why don't you take a minute to pull yourself together, and I'll make you some coffee. If you drink coffee."

I looked up at him, taking his measure. He looked amazingly vital for someone who had been dead for three weeks. He was wearing a dark-gray T-shirt with the Air Force logo, jeans covered with sawdust, and heavy work boots. He had a close-cropped fringe of gray hair and kind eyes. His nose was permanently bent to the left.

"I don't want your coffee," I said. The last thing I needed right then was a stimulant. "I want you to tell me why, in the name of God, you thought any of this was a good idea."

"That's a long story," he said.

"You have the time to tell it. You don't know it yet, but you're coming with me. We are getting in my car and driving north out of here."

"I don't understand," he said. "Why would I want to do that?"

"You wanted to see Emily Thornhill? You're going to see her. Today. What she decides to do with you is her business." Mother would never believe me if I just called her and told her that Sheldon was alive. But if I brought him to her, in the flesh, she'd have to believe me. And I had no doubt that she would find a way to settle Sheldon's hash for pulling this stupid stunt.

"I don't think that you and me driving up there would be a good idea," he said.

"You don't get a vote," I said. "You were perfectly willing to get her here and surprise her, by which I mean scare her out of her mind, because that's what you did with *me*. I don't see any problem with driving up there and letting her know that you are alive, in person."

"Don't get me wrong," he said. "I want to see her. That's the entire point of the plan. But I was hoping that she would come down here. Maybe you could call her and have her drive down tomorrow?"

"Oh, no," I said. "You are not getting out of this that easily. You can't scare me that badly and expect me to fetch my mother down here for you."

Sheldon threw up his hands in frustration. "I said I was sorry. I never had any intention of scaring you. I was up on the third floor, sanding the baseboards. Hence all the sawdust. I thought I heard someone moving around down here, so I came down to check it out. For all I knew, you were looking to buy the place. With all the work I've put into it, I ought to turn a pretty decent profit."

"You were the one to do all this, then," I said.

"Pretty much. Would you like to take the grand tour?"

Another pinpoint of realization sparked in my brain. *Sheldon wasn't dead.* If Sheldon wasn't dead, then the question of who would inherit the house was moot. Sheldon would retain possession until his death. And the codicil wasn't operative—chances were that it had never been operative. Likely as not, it was just an impressive bit of window dressing designed to lure Mother to the house on a false pretext. That meant that I didn't have any reason not to see Adam. Ethically speaking, I was off the hook. We could go out to dinner tonight to celebrate his uncle's return from the dead, assuming that Mother didn't kill Sheldon dead between now and then.

"You faked your death," I said. "You have to undo that. My mother deserves to be the first to know, and you owe it to her to tell her in person. After that, we can tell everyone else."

"I was going to tell her. I was planning on telling her the day of the funeral. I had it all planned out, and it would have worked, if Danny showed up when he was supposed to and done what I had told him to do. All he had to do was give her the codicil that he drafted, and then walk her over here. I spent the whole day cooling my heels in the foyer, waiting on her to open the door."

"By Danny, you mean the lawyer? Mr. Miller? He told me he had a family emergency, and that's why he didn't go to the funeral," I said.

"Is that what happened? I had no idea. Do you mind if I get a chair real quick?"

"Go ahead. Knock yourself out."

"As long as you don't knock me out. Just a sec."

I took my hand out of the towel and shook it. It was starting to get numb, but not quite there yet. I redistributed the ice and wrapped it back up. My breathing was finally normal, and my heart rate was down to where it had been before I went upstairs.

Sheldon came back from the kitchen with a chair, and sat in it with the back of the chair pointed towards me. "So why didn't your mother want to come see the house?" he asked. "You were down here anyway. I would have figured anybody who inherited a house would at least have been curious about what they inherited."

"You will have to ask her," I said. "I would do that right before she tears you into little ribbons. And I want to be there to see that."

Sheldon reached behind his head and rubbed the back of his neck. "Your mother will be very angry with me," he said. "I get that. If you break it to her gently, though, it might not be so bad. Who knows, maybe she's mellowed out in the last fifty years."

"You didn't see her after the funeral. She was not mellow. She was the farthest thing in the world from mellow. She was extremely unhappy. She was spouting *poetry*."

"Oh. That doesn't sound good." His face twisted into a scowl. "If she's going to be that angry with me, I can't say I don't deserve it. But I never meant for this to go on this long. It was supposed to be over by now."

"Mother is going to tear a giant strip off your back and beat you over the head with it," I said. "And she's not alone. Think of everyone else who went to the funeral. All those nice people at the wake, from your retirement community. You have to tell them, too. You have to explain this lunatic idea of yours to fake your death."

"Everybody else already knows," he explained. "Danny knows; he was the one who filled out the phony death certificate. The minister at the church knows; he didn't care so long as I threw in an extra thousand dollars as a donation. A guy I knew in the Air Force runs a mortuary in Philly; he took care of that paperwork for me, even threw in an urn for free. I filled it up with dust from my Shop-Vac, and then I told my bush pilot friend in Alaska it was coming. Ed and Hans and Paulie set up the reception; they were supposed to steer Emily over here if she went there. The newspaper didn't care whether I was really dead or not. It wasn't that difficult, and of course I only expected to be dead a day or two. I never expected that your mother just wouldn't show up."

"The entire *funeral* was phony?" I asked. "All those people *knew* you weren't dead?"

"Not everybody. Some of those folks are senile, you know."

"But what about Adam?" I asked. "Why would you go through with this whole crazy, numbskull idea if you knew he would think you were dead? Why hurt him like that?"

"Oh, Adam knows I'm alive," Sheldon said. "I asked Danny to tell him after the funeral. I knew it would be difficult for him, but I'm not cruel enough to keep him in the dark all this time."

"That's not true," I said, but with a little less conviction than I actually felt. "Adam would have told me if he knew you were alive."

"Adam knows better than to say anything to anyone," he said. "I know him. He won't contact me until after I let him know it's all right. But he knows I'm alive, he has to."

I lifted my left hand and flexed it carefully. It was numb, and it had stopped throbbing and I didn't think I had a broken bone anywhere. This was good, because if Adam had been stringing me along all this time, I would need both hands to strangle him properly.

"We're getting in the car," I said. "You and me. Now. And we're going to show the world you're not a corpse."

"Can we stop and get lunch first?" Sheldon asked. "I haven't eaten yet, and it's a long drive up to your mother's."

"We can get you a burger on the way up," I said. "And we're not going straight there. We're going to Freehold first. Adam deserves to know the truth, or if he already knows, I deserve to know why he's been stringing me along."

"Adam's been doing that?" he asked. "He's a nice kid. That's unlike him."

"It's a long story," I said.

"Well, all right then," Sheldon said. "You can tell me all about it in the car."

"I don't know what the story is, anymore." If Adam had been lying to me this entire time—if he had slept with me, and let me break up with him over a will he *knew* wasn't valid—that would be impossible. But I had just thought it was impossible for Sheldon to be alive, too. A lot of impossible things seemed to be happening lately. "What I do know is that my life started going screwy when you decided to fake your own death. What the hell were you thinking?"

"I can explain," Sheldon said. "But like you said, it's a long story."

"Don't take this the wrong way, but the last thing I want to do in this world is spend the whole drive up to Freehold listening to you tell me about you and my mother and what you did to each other in 1962."

"But that's the problem," he said. "You only know half of what went on."

Chapter 26

It didn't start in 1962. That's the first thing you need to understand. I was in love with your mother when she was in seventh grade, and I was in eighth. Now, she didn't know who I was. She didn't talk to me. She didn't talk to anybody. Everybody knew who she was, and everybody knew who her grandfather was. Not that she made a big deal about being from a rich family or anything, but it impacted how you looked at her. She was treated differently because of that, and I don't think she handled it well. That's probably why they took her out of public school and sent her to prep school when she was old enough.

But I was in love with her, all the way back then. I had one class with her in high school. I'd failed freshman geometry the year before, and they made me retake it. I sat behind her, and I almost failed again because I spent the whole time smelling her hair. It smelled like apples and honey.

Once she went off to prep school, I figured I would never see her again. It didn't bother me too much. I knew it would never work out. We didn't have anything in common that I knew about. My dad always told me you didn't ever want to marry someone that was too high above you or too far below you, because it never worked out, and I guess he was right about that. Anyway, I dated other girls in high school. I had fun. But I never stopped thinking about your mother, wondering how she was doing, that sort of thing.

I saw her one time, at the King of Pizza—I guess she was home for the weekend, having dinner with her family. She sat at the table across from mine. I spent the whole time looking at her, until my mom told me to stop staring. I think her brother saw me looking at her, too. They didn't send him to prep school, because he wanted to play football and be on the swim team and just be a regular kid. Nice guy, you know, but he didn't want just anyone dating his sister.

At some point, your mother noticed me. I don't know

how it happened, but all of a sudden she's interested in me. But, being your mother, she couldn't do something as simple as ask me out. She always had to do things the hard way. What she did was find my sister's best friend and tell her she thought I was cute, and that was supposed to get back to my sister, who was supposed to tell me. It worked, although I supposed I shouldn't have.

Anyway, I was not a total idiot, so I asked your mother out, and of course she said yes. So when we went out, I played it very cool. The perfect gentleman. We went out, saw a movie, and I drove her back home. I did not lay a hand on her, not once. We had a great time, don't get me wrong, but she didn't give me much in the way of encouragement. I was fine with that. If she wanted to take it slow, I was willing to take it slow along with her. This was 1962, you remember. Girls then weren't forward the way they are now. But I didn't care. I was in love.

So the day after Thanksgiving, I was sitting in my house, doing my homework, and listening to a football game on the radio. And your mother just showed up. She came in to the house, said hello, and said she wanted to go into Philly to get pizza. I figured, hey, why not. So we went and got a slice, and we just sat there again, staring at each other, not talking. Except this time, when we were leaving, she stole the car keys out of the pocket of my varsity jacket. She got behind the wheel of my car, and I had to ride along or be stranded on the wrong side of the bridge. I was a little ticked off, because I didn't like anyone else driving my car, but I could tell she had something on her mind and I was willing to go along with it.

She drove us to this drafty deserted old house out in the suburbs, and walked inside like she owned the place. I followed her inside, because she still had my keys, and because I wanted to see what would happen. I opened the door, and your mother was standing there, in this warm shaft of autumn light. She was wearing this pure-white cardigan, and the light just folded itself around her. It was the most beautiful thing I ever saw in my life. I can still see it, if I close my eyes, and wish hard enough. And then, when she saw me watching her, she took the cardigan off, and then everything underneath it.

"Stop," I said. "Please. Just stop talking."

"Oh, come on," Sheldon said. "Your mother had a life before you were born, you know. And she had the most amazing rack back then."

"I am *serious*. Quit talking."

"Of course, you don't do so bad yourself in that department. I can see why my nephew likes you."

"Listen to me. Do you want a burger or don't you? If you want me to stop this car and get you something to eat, you will oblige me by *not talking about my mother* that way, and especially not talking about *me* that way. You two had hot, filthy, nasty sex fifty years ago. Stipulated. I don't want to hear about it."

"I could ask you what hot, filthy, nasty things you've been doing with my nephew. Is that what's going on? You sounded awfully interested in him, back at the house."

I hit the accelerator as hard as I could just then, trying to pass someone's ancient red Volvo that was wallowing in the right lane. I moved back over to the right, cutting off the Volvo, whose driver honked at me. I pulled into the closest strip mall, parking my car in the first place I could find.

"Get out of my car," I said.

"You're crazy. You can't just leave me here," Sheldon said.

"I don't intend to. Get out of the car. Now."

"What are you talking about?"

"You said you were hungry," I said. "Get something to eat, whatever you want. You are not allowed back in this car for fifteen minutes."

"All I see is a Dunkin' Donuts and a Chinese restaurant. There was a Five Guys half a mile back. If you could drop me off there, it would be a nice thing."

"If you don't get out of this car right now, I am going to pull this steering wheel off the car and beat you to death with it."

"OK, OK. I'm going," he said. "You want anything? Egg

roll? Cruller?"

"Get out. *Now.*"

As soon as Sheldon vanished inside the Chinese restaurant, I put my head on the steering wheel and cried. I am not particularly proud of this, but I needed to cry and no one can say I didn't deserve to cry. After about five minutes of uncontrolled tears, my head banged against the center of the steering wheel and the horn went off. I was still wearing my seat belt, which was good because otherwise I would have jumped through the soft top of the Audi. After that, I tried my best to calm myself down and wipe the tears off my face, but it didn't work and it made me feel even worse. I cried until my body was sore from the shaking.

It's just stress, I told myself, but I knew that wasn't all of it.

Sheldon is giving me a hard time, that's why I'm crying, I thought. But that was just, as they say in first-year law school, the proximate cause.

Then why are you crying? I asked myself.

Adam. Of course. Why else?

I didn't think Adam knew Sheldon was alive. It didn't make sense. He wouldn't have let me break up with him if he knew that the codicil was phony. And he wouldn't have been as upset as he was about the bills that were owed by the estate. It couldn't have all been an act. Could it?

If Adam was as loyal to his uncle as I was to my mother, he might have lied to me. That was something I hadn't considered. It seemed unlikely, but it was at least possible, and I couldn't think of any way to know for certain other than confronting Adam directly. If I was wrong, and Adam knew Sheldon was alive, then I could turn my back on him with a clear conscience and an aching heart. If I was right, and Adam didn't know Sheldon was alive, then everything would be all right. We could take up where we left off, without any interference from the prior generation or the New Jersey Bar Association.

But would everything be all right?

I didn't *know*, and I would find out in an hour, and I

wasn't ready to find out.

I knew how I felt about Adam, or at least I thought I did. I wanted to be close to him, to feel his warmth next to mine, to see his eyes light up when I walked into a room, to see him look at me with longing and ardor, to possess him and have him possess me.

But that wasn't the same thing as romance.

And it wasn't the same thing as love.

I hadn't let myself use that word in connection with Adam. I knew I liked him. I knew I was attracted to him. I knew I couldn't stop thinking about him. But I didn't know if I loved him. I thought he wasn't ready to say that he loved me. To be honest, I didn't know how I would react if he *did* tell me he loved me.

We'd spent so little time together, after all. And the one thing that we had in common—the one thing that had brought us together—was Sheldon Berkman.

I rubbed my eyes, blew my nose, and did the best I could to salvage my composure and my makeup. This worked until Sheldon knocked on the passenger-side window and made me jump against my seat belt.

"You doing OK in there?" he asked. "Just checking."

I shot him a look that I thought was cold and malevolent, but that he apparently thought was warm and inviting. He opened the door and got in the car.

"I ended up splitting the difference," he said. "I got crab rangoon at the Chinese place and a chicken biscuit and coffee at Dunkin'. It went together better than you'd think it would."

"I'm so pleased. I can't even tell you."

"Are you sure you don't want anything to eat? Maybe a snack or something? My treat. You look like you could use a pick-me-up."

"I don't want anything from you but for you to tell the truth about what you did," I said.

"The truth is that you're looking a little worse for wear. And I'm sorry about that. I opened up my big fat mouth when I shouldn't have. Let me make it up to you."

"You couldn't make this up to me in a thousand years of

trying, so don't. You have no idea how much you have messed up my life over the past couple of weeks."

"You're the one that's driving. I would feel a lot better if I knew you were keeping your blood sugar up. I can get you a bottle of Coke at the Chinese place; they had a whole refrigerator full of them."

"Fine," I said. "Get me a Coke, and keep your mouth shut the rest of the way to Freehold, and we'll call it a truce. Deal?"

"Deal," he said, and came back a minute later with a bottle of Coke, a Sprite for himself, and two fortune cookies. He opened his and checked the fortune. "It says, *To one who waits, a moment seems a year*. Sounds about right. What did you get?"

I ripped open my cookie and read the fortune. "*Depart not from the path that fate has assigned*."

"I guess that could mean anything," Sheldon said.

"The only path I'm following right now is the Garden State Parkway," I said. "Buckle up."

I gunned the car back onto the Parkway and headed north in relative peace and quiet.

Chapter 27

Adam lived in a pleasant house on one of the main commercial streets in Freehold, in a mixed residential-commercial neighborhood. There was a deli two doors north and a fried-chicken restaurant just to the south. The house had peacock-blue siding, a large front porch, and a collection of whimsical topiary bushes in the minuscule front yard. Adam's battered old Jaguar was parked alongside, and I pulled my car behind it.

I had meant to get the address from Sheldon, but he had fallen asleep at the turn-off from I-195. Luckily, I had brought the redwell Adam had given me, and his address was on some of the paperwork. I left Sheldon snoozing on the passenger seat and got out of the car and knocked on the front door.

There was no response.

I did a quick, surreptitious check of the mailbox, and there was a PSE&G bill for "Adam Lewis," so I knew I was at the right address. I knocked again. Still no response. The door was locked.

The front porch had a swing that looked comfortable enough, and I had no doubt I could sit there until Adam came back from wherever he was and play *Candy Crush Saga* until I ran out of lives or patience. I tried his cell number, but it went straight to voicemail. I checked his Facebook status, and he hadn't posted that he was going anywhere or doing anything.

I heard a scraping sound, and checked behind me to see if Sheldon had gotten out of the car. He still looked to be asleep, so I listened again, and the sound was coming from behind the house. I stepped down off the porch and went to check to see if there was a way into the backyard, which there was.

I heard the scraping noise again, coming from the far back corner of the house. I walked around and looked, and saw Adam's head sticking out of the ground.

"Oh, it's you," the disembodied head said. "I thought I heard someone knocking."

"No wonder you couldn't answer the door. Are you all right down there?"

"Sure," he said. "Could you hand me that caulk gun? The one with the white handle? It's about a foot out of my reach. Be careful you don't fall in."

I picked up the odd metal implement that he indicated and stuck it down in the hole where Adam was standing. "Thanks," he said. I couldn't help noticing that he wasn't wearing a shirt.

"I always heard that the first rule of holes is that when you're in one, stop digging."

"It should be that if you're digging one, make sure you can reach the caulk gun. What are you doing here?"

"I have some news for you," I said.

"I have some news for you. When you install a rainwater cistern in your house, make sure you pump all the water out over the winter, so when it gets cold enough to freeze, it doesn't crack the plastic wall and cause a leak. I've been meaning to do this all winter, but it's the first day in a long time that it's been warm enough to work outside. I have all the gravel cleaned out, I think. If you can give me a minute to caulk the leak, I can listen to whatever news you have to tell me."

"I admire your ambition and work ethic." I also admired the way his muscles rippled under his skin, but I didn't say that out loud. He was just starting to work up a sweat.

"You sound like a sidewalk supervisor," Adam said. He took a long-handled shovel from the depths of the hole and stuck it out, handle first. "Would you mind taking this? As long as you're here, you might as well be helpful."

"Not a problem," I said, taking the handle.

"Of course, you're not supposed to be here anyway. Legal ethics, remember?"

"I found a loophole," I said. "Not a big loophole, though. Maybe five-foot-four, I guess. I didn't think to measure."

"If this is a joke, I'm not getting it. Can you take the caulk gun?"

"No problem. Do you need help getting out of that hole?"

"Just stand back." He grabbed the lip of the cistern and pulled himself up, bunching his legs underneath him. With one convulsive heave, he pushed his upper body out of the cistern and onto the lawn, and then scrambled the rest of the way out. He stood up and brushed a few stray wisps of grass off his glistening torso. "Have you come here to negotiate? Because I have a rule about making any agreements unless I'm properly dressed."

"I have one thing to show you. It's in my car. If you follow me, you'll understand why I came."

"You didn't bring the stuffed giraffe all the way down here, did you? If you didn't want it, you could have just sent it back."

"Something else," I said. "Something big."

"I thought the stuffed giraffe was pretty big."

"Even bigger."

"You say so," he said. He went over to the back porch and grabbed a black T-shirt with a cartoon dinosaur on it, and put it on. "Let's go see. It better be good, whatever it is."

We trooped around the back of the house, and I walked over to the passenger side of the car and looked through the window. The car was empty.

"He got away," I said. "Let's look around. He couldn't have gotten far."

"What are you talking about?" Adam said. "Who are you talking about? If this is a joke, Wendy, it isn't the least bit funny."

"Yoo-hoo!" I said. "Sheldon! Where are you? Come out, come out, wherever you are!"

"This is a joke," Adam said. "You drove all the way down here to play hide-and-seek."

"It's not hide-and-seek," I said. "I found him. Your uncle. Sheldon. He's alive, has been all this time."

"If this is a joke, it's not very funny, Wendy. Unless it isn't a joke, and you're delusional."

"No joke," I said. I looked up and down the street. No sign of Sheldon. He wasn't on the porch, and he couldn't have gotten into the back yard.

"Uncle Sheldon is dead. You should know. You went to the funeral."

"*Your Uncle Sheldon is alive*," I said. "He was never dead. He was trying to play a sick prank on my mother. He was hiding in the house in Cape May, the one in the codicil. He was fixing it up."

"You may not be aware of this, but you're having a dissociative episode right here in my front yard. Do you have a past record of mental illness that I need to know about? Do I need to call someone to pick you up?"

Adam stood there and grinned at me, that adorable, infuriating grin that had been haunting my waking hours for the last week. I wanted to throw something at him, but I didn't have anything close at hand. The only thing that kept me from slapping him was the fact that he wouldn't tease me like this unless he really thought Sheldon was dead.

"He's alive," I said. "And it's important that you believe me. Because if I find out later that you knew he was alive all this time, you and I are going to have a problem."

"Uncle Sheldon is dead," Adam said. "I picked up the ashes from the mortuary myself. If you think he's alive, you're wrong. I know I was teasing you just now, but now you're starting to worry me. You need to stop whatever this is you're doing, because there is no way you can convince me that my uncle is still alive," he said.

"Oh, there's a way," I said. "Having said that, that's wonderful that you think so. I'd hate to think you were lying to me all this time. Now all I need to do is find out where he wandered off to, and we're set."

"Let's just suppose, just for a minute, that you're right and I'm wrong," Adam said. "Maybe you did go down to Cape May. Maybe there was someone squatting in that old house. Maybe he told you he was Sheldon Berkman, and you believed him. But he isn't, because *Sheldon Berkman is dead*. That would explain everything, wouldn't it?"

"Then let's find whoever it was that was in the car, and we'll know for sure," I said.

"If there was someone in the car, where did he go?" Adam asked.

"I don't know," I said. "You have to believe me on this one. I am telling you the truth. Your uncle is alive, and he's around here somewhere. Why don't you go down to the chicken place? I can check the deli, and we can meet back here."

"Let me explain what this looks like from my perspective," Adam said. "We went out twice, and had a great time, at least the second time, anyway. And the next morning, you tell me that we can't see each other again because of that insane codicil."

"Which doesn't apply anymore, because your uncle is not dead," I said.

"Be that as it may. Now, here you are, telling me my uncle's alive, and asking me to trust you, and you don't seem to understand why that's difficult for me right now. You are not giving me a lot of room to work with here, Wendy."

"Your uncle is alive. You have to believe me. We can find him. *He cannot have gotten that far.*"

I stood there for a long moment. I felt tears streaming down my face for the second time that day. The first time, the tears had come from stress and anxiety and uncertainty. These were different. They were hot tears, from anger and disappointment. *It isn't fair*, I thought. *Sheldon is alive. You have to believe me. We can be together again. All you have to do is listen to me.*

But I didn't say anything, because life wasn't fair and Adam didn't trust me and I was losing him and there wasn't anything I could do about it. And anything I could say would be so terrible and final that I couldn't ever take it back.

And then, at the depth of my despair, and right on cue, Sheldon opened the front door of the house and stepped onto the front porch. "What are you kids talking about?" he said. "Hope I haven't interrupted a lovers' quarrel."

Chapter 28

The look on Adam's face was a combination of shock, amazement, and utter consternation. "*Holy shit,*" he said. "Where did you come from?"

"Hello, Adam," Sheldon said. "Good to see you. You've done a lot of work on this place since the last time I was up here. Did you pick out this blue for the siding?"

"Holy shit," Adam said again. "You *are* alive. How? Why? What the hell is going on?"

"How did you get in the house?" I asked. I tried to keep the edge of anger I was feeling out of my voice—mostly because I was so happy that I didn't have to spend the afternoon looking for Sheldon to prove to Adam that I was right—despite the fact that I still wanted to wring his neck.

"I was in the car and I woke up and it turned out we were here," he said. "I didn't know where either of you were. I had a key, so I went inside. And I'm an old man, and I had that bottle of Sprite on the drive up here."

Adam rubbed his face with his hands. "This is not happening," he said. "Why? What in God's name did you think you were going to accomplish?"

"Didn't Danny tell you about the plan?" Sheldon asked. "He was supposed to, after the funeral."

"Tell me what?" Adam asked. "That you weren't really dead? That you were pulling an insane stunt?" There was an edge to his voice I hadn't heard before. I'd expected Adam to be unhappy about being proven wrong, but he sounded as though he was angrier at Sheldon than I was, and I wasn't sure that was possible.

"Maybe we can talk about it inside? Sitting down? Instead of, you know, out here in the front lawn?"

"Uncle Sheldon, do you have *any* idea how much stress and pain and aggravation you've caused me the last few weeks?" Adam turned to look at me just then, and he saw the grim look on my face, and the tracks of the tears still warm on my cheeks. "Not to mention what you put Wendy and her mother through," he added, the last few words trailing off.

"I am starting to realize that my strategy may not have been incredibly effective," Sheldon said.

"That's the understatement of the year," I said.

"I'm sorry. I am," Sheldon said. "Danny was supposed to tell you I was alive. If he hadn't screwed up, we wouldn't be having this conversation."

"This is crazy," Adam said. "I don't know what to do now. I mean, there's not a rational way to handle this."

"Well, then, let me explain," I said. "We are going inside. Adam, you are going to explain to your uncle exactly how hurt and embarrassed you are by his deception. He is going to explain his entire stupid plan, in all its insane complexity. And then, I am going to schlep Sheldon up to see my mother, so that she can settle his hash properly. That, and one more thing."

"Which is?" Adam asked.

I drew myself up to my full five feet eight inches and stood right in front of Adam and gave him the sternest lecture I could manage short of actually poking him in the chest with my finger. "You are going to apologize to me," I told him. "You are going to make the most abject, the most heartfelt, and the most meaningful apology that any man has ever made to any woman in the history of the world. And it is going to be real and honest and sincere and if you don't do it, you are never going to see me again."

Adam responded with a slight sheepish cringe that indicated that he was beginning to realize just how much he had fouled up the last few minutes of his life.

"Don't take this the wrong way, but you really do remind me of your mother," Sheldon said.

"Inside. Both of you. *March.*"

It was clear from the inside of the house that Adam was undertaking a serious renovation project. A large workbench sat in the dining room, complete with circular saw and a drop cloth to catch sawdust and little bits of crown molding scattered on the floor. What furniture there was looked basic and utilitarian, including two lower-end IKEA loveseats in the living room that bore the scars of being dragged in and out of a series of low-rent apartments. I sat in one, and Sheldon sat in the other, and Adam grabbed a chair from the kitchen and found a spot between us. None of us wanted to get closer to the others, because we had hurt each other so recently.

"I admit it. I did a stupid thing," Sheldon said. "But I don't get why you're so angry with me. I thought you'd be glad to see I was alive, at least."

"That's because you haven't been getting your credit card statements," Adam said. "I paid all of your credit card bills, figuring I'd get reimbursed once the house was sold. I canceled the cards, but then all these new statements with these new charges started coming in. I thought it was identity theft, that someone had stolen your name and was buying all the inventory from every home improvement store in South Jersey. But it was you all the time. What the hell have you been up to?"

"I haven't had anything else to do," Sheldon said. "Being dead isn't all it's cracked up to be, you know. I've been working on the house, trying to make it as perfect as I could. I figured her mother would show up eventually, and if things didn't work out with her, I could flip the house and pay for all the renovation costs. You should see it. It looks fantastic. Wendy here can tell you all about it."

"Uncle Sheldon, for God's sake," Adam said. "I have fraud investigators from three different credit card companies chasing after you, did you know that? And on top of everything, you went and gave that house away to someone you hadn't seen in fifty years. Do you have *any* idea what the last few weeks have been like for me?"

"They haven't been all that great for me, either," Sheldon said. "But I got a lot accomplished on the house. You'd be surprised what you can do when you have enough spare time. Are you going to put the crown molding in here, or just in the dining room?"

I could see the veins bulging in Adam's neck. "You can't kill him," I said. "I understand. I have wanted to kill him ever since Cape May. But it's not a good idea."

"No jury would convict me," Adam said.

"If you kill him, it brings the will back into play. And the codicil, for all I know. We'd be back to Square One."

"And the financial stuff is just the tip of the iceberg," Adam said. "Then there's the chaos you unleashed on my personal life. Wendy's, too. What is wrong with you?"

"It was a good idea," Sheldon said. "It would have worked, if all of you had done what you were supposed to have done."

"Instead, it did the exact opposite," I said. "You scared the hell out of me, and caused poor Adam here weeks of grief. And you have also messed with my mother, and you have no idea what pain is still in store for you."

"About that," Sheldon said. "It's already been a long day. Maybe we could put that trip off until tomorrow? You know, stay here tonight, and get a fresh start in the morning. We also need to think about dinner. There's that Mexican place we went to that time."

"You don't get a vote," I said.

Adam looked at me quizzically. "What happens if your mother kills him? Wouldn't that trigger the codicil?"

I thought for a second. "If she's convicted of murder, she wouldn't be eligible to inherit, and the house would go back to the estate. But no jury would convict her. Maybe we should be careful."

Adam nodded. "Or we could all kill him, like in *Murder on the Orient Express.*"

"Can we please not talk about how you want to murder me?" Sheldon asked. "I would greatly prefer a civilized discussion, if that's not too much to ask. Perhaps over a nice dinner."

"If you want a civilized discussion," Adam said, "you can start by explaining why you initiated this insane, crack-brained scheme. That's all I want right now. Tell me why you did this. Tell me why you thought this was a good idea. Tell me what you thought you would possibly get out of this other than upsetting me and Wendy and all the nice people at the senior-living complex."

"I didn't mean to upset anybody," Sheldon said. "I didn't

mean to cause anybody any grief. What I did, I did because I loved Emily and wanted to be with her. That's all."

"Then why not call her?" I said. "Send her a letter. Be her Facebook friend. You didn't have to go through this charade to get her attention."

"You don't understand," Sheldon said. "It's not your fault. You're young. You have the rest of your life ahead of you, as they say. I am old, and I am lonely, and I am deathly afraid of spending the rest of my life alone. That's something that's hard for me to admit, even to myself. If I just went up to Emily and tried to contact her out of the blue, there was a good chance she wasn't going to want anything to do with me. I had one chance with her and I needed to make the most of it."

"How'd that work out for you?" I asked.

"It was a good plan. I knew she would come for the funeral. She would ignore every other thing I tried to do, but she'd promised to come to my funeral when I died. So all I had to do was die and that was easy enough."

Adam snorted at this, and managed to be adorable. I had to remind myself to be mad at him.

"Then all I had to do would be to come back to life, in just the right way. And I thought that if Emily saw me alive again, in the house where we'd spent our honeymoon, with it restored to be as beautiful as it was back then—well, it seemed romantic to me. It was a big risk to take, and it didn't pay off the way it should have, but it seemed like a risk worth taking, to me. Especially since the alternative was just spending the rest of my life sitting around Victorian Cottages, growing old and moldy and sad and lonely."

"I talked to those old women at Victorian Cottages," Adam said. "There were at least three of them who would have snapped you right up, if you'd asked them."

"But that's not what I wanted," Sheldon said. "I didn't want to shack up with someone I hardly knew, just to have a fling. You have a lot of free time when you're retired, you know, and I spent a lot of mine going over my life, trying to figure out how I got to where I am—all the choices that I made. And the one thing I really regretted was not trying harder to work things out with Emily. I wanted to fix that. I'm good at fixing things, you know, and this was the one thing I never managed to repair. And now, it looks like I broke some other stuff that I hadn't intended to, and I'm sorry."

"I'm glad to see you're still alive, at least," Adam said. "Next time, when you plan something this crazy, could you maybe ask me for help or something? If I had been in the loop on this, I could have maybe made it work for you."

"I couldn't tell you, Adam. You're a reasonable guy. This was not a reasonable thing to do. You would have talked me out of trying the grand romantic gesture."

"But that's not what you were doing," I said. "You were trying to trick my mother into spending time with you. If you cared anything at all about her, you wouldn't have tried to win her over by deceit. And if you knew her at all, you should have known that she wouldn't sit still for you to try to manipulate her. If it had worked out like you wanted, she would have squished you like a bug. She's probably going to do that anyway."

"Maybe she will," Sheldon said. "But we loved each other, once. She might have been mad at first. But we always cared about each other, even when we were fighting, and I thought if I could just get her to fight with me, one more time, I might have a chance to win her over. I know how stupid it sounds now, but when I was planning it, it seemed like a real possibility. And even if it failed, at least I would have seen her again, even if it was just long enough for her to try and tear my head off. That would have been something."

I got up off my loveseat and went over to Sheldon, who was hunched over, with his chin in his hands. I sat down next to him and patted his shoulder, largely because I didn't know what else to do. He took a couple of deep, sighing breaths and then stood up.

"I'm going to go outside for a minute," he said. "Adam, you don't happen to have anything that needs doing out back, do you? I need to get some fresh air and clear my head."

"I was just fixing a leak in the cistern," Adam said. "I

need to put the lid back on and clean up. You're welcome to take a look at it."

"I told you not to go with the plastic on that thing. Concrete wouldn't have leaked on you like that."

"Should have listened," Adam said. "Live and learn."

"It's good to see you, Adam. I'm sorry I didn't tell you what I was doing."

"It's all right, Uncle Sheldon. See you in a few."

"And don't wander off," I said.

Chapter 29

"In case you were wondering," I said, "now would be an excellent time for that abject apology. The sooner you grovel at my feet, the happier you will be in the long run."

"I am not about to apologize to you," he said. "You can't come to my house and spout nonsense to me about my uncle being alive and think that I am just going to accept whatever you say unreservedly."

"But it wasn't nonsense. You see that now. I was *right.*"

"How was I supposed to know that? If anything, you owe *me* an apology for sandbagging me like that."

"You cannot be serious," I said.

"You could have just called and put Sheldon on the phone. That way, you wouldn't have come across as a crazy person."

"It doesn't matter what I did or didn't do," I said. "You were *rude.* You were *dismissive.* You *hurt my feelings.* Maybe I should have called or done something else different, I don't know. But the whole way up here, I was thinking about you and how much I wanted to be wrong about whether you knew he was alive or not. I was willing to give you the benefit of the doubt. And you weren't willing to show me the same courtesy, even though *I was right.* And now *you* want to break up with *me* because you were *wrong*? Do you know how ridiculous that sounds?"

"We are not breaking up," he said. "We were never together. We are not in a relationship. We barely know each other. We've had two dates. We don't live anywhere near each other. We don't have much of anything in common. If you look at it analytically, dispassionately, we should both be able to walk away and still be happy about it."

"Is that how you look at relationships?" I asked. "Analytically? Dispassionately?"

"It's the sensible approach. We had what we had that night in Point Pleasant and it was nice. It was wonderful. But everything else has been frustrating and stressful. At a certain point with any investment, you have to think about cutting your losses."

I looked at him just then, sitting on that battered old loveseat in that ridiculous dinosaur T-shirt, and it occurred to me that he didn't look stressed. He didn't look frustrated. He looked anxious and pale, and I could see the muscles in his jaw twitch.

"You don't believe that," I said.

"I don't believe what?"

"You don't believe everything is all about facts and analysis and looking at things dispassionately. You don't believe in the sensible approach. Deep down, you're a romantic."

"You can't just ignore facts," he said, and there was a ghost of that infuriating, maddening grin on his face. "Facts are important. The sensible approach has a lot going for it."

"But that's not the most important thing, is it?"

"It can be. It depends. I'm not saying that romance isn't important, but practical considerations have to be taken into account, too."

"Here's a practical consideration for you," I said. "You sent me a giant stuffed giraffe."

"What if I did?"

"Not flowers, which would have been a normal thing to do. Not candy, which would have been nice. Especially Godiva. For future reference."

"Noted," he said.

"You didn't do any of that. You, Adam Lewis, sent me a giant stuffed giraffe."

"So?"

"Why?" I asked.

"Does it matter?"

"The giant stuffed giraffe means something. What it means, I don't know. I didn't bring my magic decoder ring to the office that day. But it means something to you. More importantly, it means that you're not just operating on a factual, analytical, dispassionate basis. You sent me that giraffe for a reason. I want to know what that is."

"Who says it means anything? Maybe I had a coupon."

"It means something. Spill."

He leaned back in his loveseat and stretched. "You've seen giraffes up close, right? At the zoo, I mean."

"Sure."

"Giraffes in the zoo are clumsy and awkward," he said. "They look like they were put together by a committee. But everything about them is basically functional. The spots are camouflage. The long necks are for getting leaves off the tall trees. As a package, the giraffe *works*, but it's not what you would call *charismatic*, the way that lions and tigers and elephants are, or, you know, *cute*, like penguins or koalas or babies are. The giraffe is not romantic, if you follow me."

"So, the giraffe is meant to be, what, an ironic comment on your own character?" I asked. "That's the most cryptic thing I've ever heard. Do you have a secret decoder ring I can borrow that explains all of this?"

"Are you going to listen to the explanation, or just make sarcastic comments?"

"Sorry. Go ahead. By all means."

"We only think that the giraffe is not romantic because we see the giraffe in the zoo, where there's no room for them to roam. But in their natural habitat, the giraffe can run, and all that awkwardness, all that clumsiness, just goes away. In the wilds of Africa, the giraffe is graceful. It's beautiful. It's inspiring, almost. And that's what I want to be. And for a while there, with you, that's what I was."

I looked at Adam, sitting on that loveseat. He didn't look like a giraffe. He looked like a wolf coiled up in his den, dark and dangerous.

"If you really felt that way, why would you want to give up on that?" I asked. "Why wouldn't you want to keep feeling that way, if you could?"

"I want to have that feeling again. I want to feel the way I felt when I saw you walking towards me in that red dress and those ridiculous high heels. It's just that a relationship has to be based on something more than just how you feel about each other, or how you make each other feel. There has to be a logical basis to it, or it won't last. And when I look at you, everything that's logical and reasonable in my life becomes that much less important. It's like the ground is slipping from under my feet. And even now, even though we're upset with each other, even though both of us are ready to walk out of here and never see each other again, I can feel that attraction, that passion, and it's pulling me towards you. And that scares me."

"It scares me too," I said. It wasn't the least bit true, but I said it anyway. "But I think that being scared like that is a feeling worth having. And if nothing else, it's something that we can build on. If you feel a certain way towards me and if I feel a certain way towards you, we at least have that much in common. Don't we?"

I was sitting on the edge of my loveseat, as though Adam was pulling me towards him, slowly, imperceptibly, as inexorably as a glacier moving downhill.

"We have something," Adam said. "Something big. And no, I don't want to throw it away, or give it away. But I don't trust it, not yet."

"I understand that," I said. "Believe me. But the main impediment all this time has been your uncle's will, and now he's alive. There's no reason for either of us to distrust each other."

For the second time, I saw Adam's face turn thoughtful, and saw that feral glow shine out of his eyes. "I want to try," he said. "I think we owe it to each other to give ourselves a second chance. We might want to take it a little slower this time, though."

"If you say so." I didn't believe for a second that going slowly was what he wanted, but I was willing to go along with it if he was.

"Having said that, I would come right over there and give you a big, wet kiss on the lips right now, if it wasn't for one thing."

I looked at Adam for a long moment, waiting for him to grin, waiting for him to tease me, and then I realized he was being serious for once. "Because your Uncle Sheldon is standing out on the back porch eavesdropping on us," I said.

"No, I'm not," Sheldon said.

Chapter 30

Adam insisted that we call Mother and let her know about Sheldon being alive before we drove up there. "Speaking as someone who had it happen to me just now," he said, "I can't recommend the experience to anyone else. It's not a good kind of surprise, you understand?"

"But it would be so much fun the other way," I said.

"I have no doubt that it would be an entertaining and edifying spectacle," he said. "And I wouldn't mind witnessing it from a safe distance, like you do with wrecks in car racing. But I think maybe everyone has had enough agita for one day."

So I gave him my phone and he called her and explained things to her. Adam made several quite interesting faces, including one that made him look like he had a baby moth trapped in his ear. "OK," he finally said, after listening to the initial blast. "Here's Wendy." He handed me the phone without a word of explanation.

"Coward," I said.

"Even the bravest man can only stand so much before he breaks."

I think Mother took the news that Sheldon was alive about as well as anyone who found out that they just lost a quarter of a million dollar inheritance would take that news, by which I mean, not well. On top of that, it took me quite some time to reassure her that we were not playing an elaborate practical joke on her. "We know he's alive," I said. "He's sitting in Adam's house, right across from me. I drove him up here from Cape May. He's drinking a diet ginger ale and refusing to talk to you on the phone."

"Oh, for heaven's sake, Gwendolyn Rose. You can't possibly expect me to believe this nonsense."

I ignored her provocative use of my full name. "This is a special kind of Sheldon Berkman nonsense. It's true, what Adam told you. I drove down to the house in Cape May, like we talked about, and Sheldon was there, fixing it up. He'd been waiting for you all this time. The funeral was a fake, designed to get you down there. It was supposed to be romantic."

"Am I to understand that the plan was for me to attend the funeral, to undergo the ordeal of thinking Sheldon was dead, and then to walk into that ugly house that we drove past, and then have him jump out of a closet and frighten me to death?"

"He never intended to frighten you to death, no, but the rest of it is accurate. He nearly gave me a heart attack this afternoon, though, but that was because he thought I was you."

"He's gone blind, then," she said.

"No, just cranky, annoying, and demanding. It seems to be common for people his age. Of course you wouldn't know about that."

"I want to talk to this man," Mother said. "In person would be best, if the coward has the nerve to face me. I want to explain to him how badly he has miscalculated."

"I am driving him up to see you so that he can apologize in person," I explained. "I had planned to just dump him on your doorstep and watch the fireworks, but cooler heads prevailed."

"Just as well, I suppose. You'll call me when you get close?"

"Sure," I said. "It shouldn't take but an hour to drive up there."

"Neutral site," Sheldon said.

"Hold on a second, Mother," I said. "Sheldon, what do you mean by 'neutral site'?"

"I want to see her, but I am not giving her home-field advantage," Sheldon said. "I will meet her someplace out in public. Very public. So she doesn't shoot me, the way you two keep threatening to do."

"That won't help you if she claims temporary insanity," Adam said. "We can stop and get you a bulletproof vest, I guess."

"He wants to meet somewhere public," I explained to

Mother.

"Oh, how tiresome. Very well. I suppose the mall will do."

"Where do you want to meet in the mall?" I asked. "I can't think of anywhere except the food court on the top floor, as long as you promise not to throw him over the railing."

"Yes," she said. "I think that has possibilities. I will meet you there in one hour."

We piled into Adam's Jaguar and headed north on Route 9, headed for I-287 and the Bridgewater Commons Mall. We made good time, driving most of the way in silence. Sheldon was too traumatized (or excited, it was hard to tell) to say anything, and there wasn't anything that Adam and I had to say to each other that we wanted to say in front of him. Adam had the satellite radio in his car set to the all-Springsteen station, so we listened to that until we got to the highway, at which point I got tired of listening to sad ballads about the decline of the Northeastern industrial corridor and flipped over to the '80s station.

"You know where we're going, right?" Adam said.

"You want to be over to your left and then take the exit for Route 22 and then follow the signs for the mall," I said. "We'll be there in a few minutes. Try to find a space in the top level of the parking garage."

"Doesn't sound hard. Are you sure you are going to be OK driving back with me to Freehold tonight to pick up your car, and then going back home? That's a lot of driving in one day."

"I think I can figure something out," I said. If worst came to worst, I figured that I could always find a motel in Freehold somewhere and drive up to Morristown in the morning. I was certainly hoping that it wouldn't come to that. I wondered if Adam had finished the renovation on his bedroom, or if it was six inches deep in sawdust.

"I don't think I'm going to feel like driving all the way to drop Uncle Sheldon back to Cape May," Adam said.

"You better not ditch me, kid," Sheldon said. "You still

have all my stuff in storage from when you cleaned out my apartment. I need to rent a truck tomorrow and drive it all back."

"Don't take this the wrong way," I said, "but if you are counting on me to help you load it back again and drive back to help you unload it, you are sadly mistaken."

"It's not that difficult," Sheldon said. "Once you decide to put your life back together, everything else you need to do after that is just putting in the work. Getting started is the hardest part."

Adam took his right hand off the steering wheel. He squeezed my knee, and I took his hand and held it. It felt warm and comfortable.

"This is what I want to know," Adam said. "You did this, all of this, in order to talk to this woman you hadn't talked to in forty years, right?"

"So?" Sheldon said.

"So, why did you leave her in the first place?" Adam asked. "If she was your one true love and all."

"I told Wendy's mother that it was another woman," Sheldon said. "If memory serves."

"That's what she told me," I said.

"So was that why?" Adam asked. "Who was she?"

"There wasn't another woman," Sheldon said. "I said that there was, but that wasn't true. I knew she wouldn't have believed the real reason."

"Which was?" I asked. "Assuming you think that we'd believe you."

"I fell in love with Alaska," Sheldon said. "Oh, and the Air Force, too, but mostly Alaska. I'd never been anywhere outside of New Jersey before basic training. Alaska was big and wild in those days—still is, but not the way it was back then. I learned to hunt and fish and climb mountains. Every day that I worked was a challenge, and every day I had off was an adventure. And the only thing missing was Emily, and I knew she'd never want to join me there."

"So you just gave up?" I asked.

"I made a mistake," Sheldon said. "I didn't realize it at the time. I thought I was doing the right thing by ending the marriage. We were different people who wanted different things out of life. She wanted to be a big wheel in politics. I wanted to work on airplanes and serve my country. And we both thought those things were important."

"The things you want are always important," Adam said.

"But sometimes, what the other person wants is more important," Sheldon said. "Especially when that person is the most important person in the world for you. I forgot that. I let myself forget it. That's what I wanted to tell her. That's why I did what I did."

I looked at Adam, but his eyes were on the road. How important was I to him? How important was he to me? I didn't know the answer to either question.

"Here's the exit," I said. "We're almost there."

We walked past the movie theater and the sporting goods store and the little cart that sells the bejeweled smartphone cases and headed towards the food court. I spotted Pacey standing in front of the Hollister store. Simon and Benjy were gnawing on soft pretzels the size of their heads and were not noticing another thing in this world.

"Are you Mr. Berkman?" she asked Sheldon.

"That's me," he said.

"Good. I am Emily's other daughter, Patricia. You can call me Pacey, everybody else does. These are my kids, Simon and Benjy. Say hello to the nice man, kids."

"Horseradish," Benjy said.

"Benjy. Stop that. Never mind him, he says that to everyone. You will find my mother sitting in front of the little Japanese place, over on the left. I will not be joining you, as I am afraid that words will be used that I don't want my kids to hear."

"Horseradish," Benjy repeated.

"Quiet, dear. Adam and Wendy and I will wait here until Mother is done with you. Keep in mind that I have had to hear her opinions on you, nonstop, for the last hour, so I am not very pleased with you myself at the moment. My recommendation is that you start by groveling at her feet."

Sheldon's lips quivered. He said something that was too

quiet for me to hear but which might have been, "It's not fair."

"Keep to your left. I would hurry, if I were you. Or you might want to savor your last moments on this planet. Up to you, really."

Sheldon slouched off to his doom and Pacey motioned us over to the right. We followed her to a wooden divider that was topped with plastic bushes. "We don't want to get too close," she said. "But this is a good vantage point."

"What are you doing here, Pacey?" I asked.

"You know me. I never want to miss a good show," she said. "And Mother said her car was on the fritz."

"You believed that?" I said.

"No. Quiet. It's starting."

Mother was sitting all alone at a table, with her arms folded. She looked as though she had swallowed all of the sour pickles in the world. In front of her was a large paper cup with words on it that I couldn't quite make out. "What does she have in there?" I asked. "It's not coffee, is it?"

"Milkshake from Haagen-Dazs," Pacey said.

"I didn't think she liked milkshakes," I said.

"She doesn't. And you'll notice there's no lid."

"Oh."

"Not to change the subject," Pacey said, "but are you Adam? I'm sorry I didn't introduce myself before."

I rolled my eyes. I hoped Pacey hadn't made the trip just to check out Adam for herself, but that seemed like the best explanation.

"That's OK," Adam said. "Good to meet you."

"I have heard a lot about you," she said. "Good things. Mostly."

Adam just stood there looking uncomfortable, like someone had just put some tiny rocks in his shoes. Benjy and Simon were at his feet so you couldn't rule that out, of course.

"I think she's going to let Sheldon sit down," Pacey said. "I don't know if we'll be able to hear her from here." She took a step back, where Adam couldn't see her. "*He's cute,*" she mouthed. "*Nice bone structure.*"

"*Stop it,*" I whispered back.

"She's getting up," Adam said. "She's doing something."

"And here we go," Pacey said, as Mother dumped the contents of her milkshake into Sheldon's lap.

"Thank God she didn't get the coffee," I said.

"She wanted to," Pacey said. "I talked her out of it. The risk of damages, you know."

Sheldon, to his credit, didn't flinch. Years of military training and living in Alaska, I suppose. Mother started shouting at that point, and Pacey knelt and covered her sons' ears. Then Mother slammed her fist down on the table and upended it, sending it clattering. This aroused the attention of a couple of mall security guards, who began edging their way over.

"Uh-oh," I said. "I should have stopped and gotten cash out of the ATM for bail money, come to think of it."

"She'll be fine," Pacey said. "You might not know this, Adam, but my dear sweet mother has an arrest record as long as your arm. Protests, you know. Nuclear freeze. Stop the war in Iraq. Save the whales, that sort of thing. She knows how to handle herself around law enforcement." And, indeed, Pacey was proved correct, as the mall cops helped turn the table back upright and walked away.

Mother said a few more words to Sheldon, who was still sitting in his chair. I thought she was going to slap him, but something seemed to hold her back. She turned away, and then stalked off in our direction.

"The nerve of the man," she said. "Astonishing. He's lucky I didn't stab him through the liver."

"Nice seeing you too, Mom," I said.

"Hello, Wendy," she said. "And hello again to you too, Adam. You may pick up your miscreant uncle whenever you like."

"I think I'll get some napkins," Adam said.

"That would be a merciful act and more than he deserves. I take it you had no part in this charade?"

"None whatsoever," he said. "Thank you for returning him in one piece."

"I was tempted to break him in half," she said. "I mean,

the *effrontery* of it all. You will explain to him that I have no interest in inheriting that house, should he manage to expire on his own?"

"Not a problem," Adam said.

"So, are you done then?" I asked. "Or should we expect another form of retaliation?"

"He deserves much worse than a lap full of ice cream, but I don't have the time and the energy to spend on him. And I have kept your sister here from the comfort of her home and hearth long enough. Thank you, Pacey dear, if I haven't said so before."

"Not a problem," Pacey said. "Get that napkin out of your mouth, Simon."

"Do you need a ride anywhere, Wendy?" Mother asked. "We might go get dinner somewhere, too, I suppose."

"I'm good," I said.

"Very well. I will leave you to scrape poor Sheldon out of his chair. Safe travels to you both." She took Benjy's hand, the one that wasn't full of soft pretzel at the moment. "Come, dear. Grandmama is ready to go get dinner."

"*Call me,*" Pacey whispered. I glowered at her but didn't respond.

Adam came back with a double handful of napkins. "I'm going to try to get Sheldon cleaned up," Adam said. "Do you want to help your sister get her kids in the car or anything?"

"I'm good," I said. "If you let me know his size, I can run into the Gap and buy him a new pair of jeans."

"I don't know, but we can go ask. It would be a good idea anyway. I don't think he's bought any new clothes since 1997. After that, maybe we can get a sack of burgers or something else to eat on the way home."

Sheldon was still sitting there when we made our way over to him, with the table hiding the stain on his pants. "She's still beautiful," he said. "Just as pretty as the day we met. But maybe a little more aggressive, come to think of it."

Chapter 31

We filed out of the mall slowly, with me carrying Sheldon's soaked jeans in a plastic bag from the Gap. We got back in Adam's Jaguar for the long drive back down Route 9 towards Freehold. Nobody said much of anything. It was starting to get dark and Adam was concentrating on driving and I was borderline exhausted and Sheldon was still floating on his beatific vision of my mother. I was out within five minutes after I finished eating my burger. I slept the sleep of the just, untroubled by the resurrection of love-struck aviation mechanics or the state of my relationship with Adam, whatever that may have been at that point.

When I woke up, the Jaguar had made its way down to a cluster of big-box stores in Manalapan. Sheldon was snoring in the back seat. I yawned, wide enough to nearly unhinge my jaw. Adam didn't acknowledge that I was awake, so I fished my phone out of my purse and checked my e-mail. I had three different coupons in my in-box from three different shoe stores, which was probably something I didn't need to share with anyone else. I deleted two of them but kept the third, just in case I ever had something to celebrate. I switched over to Facebook, which had the same banal stuff it always did. A friend from law school had posted some inane celebrity drivel from the *Huffington Post*. The girl who had beaten me out for valedictorian my senior year at high school was linking to a bunch of cat videos.

Pacey had posted something snarky about getting to meet my boyfriend at long last, so I opened the Amazon shopping app and looked around for the most annoying toy I could find. I found these horrible-looking plastic kazoos that were guaranteed to be extra-loud. I ordered two.

"What are you snickering about?" Adam asked.

"I was snickering?" I asked. "I hadn't realized."

"Yes, but why?"

"Revenge. A cheap revenge, but I hope it will be effective."

"Is that like a family tradition, or something?" he asked. "Because it seems to be."

"It's not directed at you."

"Oh, good."

"I mean, this time, anyway."

Adam changed lanes and accelerated to get around someone in a maroon minivan. "Have you decided if you're driving home or not?" he asked.

"Why do you ask?" I employed just the slightest coquettish simper, just to see where he was heading with this.

"You realize I'm in the middle of a renovation project with the house, right?"

"I may have noticed a few things seemed slightly askew."

"Sarcasm. Great. Just what I was looking for. Anyway, you didn't go upstairs, so you didn't see the guest bedroom. It's not in great shape."

"Like six inches of sawdust all over everything?" I asked.

"Like, not having a floor."

"That sounds problematic," I said.

"I'm not exactly set up for house guests right at the moment. I know Uncle Sheldon doesn't have any place to go, but I can put him on the love seat downstairs. He's not finicky."

"Are you calling me finicky?" I asked.

Adam said something under his breath that I couldn't quite catch but sounded like *serenity, serenity, serenity*. I decided not to press the issue, but if he was going to tease me, he needed to learn to handle teasing better.

"I didn't say that," he said. "What I was thinking was that the best answer would be to put Uncle Sheldon up in a motel for the night. There's a nice place that just happens to be across the street from the storage place where I put all his stuff. He likes to get an early start in the morning; he can walk over there and have everything loaded on a rental truck before breakfast."

"Where does that leave me?"

"That's kind of up to you, isn't it? Like I said, it's a nice motel. If you want, I can drop you off there. You can get a room, and Sheldon can give you a ride back to my house, if that's what you want."

"That's not what I want," I said.

"So you're driving home?"

"That's not what I want, either."

We dropped Sheldon off without too much in the way of grumbling. He'd had a long day, and wasn't averse to the idea of going straight to bed. Adam left him the keys to the storage unit, and a credit card for the truck-rental place. It was a short drive from there to Adam's house, but not a long enough drive for me to figure out what it was I wanted to do next.

I saw Vanessa before Adam did. She was sitting in her car, which she had parked in Adam's driveway, blocking my car. I told him to keep driving, and he did as he was told, which I thought was a very good sign indeed.

"What do we do now?" I asked.

"Simple," Adam said. "We find someplace to park, and go in the back door. Eventually, she'll go away."

"You don't know Vanessa. She has something she wants from me. For all I know, she's been following me all day. She's relentless."

"I don't want her in my driveway, either, but I'm spending tonight in my own bed. Under the circumstances, you're welcome to join me."

Every time I think he can't get any less romantic, I thought, *he surprises me.*

"I thought you wanted to take this slowly," I said.

"It's your decision," he said. "You can come inside with me, or you can have it out with Vanessa. I know what I'd prefer, but the alternative should be entertaining as well." It was too dark for me to see his face clearly, but I knew he had that irritating grin on his face.

He parked the Jaguar in an empty space in front of the house that was directly behind his. He crept softly through the yard, all the way to the back fence. I followed him, checking nervously over my shoulder to see if anyone was stirring in the house.

"There's not a door in the fence," Adam said. "So we need to go over. I can go first, and then help you over, but we have to do it quietly."

"You're not serious," I said.

"Shush," Adam whispered. "And keep it down. Voices carry, you know. I hate to ask you this, but you need to trust me."

"You want me to trust you? You want *me* to trust *you*?"

"Well, sure. I mean, it's not all that high of a fence. Let me show you." He took a leap at the fence, hooked one of his feet in the lattice, and managed to vault over it without injuring himself. "See?" he said, as he picked himself up off the ground. "No trouble at all. And I can help you over."

"This is not about whether you will catch me should I try to make it over this fence, which I am not about to do. This is about me not trusting you because you don't trust me."

"We can have this discussion later," he hissed. "Right now, you need to go up and over."

"You are out of your mind, Adam."

"You want me to apologize? Is that what this is about?"

"All I asked you to do was believe me when I said your uncle was alive. You're asking me to climb a fence in the middle of the night, for no good reason. I think there is an imbalance here."

"If you want to try and see if you can get in the front door before your friend Vanessa tackles you, go right ahead," Adam said. "This felt like it was maybe a little more dignified."

"There is nothing dignified about making me climb this stupid fence," I stage-whispered.

"You're worried about being dignified?" he asked. "I've already seen you naked."

"Do you want to see me naked again?"

"Yes. Very much so." I could just see the wolf-like glint in his eyes through the darkness.

My alternatives, as I saw them, were to try to climb the stupid fence, or pull my phone out and see what kind of cab service they had in Freehold, New Jersey, this late on a Saturday night. I said something caustic and horrible under my breath.

"Whenever you're ready," Adam said.

"If you think this is adorable and romantic," I said, "you are sadly mistaken."

"All I'm asking is for you to meet me halfway," he said. "You'll see."

I took a deep breath and asked the universe to suspend the law of gravity just long enough to get me over this stupid fence. I put my feet in the lattice, one small step at a time, and inched my way up. The structure started sagging under my weight. I applied forward momentum and managed to make it halfway up before I stalled. As I mentioned before, I am a little top-heavy, and I started to tip forward. Adam took my arms and started dragging me over, but my belt snagged on the top of the fence.

"Wait. *Wait*," I hissed. "I am *stuck*."

"Quiet," he said, and kept pulling.

"*My pants are coming off!*"

He reached over, grabbed the back of my belt, and lifted me bodily over the fence as I kicked and flailed. He overbalanced and fell to the turf, with me on top of him.

"Ow," I said. "Bastard."

Adam hooked a thumb towards the house, and started walking up to the back porch, and tried a small door on the right side. It was locked.

"Unbelievable," I said.

"Patience." He got his wallet out and extracted a credit card. He slid it into the latch and the door popped open. A staircase led up to the second floor.

"After you," he said.

The room at the top of the stairs was large and tastefully decorated and had a gas fireplace roaring happily away. A king-size bed sat in the far corner, with high-thread-count sheets and a down comforter, with a door beyond it that looked like it led to a private bath. In front of the fireplace, there was a bright-red Persian rug and a cushy sofa with dark maroon leather.

"Did you do all this?" I asked.

"Every bit of it. It's nice, don't you think?"

"It's gorgeous," I said. It looked every bit as stunning as what Sheldon had done with the house in Cape May.

"I have the fireplace synched up with an iPhone app. I turned it on when you were getting dinner at the mall. I was hoping that you'd want to come up here with me, and here you are."

He's trying to seduce you, I thought. *And it's working.*

"It's been a long day," I said. "And I have to admit, it would be nice just to sink down on that couch and watch that fire for a while, sitting next to you. But first, I would like to know where we stand, you and I."

"We don't need to stand," he said. "Sit. Relax. Be comfortable."

"You asked me to trust you, and I did," I said. "But it has to be a two-way street. You still owe me an apology. And unless I get it, you're going to need to find somewhere else to sleep tonight."

Adam sank down on the couch. "You're right," he said. "It has been a long day."

"If you want to grab a blanket so you can sleep more comfortably downstairs, I would be all right with that," I said.

"I'm not going to grovel, if that's what you're waiting for. If you're looking for someone who does that, I guess you can keep looking. I know I screwed up today. I know I overreacted when you said Sheldon was alive. This has not been the best day I've ever had, or the best week I've ever had, but that's not an excuse. Sometimes I am a jerk. But not often, and when I'm not, I'm actually a pretty decent guy, if you give me a chance. That's if you want to give me a chance."

"If you can't be honest with me, I can't give you a chance."

"Then I'll be honest," he said. "I like you. I think you're smart and attractive and sexy. You don't put up with bullshit or dish it out. I want to try to make this work, and I hope that you do, too."

"I want to try," I said. "But I can't be with someone I don't trust, and who doesn't trust me. We have to build that, together, and maybe we're not there yet."

Adam took a long look into the fireplace. I took a step towards the fire, feeling its warmth on my hands and radiating up my body. I was suddenly conscious of just how warm the room was at that moment. It would feel good to be warm all over, I thought, to be under the thick covers on the bed.

"I made this room for you," he said. "I mean, I didn't know who you'd be at the time. But I did everything in here myself. I laid the bricks for the fireplace. I sanded the floors. I nailed in the crown molding. I wanted this room to be special, because I knew a special girl would come along who would want to be here, alone with me, and sit by the fire. I trusted that you would come along, and you're here, and I'm here, and the fire is warm. I think we can build on that."

I shouldn't do this. I should walk out of here, like he said. Teach him a lesson.

In his own clumsy, backwards way, he is trying to be romantic.

He's not Prince Charming, and he never will be.

But he's smart, and he's handsome, and when he smiles he makes me feel warm and soft inside. And when he touches me that warm softness blazes into something hotter than that fireplace.

What was it Pacey had said? "Romance is the socialized expression of frustrated sexual desire." By that standard, I was feeling romantic as all hell. And Adam was standing there, looking at me in that lascivious, carnivorous way of his, like I was a treat he was just waiting to unwrap.

Adam was right, I thought. *He wasn't being mysterious. This is someplace warm, and it's not just the fire.*

I took a step backwards, towards the leather sofa. I sat down at what I hoped was an inviting angle. It must have been, because Adam pressed his body closely against mine and leaned in for a kiss. His mouth felt hot and salty against mine. He smelled like smoke and coffee and desire.

He thrust his tongue deeply into my mouth, holding it there for a long, delicious moment. Then he lifted himself off the couch and knelt on the floor in front of me. He started nuzzling my neck, while one hand worked its way down my body to my belt buckle, which he started to undo.

"I thought you wanted to go slowly," I said.

"I do," he said. "Later."

I woke up the next morning happy, content, and wreathed in Adam's arms. The sun was peeking through the lace curtains. It was the start of a new day, one that we would spend together.

Chapter 32

Vanessa's car was still in the driveway when I woke up. I had no idea why she was there, unless she wanted to torment me. I didn't have an idea of how much food Adam had in the house, so it might not be possible to starve her out. There was also the possibility that he didn't have adequate stores of coffee, which would have been an unquestioned disaster. Something had to be done.

I decided not to wake Adam up right away. He'd had a hard day, and I noted that he looked very fetching when he was asleep. That had to do, I reasoned, with the fact that he wasn't teasing me. I got dressed, did the minimum I needed to do to make myself presentable, and went downstairs to the kitchen. It turned out that Adam had one of those single-serve coffee makers, and a Costco-sized box of pods to go with them. I was going to be able to withstand a lengthy siege.

I was checking Adam's pantry to see if his taste in alcohol ranged anywhere beyond light beer when the doorbell rang. I had no intention of answering it, but I also didn't want Adam to wake up just yet. I glanced at the front door and saw that it had a chain on it. I hooked the chain up and opened the door a crack.

"Go away," I said.

"I just need a very quick moment of your time," Vanessa said. "I promise."

"I do not believe a single thing you say," I said.

"I hate to ask you. Really, I do. But it will be quick."

"You are not supposed to be talking to me at all. You shouldn't be here. You should leave. Now."

"I can't leave," Vanessa said. "Not right this minute."

"What is your problem?" I asked.

"I need to pee," she admitted. "Please."

"Try the deli," I said.

"Wendy, I know you're upset, but if you make me wet my pants, I will take it very personally."

"You just spent the night in your car so you could block my car. That's stalking, technically. I take that very personally."

"I am begging you," she said.

It would be a petty revenge to make her wet her pants on Adam's front porch, but I knew I would have to clean it up. I undid the chain. "Quickly," I said. "Don't make me regret being nice to you."

"Thanks loads," she said. "Watch out that I don't hit your foot with the cane." She was wearing a ridiculously oversized walking boot, and wielding one of those canes with four legs that extremely elderly people use to get around. Her equipment didn't seem to inhibit her pace as she raced to the downstairs bathroom.

The way I figured it, it was about fifty-fifty that Vanessa had tracked me down in order to try to extort a quick settlement for her lawsuit. That was the best-case scenario. Otherwise, it meant that she had come up with some other clever idea to torment me. I just hoped that, whatever it was, it was ill-advised enough that I could use it against her somehow. I couldn't hit her, or even touch her. All I could do was let her do whatever she came to do, and then drive home and amend the pleadings I had prepared if I needed to do that. I was going to win this confrontation in the end, so long as I kept my cool.

She stumped her way out of the bathroom a few minutes later. "I am quite grateful to you," she said. "Honestly. We may have our little disagreements, but we can still be civil, can't we?"

"That's rich, coming from a woman who's just spent all night in her car so she could block mine in the driveway. Actually, if you don't mind, I'd like to get a picture of you behind the wheel. You know, for evidence in the countersuit."

"You do say the drollest things, Wendy. But it's your picture I've come to take."

"I can't imagine why," I said. "I'm not the least bit photogenic."

"Perhaps not," Vanessa said. "But your boyfriend is. Or, at least, that's what I'm hoping the state bar association will think."

"Is that your little plan? It's not enough to get me suspended from my job, but you want to get me disbarred as well?"

"It wouldn't be me doing it, you understand. It would be the state bar association. You're not supposed to have a sexual relationship with the opposing party in a pending case. They frown on such things, or so I understand."

I had another one of those flashes of realization, but this was a soft glow. A very warm, soft glow. "Won't you sit down," I said. "Your supposed injury must be very tiring for you."

"That's very tempting," she said. "I will take you up on that. It speaks well of your character that you should be so accommodating." It took her a moment to settle on the love seat. I sat down opposite her, with my hands folded neatly in my lap.

"I can see that you've been busy," I said. "So have I. I have an e-mail sitting in my drafts folder. It's complete, just not sent yet. It will go out right after this conversation is over. I'm sending it to everyone I can find at Gawker Media, and copying it to all the daily newspapers in the Northeast. I'm hoping that's all I have to do to help it go viral, but I can certainly send it elsewhere if the need requires."

"That's a remarkably feeble threat, Wendy," she said. "An e-mail. I'm quite frightened."

"The e-mail will allege that you colluded with one Sheldon Berkman to forge an obituary of his alleged death, which you then hawked to Gawker Media in order to get a job of some sort. They bit on it without checking to see if he were actually dead, which he isn't. You helped perpetrate a hoax, and they fell for it. They'll be embarrassed enough to retract the whole thing."

"Embarrassed?" she snorted. "You don't know anyone at Gawker, do you?"

"I know enough to know they like pointing out hoaxes a lot more than being hoaxed themselves. And they won't forgive you for trying to fool them."

"But it's not true. You have no proof. You can't make anything like that stick."

I sat quietly, with an impassive look on my face.

"You're bluffing," Vanessa said. "And it's a bad bluff. Wendy, I'm disappointed in you."

I waited for a long moment. I knew Sheldon didn't have any money, and I knew he needed coffee. Adam said he was an early riser. And sure enough, I heard the squeal of badly maintained rental truck brakes from outside.

A moment later, Sheldon walked in the door. "Good morning," he said. "I'm sorry, who are you?"

"Vanessa Sullivan," I said, "I would like to introduce you to Sheldon Berkman."

Vanessa jumped to her feet. "This is outrageous," she shouted. "Sheldon Berkman's dead."

"A lot of people thought that," Sheldon said. "I was much more convincing than I thought I was going to be."

Vanessa stomped over to the doorway where Sheldon was standing. "Who are you, really?" she asked. "An actor or something?"

"You forgot your cane," I pointed out, helpfully. "Wait, can you do that again? The walking thing. I want to get it on video."

"This is a shabby stunt you are trying to pull, Wendy," she said. "Even if this is Sheldon Berkman."

"It is Sheldon Berkman. Believe me, I was just as surprised as you were. But you'll never be able to convince anyone that you didn't know that ahead of time."

Vanessa wasn't wearing the pale makeup she favored, so I could watch the color drain out of her face.

"You can't send that e-mail," Vanessa said. "Even if that is Sheldon Berkman, the collusion part is not true."

"Says Little Miss Walking Boot," I said. "Do you mind if I keep this cane? You know, for evidence, at trial. Speaking of trials—they're very expensive undertakings, you know—did you know the most important factor is credibility? I wouldn't want to call a witness who had been exposed as a hoaxer by a large media outlet, even if it was just Gawker."

I was waiting on Vanessa to give me a snappy comeback. Anything would do, so long as I could throw it back in her face. But she didn't. She walked back to the love seat and started to unbuckle the walking boot she was wearing. "I hate this thing," she said. "It's uncomfortable, and hot, and I'm afraid I'm going to trip over something and break my neck."

"What a tragedy that would be for journalism," I said.

"Says Little Miss Snappy Comeback. All right then," she said. "Cards on the table. Do you want to make a deal?"

"We start with unconditional surrender," I said. "We can work on the details after that."

Adam came down the stairs just then, unshaven, wearing sweat pants and an orange T-shirt that celebrated the 2005 Big East Championship, whatever that might have been. I made a mental note that I needed to work on having him improve his wardrobe.

"What's going on?" he said.

"Peace negotiations," I said.

"Will they be concluded before I've had a chance to drink some coffee?" he asked.

"Not a chance," Vanessa said.

"You might want to take that to go," Sheldon said. "We're burning daylight as it is."

"Gotcha. Wendy, can I talk with you in the kitchen, please?"

"You mind?" I asked Vanessa.

"Is there coffee in it for me?" she asked.

"You're lucky I let you pee," I said. "This will just take a minute."

I followed Adam into the far corner of the kitchen and gave him a slow, lingering kiss.

"You realize I have to go help Uncle Sheldon today," he said. "It can't wait."

"Neither can this thing with Vanessa," I said. "I have her over a barrel. I may just be able to save my job, at least for a little while."

"How's that again?" he asked.

"That's right. I never managed to get around to telling

you that part. It's not important. But I can handle this. You go do what you need to do, and I'll get rid of Vanessa, and I'll meet you back here. If that's all right."

"I don't have a problem," he said. "I trust you."

"I'm glad to hear that," I said. It sounded wonderful to hear him say it.

"Do you want to go to dinner tonight?" he asked.

"Sure," I said. "Where do you want to go?"

Adam smiled. "Let's go someplace romantic," he said.

My heart soared. I was getting through to him at last. I had found a wonderful, adorable man, and we were falling in love with each other, and everything was going to be perfect from now on.

"I know this great little place on Route 9," he said. "And I have a coupon."

"Great," I said. "That's just what I wanted to hear."

Epilogue

Adam asked me to marry him at midnight on Christmas Eve, out in front of the big tree at Rockefeller Center. It was a beautiful, heartwarming, romantic moment, and it only happened because I had dropped several broad hints regarding how I thought he should propose. I had determined that Adam was, after all, capable of the occasional romantic gesture, if subtly led in the right direction.

It was a perfect evening. I wore the garnet dress I had worn on our first date. He knelt down and asked me to marry him, and I said yes. I think I heard sleigh bells ring when he put the engagement ring on my hand, but I couldn't testify to that.

We told our respective families at a New Year's Eve party at Pacey's house. My brother Greg drove up from Philadelphia and brought a young, attractive Indian woman with him. Her name was Dayita, and she was an orthopedist that Greg had met at the hospital—which was fortunate for him, because he'd never meet anyone any other way. I was glad that he was seeing someone, but annoyed to lose my long-term bet with Pacey about whether the first person Greg would bring to a family gathering would be male or female. She was very charming and gracious, and I liked her right away. Unfortunately, Greg forgot to warn her not to talk politics with Mother. They got into a protracted discussion about immigration and affirmative action, and I finally had to break things up and take Dayita aside and plead with her not to say anything inflammatory about health care reform or Rush Limbaugh or Altamont.

Adam's mother drove up from Point Pleasant, after Pacey and I had spent the last several days assuring her that there would be something gluten-free for her to eat. And Uncle Sheldon tagged along, although I hadn't wanted to invite him. Adam, sensibly, pointed out that we wouldn't be together without him and I couldn't disagree. I did insist that he bring a change of clothes in case Mother decided to throw something else at him.

Pacey had taken the sensible step of hiring a caterer, for which everyone was grateful. We made our announcement just before dinner, and nobody was the least bit surprised except for Pacey's husband and Greg's new girlfriend. Pacey did let out an approving squeal once she saw the engagement ring, which was all I wanted to hear. We all sat down and heaped our plates with (gluten-free) gnocchi and roast beef and ginger-cilantro chicken, and I made a note to get the name of Pacey's caterer.

At dinner, I made my other announcement, which was that I had quit my job in Morristown and was moving to Freehold. I'd had Mother pull a couple of strings in her South Jersey network, and one of her friends had gotten me a job clerking with a county probate judge, with an eye on me taking over the judgeship on his retirement.

We were almost done with the renovations on Adam's house. We had decided against flipping it, at least for the time being. That left the wedding to plan. I had three different sites picked out so far, but Adam was trying to convince me to get married on the beach at Cape May. I was looking forward to ironing out all the details over the next few months. We both wanted to get married in October, and honeymoon in the Caribbean after hurricane season had blown through, and after that we would spend the rest of our lives together.

After dinner, I ended up on the overstuffed leather couch in the family room, with a glass of chardonnay in one hand and a Mo Willems book in the other, doing the funny voices for Elephant and Piggie for an adoring audience of two. When I was done with the book, Adam sat beside me and whispered in my ear. "Is there someplace we can go?" he asked.

"Pacey says there's Linzer torte," I said. "I am not going anywhere, unless you count maybe getting a chardonnay refill."

"I mean, just for a short time," he said.

"Seriously? Here? In my sister's house?"

He explained, very quietly and discreetly, what he had in mind.

"Oh," I said. "I see. Well, the basement is furnished, so that might work, if we're careful."

"That sounds fine," he said.

"As long as we're back upstairs by the time she's ready to serve the Linzer torte."

"I promise."

The steps down to the basement were creaky, so I went down slowly, trying not to make a sound. Adam followed my lead. The light was on downstairs, which I attributed to one of the twins having left it on. I didn't hear the voices until I got to the bottom step.

"Are you sure we should be doing this?" I heard Sheldon say.

"Relax, dear. Everyone is thinking about the lovebirds upstairs. They've forgotten we're even here."

My body froze in shock.

"They do make a cute couple," Sheldon said. "It's the one nice thing that's come out of all of this."

"Not the only nice thing," Mother said. "Come here. This sofa folds out, you know."

I looked back at Adam, whose shocked face must have mirrored mine.

"Oh my God," I whispered.

"Back upstairs," he mouthed. "Now."

We made our way back upstairs as quietly as we could, and then closed the door behind us. Adam started making a horrible hacking sound, which resolved itself into a most unmasculine giggle.

"Stop doing that," I said. "This is not funny."

"Seems funny to me," he said.

"Quit it. This is serious. What if they start dating again?"

"Well, then, good for them."

"What if they get married before we do? Then we'd be related. Or something."

"Relax. They're not going to get married. They're just, I don't know, feeling romantic."

Romance is the socialized expression of frustrated sexual desire, I thought. "The whole thing is just creeping me out," I said.

"I understand," he said. "But that's not important. The important thing is you and me. And a whole new year to spend together."

"And midnight. And a kiss."

When the party was over, we walked out the front door of my sister's house, hand in hand, into the welcoming night of the old year that was past and almost gone, into a new year that was bright with promise, and fulfillment, and love.

About the Author

Curtis Edmonds is a writer and attorney living in central New Jersey. His work has appeared in *McSweeney's Internet Tendency, Untoward Magazine, The Big Jewel, Yankee Pot Roast,* and *National Review Online.* His book reviews appear on the *Bookreporter* website. Other short fiction appears online at his yet-to-be-award-winning website, http://www.curtisedmonds.com/. His first novel, *Rain on Your Wedding Day,* was published by Scary Hippopotamus Books in March 2013.

A Brief Factual Appendix

In reading this book, you may have noticed that, at times, Wendy Jarrett's story takes on the character of a country-western song. This is not an accident. Anyone who is an adept of country music will hopefully have noticed that the story makes specific references to various George Jones songs.

On April 26, 2013, the day that George Jones died, the critic Terry Teachout tweeted a recommendation for a book about George Jones, written by Jack Isenhour. I read the tweet and checked out the book on Amazon, which, as it turned out, was entitled *He Stopped Loving Her Today: George Jones, Billy Sherrill, and the Pretty-Much Totally True Story of the Making of the Greatest Country Record of All Time.*

I am not the kind of person who can resist that kind of title.

About a month or so later, I was sitting in the Spartan waiting room of my car dealer, waiting on them to figure out, once and for all, why the God-damned check engine light in my mini-SUV kept going on. I had Isenhour's book on my Kindle while listening to classic George Jones on my iPod. Isenhour is a talented writer, and the book is a careful deconstruction of both the concept of "authenticity" in country music and the classic work of art that is "He Stopped Loving Her Today." I read the book, and reread it, and evolved the concept of writing a novel based on the song.

"He Stopped Loving Her Today" has a very powerful, evocative story. (If you're not familiar with the song, feel free to take a moment and check it out on YouTube.) A man falls in love with a woman, who breaks off the relationship. He spends his days unhappily brooding over his lost love. Finally he dies, and his friends breathe a sigh of relief that his romantic suffering is at last over. At the funeral, everyone wonders if his lost love will show up, and she does. In a three-minute song, you've got love, romance, heartache, pathos, death, and a final dramatic reveal, and three memorable characters. That's not a bad structure to work with, and build around.

The initial problem I had was finding the right protagonist to work with. "He Stopped Loving Her Today," as told from the dead man's perspective, is simply too depressing to tell—and having written a very depressing novel (*Rain on Your Wedding Day*) just previously, I decided to do something that was at least a wee bit lighter. The narrator's perspective isn't much easier to work with—he's just a passive observer who watches his friend die by inches, and then goes to the funeral to mourn, and we never learn anything about him at all.

The next logical place to start is with the character of the woman who shows up at the funeral, the love of the dead man's life who left him and caused him years of suffering. Her character is a bit more interesting, and compelling. However, telling her story posed me with a small problem.

One of the reasons it was so appealing for me to adapt the story of "He Stopped Loving Her Today" into a novel is that the scope of the story is universal—the people involved could be almost anyone. To give you an idea of what I'm talking about, the great songwriter Guy Clark, years before "He Stopped Loving Her Today" was written, wrote a similar song called "Let Him Roll." The story of Clark's song (again, feel free to check it out on YouTube or Spotify) is exactly the same—there's a dead man, a narrator, a funeral, and a lost love showing up at the funeral. But Clark's dead man is a homeless wino, and the mystery woman had been a prostitute. You could tell that story—although not so well as Clark does—but it wouldn't be as adaptable, and it almost certainly couldn't be a contemporary romance.

The thing that tripped me up, initially, about "He Stopped Loving Her Today" is that there is exactly one telling detail in the lyrics. According to the song, the man and the woman were in love during 1962. (There's no particular reason why that is, except that "1962" rhymes with "I love you.") I wanted to preserve that data point, but I also wanted to set my story in the present. In order to tell the story of two young adults in the 2010s, I had to reach back and also tell a story of teenage romance in the early 1960s. I think that I managed to do justice to both stories, but the reader of course will have to judge how well I did.

Isenhour talks about how the producer of "He Stopped Loving Her Today," Billy Sherrill, mixed in a passage of string music towards the end of the song. As Isenhour tells it, the string music is supposed to symbolize the soul of the dead man rising up to heaven. For a country song, this almost qualifies as a happy ending. I chose to have two happy endings in WREATHED, and while that may not be true to the spirit of "He Stopped Loving Her Today," I think that the novel still manages to convey that feeling of redemption and hope.

I tend to set a lot of scenes in restaurants. I like restaurants. They're good places to eat and meet people and eat and have important discussions and eat. I don't think I mentioned specifically any of the restaurants where Adam and Wendy go on their dates, but they're real places and you can go there. Delta's in New Brunswick has excellent Southern food and questionable parking. Jack Baker's Lobster Shanty weathered Superstorm Sandy (rather better than I did, all things considered) and has good seafood and a kids' menu. I am (sadly) much more likely to be eating at the generic chain place where Wendy and their mother have their memorable dinner to start off the novel, though.

Acknowledgments

This story would not be possible without the late, great George Jones. I have been a fan of George Jones's music since early childhood, listening to his lonesome baritone ripple across the North Texas prairies on WBAP-820 out of Fort Worth. Thanks to Terry Teachout for recommending Jack Isenhour's book, and Jack Isenhour for writing his book, and the nice folks at Twitter and Amazon that helped steer me towards the book.

Thanks of course to my wife and my twin daughters (who, at age five, are finally sleeping well enough for me to finish this novel in a timely fashion). And thanks to the rest of my family, either here in New Jersey or in Texas, who read the last book and helped get the word out.

Thanks to Carin Siegfried, who was again willing to work with me and edit this manuscript and set me straight about my near-total lack of understanding regarding women and the clothes they wear. She is a joy to work with and has helped make this manuscript better than it had any right to be.

Thanks to Christine LePorte, who proofread the book and was an immense help in catching the continuity errors that persisted after a couple of major rewrites and realignments to the middle part of the tale. I can only apologize for not including the five-page lyric poem about Whataburger that I promised her. Any errors that remain are my responsibility (although I hope that there aren't any, or if there are, they aren't as egregious as the one about IHOP in my last book.)

Thanks to Doug Niday, who did the calligraphy on the dedication. One of the few things I enjoy about self-publishing is doing things my own way, and using calligraphy on the dedications of my books is something I enjoy (and which a traditional publisher would probably not let me get away with).

Thanks to the wonderful and talented (and anonymous) artists of Dangerdust (https://www.facebook.com/ddccad), who designed and chalked the beautiful cover. You can follow them on Instagram or Tumblr, and buy their stuff on Behance or Etsy.

Thanks to Nathan Bransford, whose terrific blog and book on novel-writing has been a big help this far in my career, and who helped me get my query letter in shape. (It is not his fault that this book is self-published, a fact about which I refuse to say anything further.)

Thanks to everyone who read and reviewed *Rain on Your Wedding Day*, including fellow authors John Shors and Markham Shaw Pyle. Thanks to everyone who's retweeted me or let me write for their blog or done whatever needed to be done to help get more readers for that book, and I hope I can count on you to do the same thing for this book.

And, of course, thanks go to you, the reader, without whom the entire enterprise is based on sheerest folly. I am pleased beyond measure that you've read this far, and I hope you've enjoyed the book and that you'll tell a friend. God bless you and keep you safe from harm.

Curtis Edmonds
Duckthwacket, New Jersey
October 2014